"I highly recommen

likes to read espionage novels. It is full of action and so immersive that you'll feel like a spy yourself! The writer hasn't tried to glorify anything, and that makes the story seem real. The book is smartly written, and the story moves at a fast pace. My rating for *The Spy, the Renegade, the Rogue* is **4 out of 4 stars**. It is not your usual spy stuff. It goes deeper than general conspiracy theories and provides a critique of the political influence on intelligence agencies."

OnlineBookClub.org

Official Review

Robert de Casares

The Spy, the Renegade, the Rogue

E-mail for all enquiries: rdecasares@gmail.com

This novel is based on a true story; however, all the names of the characters, as well as some organisations, are fictional. So are the events depicted. All and any coincidences are accidental, and the author does not assume any responsibility for such.

Contents

PROLOGUE

In Summer 2008, a hunter from the Baniwa indigenous tribe found a wreckage of a small Piper Cherokee aircraft deep in the rainforest, eighty miles to the west of the Brazilian city of Manaus.

It was almost intact, just one wing had come off during the crash; he used his machete to cut the lianas and roots that had grown all over the body of the plane, and climbed inside the cabin. There he discovered a skeleton. The fabric of its clothes had rotted away; the bones were clean, every shred of flesh eaten away by the ants, millipedes and other creepy-crawlies that swarmed these parts.

The carcass was fixed to the pilot's seat, hanging in the harness. It looked like death was instant: there were no signs of attempts to release him- or herself after the impact. On the cabin floor lay the pilot's bag.

The hunter picked it up and brought it to his village, deep in the Amazonia forest; there, he gave it to a British anthropologist who had been living among the natives for a few months, studying their way of life, collecting data for his thesis.

The anthropologist heard the hunter's story and inspected the bag: nothing special, some private belongings and the pilot's documents. Not a Brazilian, a European. There was an envelope inside, too, addressed to a Mr Jeremy V. Ashton-Miles, Esq., a London solicitor. It was only slightly damaged.

The anthropologist took the bag to the police station on his next trip to Manaus. He handed it over, with the Piper's coordinates, but kept the envelope. Being conservative, a man of traditional beliefs, and knowing the local police well, he felt it was his duty to the dead man to make sure the letter found the addressee.

He posted the letter when he returned to London a few months later.

The Manaus police concluded that the plane was the same Piper Cherokee that was stolen from an airfield in the state of Mato Grosso three years previously, and began a half-hearted search for the dead pilot's relations, friends and associates. They found none.

The envelope found the addressee, though; the London solicitor opened it, read the covering letter, and added it to several others in a folder in his safe.

The envelope stayed there a few more years, until the lawyer decided that the time had come. Then, in accordance with the instructions that the letter contained, he published the contents of all the envelopes on the Web. They made up the story that follows.

Introduction:

THE FORGOTTEN SHADOW

I am a professional intelligence officer, or a spy, if you wish. Depends on which side you are on. Frankly, this is something that I myself could not be sure about for years.

I have worked successfully and for a long time. I have deceived, manipulated, blackmailed, broken lives, stolen and killed. These are the normal methods of our work. No intelligence service can exist without them, or else it would not be an intelligence service, but something completely different. Of course, officially these methods are exclusively referred to by less disturbing terms: cultivate, recruit, mislead, influence, obtain, acquire, neutralise and liquidate.

At all times, until my life path reached the Watershed and changed beyond recognition, I was driven by the highest of motives. High motives are the only justification for work that is essentially dirty. When one of my colleagues tells you that he is unsullied, do not trust him. This is disingenuity. Even if he didn't personally participate in the deed, but knew of it and did not raise objections – how is he different? 'If you walk along a dirty road, you cannot help soiling your feet.' That is how Nautilus, my favourite band, put it in their famous song.

Like a drug, dirty work can be healing or poisonous. However, this again depends upon which side you are on. *A la guerre comme a la guerre.* Honesty, decency, integrity and nobility have not won a single war, from Trojan to modern times. And OUR war is forever in twilight; it is endless and goes on continuously, when cannon roar and when there is peace and quiet: permanent, covert, undetectable by ordinary people.

Over the course of my career, I have achieved a lot. And lost everything. Not only money, home or my loved ones, although I lost them all; but immeasurably more. Myself. From a man, I have turned into a shadow.

People and objects cast shadows. But not only that. Events are capable of casting shadows, too: large and small, one or many, depending on the scale of the event, on how outstanding it is, and on how impressive to those who witness it. To what can one compare the impact of the collapse of the USSR in 1991: the fall of the largest superpower on Earth, bigger than Europe and the USA combined, followed by the global redistribution of territories, resources and power?

It may happen that an event has occurred and passed, it is no more, but its shadow lingers on. Not metaphorically, in memories or as history. Quite literally. In my world it is quite possible that the shadow is physical, tangible, and exists on its own, independently of its source. For on the brink of the nineties this world changed so abruptly, leaped into a new reality so suddenly, that a huge mass of people simply stayed on to live in the old dimension, unable to comprehend what was going on around them.

And what about those who were an inherent part of the machinery that ruled the world that had gone, tied to its masters by sacred ties, by oaths of allegiance? What about them, those people who carried out any order, risked life and limb, forsaking all morals, ready to sacrifice themselves, their homes, their families for the sake of sacred Duty, at the first command of their supreme masters? Many did not survive. Many transformed themselves and became mutants. Many were able to adapt, or found the fortitude and the patience to survive these egregious times.

And some turned into shadows. Anchorless and rudderless, long since forgotten about; but they shall remind the world of themselves one day…

But enough of philosophy and deliberations.

This week I have to do something that my heart and mind have secretly desired for many years. When I finally became conscious of my destiny, the rest was easy. I just switched into professional mode: specified the target, the task and the opportune ways to achieve my goal. Then came the preparation stage: I worked out every detail thoroughly, having spent several months gathering information and thinking through the logistics.

I have no way of knowing how it could end. Quite possibly, it will be the end of me. But I know how it all began. That is why I have decided to write these notes while I still can. I shall spend a few nights at my computer and leave the typescript in a sealed envelope with instructions to my lawyer. He is a smart chap, and a good friend. If I were to go where there is no returning from, let him publish what I have scribbled. *Littera scripta manet*. The written word stays… These notes will explain something to those I love and have not seen for a couple of decades. Of what I lived through and could never share; of what only shadows like me could understand.

I do not care about the rest.

Chapter 1. THE OUTSET

Dzerzhinsky Square basked in bright summer sunshine. As I came out of the massive building of the KGB Headquarters and went down Marx Avenue, my head was spinning. It was too late to return to the office and too early to go home. I had to sit down, have a drink, calm down and think. There was a cosy lounge bar that had just opened in the Khudozhestvenny Drive, a private one: market reform ('*perestroika*') was in full swing and its creations mushroomed everywhere.

Having swallowed a shot of vodka in one gulp, I relaxed a bit, the nervousness lifting, my brain clearing. What on Earth had happened? Today they had made me an offer that I could have refused. They'd given me three days to think it over. Were I to agree, I had to confirm the meeting with Sergey Vladimirovich (an alias, surely) by telephone. If I refused, there would be no negative consequences for my career and I would be posted abroad as planned. They assured me of this, but God knows what would really happen. They played very intricate chess games, impossible to see through or figure out. There were too many unknown variables in the equation for it to be solved.

When I was summoned to see the Deputy Chairman of the KGB (the Committee of State Security), I was very much surprised. The level was far too high for a simple formal blessing before my posting. After all, who was I? A mere Captain of the First Chief Directorate of the Soviet KGB, that is, Foreign Intelligence. My boss, the section head, had told me that it might be part of the new approach adopted by our leaders: more personal attention to the personnel.

Well, this could be true – the country was struggling with reforms, changes were apparent in every walk of life, and down-to-earth, democratic and humane attitudes to subordinates was becoming the 'in' thing at the top.

So, here I was, in the spacious office of the Deputy Chairman: the inevitable portrait of the Iron Felix[1] on the wall, large windows draped in heavy net curtains and a cut-glass carafe full of water on a large desk stacked with a dozen telephones and a small switchboard.

'Well, Dennis Petrovich.' The Deputy coughed to clear his throat and looked at me from beneath his heavy bushy eyebrows. 'We are finished with the formal part. You are ready for your posting.'

'Thank you for your trust in me, Comrade Colonel-General.' I stood up from my chair.

'Sit down, we are not through yet.' He pushed a button on the switchboard. 'Send in Sergei Vladimirovich,' he ordered his aide in the waiting room.

'And tea for three,' added the Deputy.

---

[1] **Felix Dzerzhinsky, the founder of the Soviet secret police and intelligence, the predecessors of the KGB**

A tall, slender, balding man of about forty-five entered the office.

'There you are, do get acquainted.'

A firm handshake, and Sergei Vladimirovich (or SV, for short) took a chair opposite me at the T-shaped conference table. The aide put on the table three glasses of tea in solid silver holders. But I didn't touch mine.

I was listening intensely. As I heard what was expected of me, my jaw nearly dropped, but I pulled myself together just in time. An hour later, the Deputy stood up and smoothed his jacket.

'Well, I hope that you will arrive at the correct decision, Dennis Petrovich.' He addressed me semi-formally, not by surname but by patronymic, and then gave me his hand to say goodbye, adding softly, 'Off you go, son. Good luck to you.'

SV rose halfway from his chair, nodded and smiled with his lips only.

And now, at a table with a small carafe of vodka and chasers for company, I was racking my brain for an answer. So far it was just swarming with question marks.

First question: Why me? There were far more experienced and skilled operatives to choose from. Here, though, it seems I had my answer: it was precisely because I was young, lacked experience and had limited access to state secrets that I had been chosen. Even if I tried, I could not damage our Service beyond repair. And if somebody tried to wring secrets out of me, they'd find little of value. What's more, my personal qualities and qualifications suited the business ideally.

Second question: What happens if all goes to plan? How long would the operation last? What happens afterwards? Well, they had outlined this in general terms, of course. It sounded all right in principle, but could I trust them? I would never find out what details of this operation would be committed to paper, what exactly would be documented. Never.

I finished the vodka, paid and left. There was a taxi rank nearby; as the green-yellow Volga cab was taking me along the Gorky Street and home, my mind kept racing.

Question three: What would happen if the mission failed? There were several options here, all of them very unpleasant. Moreover, it was unclear what could be considered a success and what put down as failure: all depended on interpretation and particular circumstances. And on two or three particular people, the only ones with access to the operation. *Will they stand up for me if I am in trouble?* The whole thing seemed to be volatile and open to arbitrary decisions. This worried me.

And the last one: What would happen to my family if things went wrong? I asked them this one at the meeting.

'We will look after them. They will lack nothing. Do not worry; we will take care of them. You know that we always look after our officers' families.'

Words. Assurances. But what can you expect from the top brass? If I were brave enough to say yes, SV would have to answer detailed questions on that account.

There was no one to seek advice from. That would be too dangerous. I did not believe in God then, so could not expect help from above, either. From a professional point of view, the mission was most interesting, however risky. It was also, it seemed to me, necessary. At that point I was a romantic still, convinced that spying was a necessary tool, which, in the right hands, could help heal the world, make it better…

Also, I enjoyed my work; risk was always present, only the degree varied. But, as they used to say in the Service, he who doesn't risk, drinks no champagne. As far as our business was concerned, it was always full of charades, and there were always more questions than answers. And, I told myself, any answer raised more questions; this was an endless quest. Therefore, by the time I had reached my apartment block in a leafy suburb by the Moscow River, my mind was made up: I would do my duty, come what may.

Three days later, I rang up SV. We made an appointment. Not at a safe flat, nor in the office – they were all bugged (this went without saying) and it was unclear who might eavesdrop. There was chaos in the country, people no longer feared or respected anything. Thus, we set up a meeting in a café near Belorusskaya tube station.

I turned up at the site a quarter of an hour before the time, having dry-cleaned it first – that is, checked there was no tail, or surveillance people, following me. No, there were no watchers, nothing suspicious detected. Soon SV arrived, said hello and took his place at the table. A minute later, a man materialised before us: roughly my age, with regular, totally unremarkable facial features. He had light brown hair, quite standard. Dressed like thousands of Muscovites. An ideal appearance for an operative designed for certain covert missions, such as surveillance, courier or special action.

'Here, shake hands.' SV called the man to approach. 'This is Andrei. Your liaison man and courier. Codename "Joseph".'

The man held out his hand. His handshake matched his appearance: neither energetic, nor slack. Neither dry, nor wet.

‘And this is Dennis, also known as “Ayden”. The two of you are going to become good friends.’ Thus having introduced us, SV nodded towards a free chair, directing Andrei to sit down. ‘Is the coast clear?’

Obviously, Andrei was watching the entrance and the vicinity, conducting anti-surveillance.

‘Everything is fine,’ he answered in a colourless voice.

‘Well, my friends, memorise each other very well. You will be seeing each other, albeit not too often, in various cities and countries. And in any circumstances, as required, come hell, come sunshine.’

SV waved to the waiter, who rushed to him holding a menu: ‘Coffee and mineral water.’ SV paused, waiting for the waiter to move on. ‘Andrei is from Department S, so you can rely on him. He knows the ropes.’

Oh yes, the Directorate of Illegal Operations, or simply Directorate S for short, was staffed with the best and toughest professionals.

'Now, with regard to the mission at hand: we,' SV grinned contently, 'call it Operation Traveller. Secrecy here is absolute and paramount. Even in the FCD, no one is aware of its existence, except you two, Andrei and Dennis. Your boss knows nothing. Your future Head of Station (KGB *Resident)* won't be told. This is a Central KGB Headquarters operation, and that is it. In HQ, only two people have access to it: myself and the Deputy Chairman, whom you have met. The immediate controller and supervisor is your humble servant.' He bowed slightly. 'From this moment, I am "Otto", by the way.

'Andy, off you go. It's time. Dennis and I will chew the cud some more. Have a look around as you leave, OK?'

Andrei left. Coffee and water were served.

Sipping coffee, we spent another hour going through every detail of the clandestine liaison system. The system looked good and reliable, and should work in both the first and second stages of the operation.

There were five pre-selected meeting sites, all in different countries – Germany, France, Switzerland, Austria, England – and a pre-arranged time. We were to call either of the two numbers, one in Amsterdam, another in Madrid. If no one answered, we should leave a message – just a meaningless phrase that contained my workname and the code of one of the countries. For example: 'Hello, this is Ayden. I will call again at three o'clock,' would mean that the 'meet' would be in Switzerland (country code three), in Geneva, on the third day after the telephone call, near the Lord Brunswick monument, at 15.00. And every first Thursday of the month, I had to check for messages from 'Joseph', in the form of a vertical red line on the wall of the house on my way from the service flat to the embassy. Having noticed it, I must go to the meeting in the Turkenschanz Park, Vienna, the following Sunday.

'Here is the plan and a photo of the signal site. Look, memorise and return,' SV said. Then we discussed some of the targets and major players. SV showed me a few more photos, and I committed to memory the names and faces. Each was accompanied by a succinct description. At the end of the briefing SV ordered cognac.

'Well, here's to those like us. They are few and far between.' He raised a glass of twenty-year-old Hennessey, a drink that had newly appeared in Moscow. 'Come on, Dennis. It's your show now. I have no idea when we shall see each other again, but remember that I am always there, keeping a keen eye on developments. When you come to Vienna, take a couple of months to settle down, and then start. Looks like we have gone through everything at hand. Good luck. Go with God!' He gestured as if releasing, or perhaps unleashing, me.

The next day I began preparing for the planned posting to Austria, my cover job being the new Third Secretary of the Soviet Embassy. Several months of internship in different departments and sections of the FCD and the Ministry of Foreign Affairs passed by quickly. In that time I heard nothing at all about Operation Traveller. Absolute secrecy prevailed... Unless contacted by my controller

Otto, I was to carry on as a 'mainstream' intelligence officer.

The New Year's Eve party was fantastic, a light-hearted, jovial family affair. We gathered at our country home about ten miles south-west of Moscow. Set among huge, century-old pines, the two-storey wooden lodge belonged to my parents: a gift to my father from the grateful government for some hush-hush achievements in the field of nuclear physics (a new type of bomb, in fact). Surrounded by deep snow drifts that shimmered in the moonlight, it looked like it came straight from a fairy tale. My wife Elena, our son Max who had just turned eight, my old man, my mother and Elena's parents gathered around a large round table, heavily laden with rich winter food, bottles of champagne and a Bohemian crystal carafe of Stolichnaya vodka in the middle.

As we toasted away the last moments of the old year, chasing vodka with red caviar canapes and waiting for the traditional greeting of our national leader at ten minutes to midnight, I was looking at Elena across the table. What was going to happen us? Where would the precarious path that I have chosen lead us in the end?

A flashback from a decade ago struck me just as Gorbachev began his New Year's address to the people of the Soviet Union.

'Stay with me. Don't go, stay!' A soft but persistent voice broke through the veil of fever and delirium. My vision was blurred, her soft fingers felt like ice: a welcome touch on my burning forehead. I was about to cross the thin line between the worlds of the living and the dead; her call brought me back from the brink. *'Stay with me!'* So I did.

After three operations and several blood transfusions, my life and my right arm were saved. When I came to, and my sight cleared, I saw the lovely oval face, the full lips, the dimples on her cheeks, and the incredible green-grey eyes under her heavy lashes. Her hair was chestnut; I could tell by a few locks coming out from under the white cap. She was a surgeon; and I was at the field hospital in Dire Dawa, a city on the border of the great Ogaden desert in Ethiopia. It was only just liberated from the Somalian invaders; I was unlucky enough to attract the attention of one of the numerous gangs of stray Somali soldiers and local cutthroats, the *Shifta.*

They attacked before dawn. There were five of us, camping for the night by a dirt road. We were on a mission: searching for a Soviet Colonel, a military advisor who had been kidnapped three days ago, together with his interpreter and driver.

The fight was fierce, but brief. The 5.45mm Kalashnikov AK 74 assault rifles that my team carried were deadly weapons, and we cut down a few scumbags. But one of them crawled too close to our small camp in a ruin of a hut, unnoticed. He threw one hand grenade, then another. The huge blast was all that I could remember clearly.

Cuban soldiers found me two days later among the rotting corpses of my comrades, hyenas and vultures devouring the grisly remains and waiting for me die. Later, I could dimly recall shooting at the boldest beasts, who grew impatient and tried to snap at my boots; through the haze of semi-consciousness, it all looked unreal… I'd lost a lot of blood, but, what was worse, my wounds had got infected. They brought me to the field hospital just in time. That was the end of my posting to Africa, but the beginning of my newfound happiness. Elena and I got married a year later.

'Happy New Year!' everyone at the table shouted, as the clock on the Kremlin Tower on the television struck twelve. Startled, I jumped from my chair and took the champagne glass that Elena was holding out to me, watching my face with a gentle smile.

In mid-January Elena, Max and I boarded the Moscow–Vienna train at Belorusskaya Station. Our compartment in the international coach was warm and cosy; steaming hot tea was served, the special railway blend brewed over coals. My wife and the boy were glued to the window, as the Moscow suburbs outside gradually gave way to endless fields and forests. A complex cocktail of feelings overwhelmed me: anticipation, anxiety, joy and grief.

At Vienna's Ostbahnhof we were welcomed by Stas, the Second Secretary of the Embassy and a friend of mine. He drove our team to an old mansion in Sternwartestrasse, in a quiet residential area. The house was populated by Soviet diplomats and their families. We were allocated a small, but very comfortable, flat overlooking spacious gardens (almost a park) that boasted ancient beeches, elms and even a volleyball court. It was so tranquil, so friendly, so cosy: it seemed to be a world apart from the stress and tension and the casual hostility of Moscow life. It would have been so easy to be lulled and let my guard slip… But it could not fool me.

Soon, I was up to my eyeballs in routine: familiarisation with my responsibilities at the Embassy and the KGB Station, presentations at the Austrian Ministry of Foreign Affairs. Luckily, the chap I took over from did a good job of handing over every useful detail and contact and introducing me to the Viennese way of life. In the meantime, Elena was busy building and feathering the family nest, going shopping with her new female friends; and Max was running around the gardens with other boys after school, shooting his newly bought toy Cobra revolver. Before long, Elena got a job as the Embassy doctor, with her own small surgery in the compound. My family seemed to love their new home and Vienna.

In those last years of the Cold War, Vienna was one of the most important and lively centres of world espionage. Austria was a neutral country; it was not a member of any political or military blocs. For this reason, it hosted numerous international organisations: from the UN's IAEA and UNIDO (United Nations Atomic Energy Agency and United Nations Industrial Development Organization) to OPEC, the petroleum exporting cartel that practically wrote the rules of the world oil markets. Besides, Vienna had long been the main platform for negotiations between NATO and the Warsaw Pact[2] on the

---

[2] **The military-political bloc of Socialist states, created in 1955 as a counterweight to NATO.**

limitation of conventional armed forces, as well as on security and cooperation in Europe

. Thus, there was more than enough room for all intelligence services worthy of their name to play in – the future world order was being formed here and penetration targets abounded. Which is to say, places where one could plant agents in order to obtain (to steal, in plain language) secret information.

A month flew by, virtually unnoticed. I saw myself being watched constantly, but this was normal in our world: the counterintelligence people always try to figure out who the newcomer really is: a 'straight' bloke or a spy working under cover.

In Austria, however, it was often unclear who the watchers were: the locals, the American CIA or the British SIS. The latter two felt at home in this neutral land; its government gave them carte blanche, so there were no holds barred. Be that as it may, by the end of the second month their interest had waned – perhaps because they failed to detect anything of interest. Just another boring diplomat.

I enjoyed my posting; my job was challenging, exciting and absorbing. My family was comfortable and happy. What more could a man wish? However, one thought kept nagging me, as the inevitable day drew nearer. The day when I would have to make good on the promise that I made half a year ago to the Deputy Chairman of the KGB. It was looming relentlessly.

After that, my life would change beyond return or repair, however inconspicuous the change might be to outsiders. Now it seemed ages ago, that day in Moscow, when, having weighed the potential risks and rewards, I entrusted myself to destiny and the High Command. I had agreed. Now there was no way back. In for a penny, in for a pound.

Following the established tradition, one Saturday morning I took Elena and Max shopping in the city centre. This time, however, there was a difference: I was the one who chose the route, not my wife.

This is why, despite Elena's protests, we deviated from Maria-Hilferstrasse, the area favoured by Soviet employees and their wives, and drove towards Kaertnerstrasse, to the accompaniment of Elena's grumbling about sky-high prices and the fact that with my salary, we could afford no more than window-shopping there.

I set down Elena and Max at the start of this famously upmarket shopping trail and drove on, pretending to look for a parking space. In fact, I left the car right around the corner. The narrow old streets of Central Vienna wove an intricate pattern, merged and opened into passages and courtyards. Not far from here, in a beautiful nineteenth-century house, lived Dudley Stephenson, First Secretary of the British Embassy. At the same time, he was Head of Station of the Secret Intelligence Service, the SIS, popularly known as MI6: the intelligence service whose very existence was not officially recognised at the time.

It was SV in Moscow who told me his street address, as well as the fact that every Saturday at 10.30 a.m. he took for a walk Jock, his Scotch terrier. I knew Stephenson personally: we were introduced at a reception at the Soviet Embassy on 23rd February, the Armed Forces Day. My impression was that he was a sophisticated Englishman who excelled at small talk; suave, pleasant and dangerous.

Here it was: the courtyard I had been looking for. And the time: half past ten. My temples were pulsating. The adrenalin was overflowing. I suddenly realised that my right hand was at my forehead, trying to make the sign of the cross, quite unwittingly. The habit must have been genetically inherited from my ancestors: in a moment of danger, or trouble, I was asking for help from 'above'…

I slowed down. *He has to appear now. But what if he doesn't? I shall have to try again, and again. Come on!*

A door opened in the far end of the courtyard. I stopped dead. A ruffled grey muzzle looked out of the doorway… Jock! The tall frame of his punctual master appeared next; he followed his terrier, walking towards me. I stepped into his path. Stephenson glanced at me, having recognised me instantly. He smiled, as if he was expecting me. Question marks flashed in his eyes.

‘Good morning, Mr Antonov.’

‘Hello, Mr Stephenson. What a pleasant surprise!’

I stepped deeper into the courtyard, knowing I couldn’t be seen from the street, and held out my hand. A handshake, and my note was now in the Brit’s palm.

‘A meeting. Sunday. All the details are there.’ I turned around and left, feeling his watchful, perceptive grey eyes follow me.

Five minutes later, I was strolling down the lively, elegant Kaertnerstrasse. I found Elena and Max outside the window of a jewellery shop, as we’d agreed. It was just beginning to rain: my wife was so absorbed contemplating the glittering gold and diamonds, that she failed to notice either the drizzle, or my tension. ‘Honey, it is so beautiful but I have seen enough. Let’s go to “Maria” – I need to buy trainers for Max,’ she said, taking me by the arm.

‘Oh well, once I am promoted, I’ll buy you that ring over there.’ I gave her a little squeeze and we strolled towards the car.

The following day, Sunday, we drove to Vienna Woods. We left the car not far from Klausen-Leopoldsdorf and walked leisurely across the picturesque rolling hills, covered by last year’s dead leaves. The weather was indefinite, vague, neither here nor there: spring was in the air, the sun’s rays penetrated the grey mist from time to time, crows and rooks croaked (I am not sure what the latter do, but clearly they do not sing). I felt vague, too. Will he come, or will he not? It was like going on a first date with a girl, really.

The path reached a crossroads. Not a living soul around.

‘I’ll catch up with you in half an hour.’ I nodded to Elena. She was aware of my main job and its peculiarities, in general terms, so she knew better than to be surprised or ask questions.

‘Be careful,’ she whispered, looking worried, and took Max by the hand.

'Are you coming back soon, Daddy?' He tried to speak like a man, a serious look on his little face.

I winked at the boy: 'You look after Mama for me.'

I turned onto the left path. In about hundred yards, down the hill slope, I noticed a green Barbour wax jacket under a tweed cap… Stephenson! He had come after all.

That meant that from now on I was to be the Traveller: the channel of 'controlled information', as Otto put it.

It took me what seemed to be eternity to walk the hundred yards downhill.

On Thursday I had a rendezvous with a man that our Station, the *Rezidentura*, wanted to recruit and was busy cultivating: a young hopeful official from the Austrian Chancellor's office. He had swallowed the bait and was firmly on the hook; from now on any meets were strictly covert, to avoid blowing his cover with the opposition. This meant that my rendezvous with Karl Gustav only occurred after a thorough dry-cleaning. It was vital to ensure that I was not being watched.

That's why, for the three or four hours before the meeting, I moved about town, stopping off at the post office, the library, a shop. Everything had to look innocent, so that no one following me would suspect that I was trying to detect them.

An obvious attempt to detect a tail is rude and unprofessional. A watcher's job is hard and often thankless. If they take offence, they can take their revenge afterwards. Such things happened. They could puncture your tyres, or smash your car – or your head. That's why detection traps, the sites where you'd definitely see watchers if they tailed you, were carefully selected, logically woven into your route. They must be outwardly innocent and effective (but elegant, without any cheap effects).

Since I was definitely not expected in our station during these three or four hours, and my absence would raise no suspicions, I decided to use this time to meet my new ‘friends’. By the way, this is how the SIS refer to themselves: ‘the Friends’ or ‘the Office’. From there, I could go straight to my official business, that is to the rendezvous with my potential recruit, now wearing my ‘proper KGB hat’.

In the beginning, such modus operandi, however secure, made my head spin. You had to play two diametrically opposed roles, without any pause or break, one right after the other.

The first role is that of an agent, being briefed and passing on intelligence.

Your controller listens carefully to your every word, the way it is articulated, intoned, watching your body language. Everything is recorded to be analysed later. Are you reliable? Could you be a double agent?

The second role is exactly the other way around: you are a recruiter, a controller. You are luring your target into the spy net, debriefing your object or eliciting information from him, checking him out. Is this a sting to set you up? Is he genuine?

It took a lot of willpower to ignore what happened an hour ago and change the tune completely. Failure was not an option. This was real life, not the theatre, and if your acting was not convincing you would pay: quite possibly with a bullet to the head. My audience was extremely demanding. And not prone to forgiveness.

After such theatre, I came home squeezed dry like an old lemon.

Thursday came at last. Having completed a part of my dry-cleaning route, I went straight to Stephenson's safe flat. It was cleverly chosen: a high-rise apartment block in a new development on the Danube's left bank. All avenues of approach could be clearly seen from the fifth-floor window and I, in turn, could clearly see any signals: curtains open – welcome; curtains drawn – walk on, no meet.

This time, as I looked up from the street, the curtains were open invitingly. I climbed up the stairs, my heart beating rapidly. On the fifth-floor staircase, Stephenson stood in the doorway and beckoned me to enter. The door was firmly shut, a double turn of the key in the lock – and my new life began in earnest.

'Dennis, we should be on first-name terms. It's an old tradition of the Office, and you are family now. Welcome on board. Join the team!' Stephenson smiled gently and gave me his hand.

I shook it firmly.

'Thank you. Yes, of course… Dudley.'

'Let us have a seat.' He pointed to a sofa and sat down in an armchair opposite. The sofa was positioned in a pool of light from the window, so Stephenson could read my face easily. On the table, there was a coffee pot, two cups and a small plate of biscuits.

'Dennis, our service is delighted with your courageous decision and is grateful for your bravery.' Dudley looked me in the eyes. I smiled and bowed my head slightly. He looked so much like George Smiley from those John Le Carré films – *The Spy Who Came in from the Cold* and *Tinker, Tailor, Soldier, Spy*. A delicate, intelligent face, gentle manners, only the glasses were missing… As if he'd heard my thoughts, Dudley put on thinly framed glasses and reached for the tape recorder.

'You don't mind, do you? We don't have much time. This is to avoid missing something. Coffee?'

'Certainly, Dudley. Oh yes, and coffee, too, please. I only have an hour.'

'Well, Dennis, tell me about yourself. And I shall put in some silly questions from time to time, if that's OK?'

What followed next reminded me very much of the interviews with our personnel officers when I was being vetted to enter the KGB. Obviously, the SIS needed to know everything about me: my pedigree, background, family and circle of friends, finances, education, my views on politics and life, tastes, preferences. All that could explain my motivation and would help them judge whether I was dependable, reliable and fit to spy for the Service. Or not. The questions would be repeated many times, differently formulated and presented, from rendezvous to rendezvous. And the tape recordings would be thoroughly analysed: are there any inconsistencies? Does the intonation reveal a lie? Single out, specify, check. All this was painfully familiar. I was fully aware that Stephenson understood that I knew the game. He, in turn, did not doubt for a minute that I was conscious of all the intricacies. Those were the rules, there was no avoiding them. Professionals don't need words or explanations… and yet they still get caught by clever traps, by the smallest of nuances!

We finished with the introductory bit, which necessarily included my stating my motivation. It needed to be strong to justify breaching the oath of allegiance and betraying my country, thus committing a capital offence. Disgust with the Soviet system; my ancestors, the nobles, who, after the Communist revolution, were deprived of their homes and possessions and later perished in Stalin's prison camps; all this combined with the thinly veiled desire for monetary reward, seemed to be strong enough. At least, my interviewer kept nodding understandingly.

Then we moved on to the details of my work with the Vienna Station. I named all the KGB officers that operated under cover in Austria. Ditto the GRU, the military intelligence, known to me. Now the trapdoor was firmly shut, with me the prey trapped inside.

I had divulged top-secret information to the enemy and caused direct operational damage to my own side. This constituted high treason, a crime that carried a very long jail sentence by Soviet law – if I was lucky. If I was less lucky, I'd be looking at a bullet through the head. This was called 'securing' in the professional parlance: the fish had swallowed the bait and could not get off the hook. Oh yes, now Dennis Antonov was a fully-fledged, secured SIS agent, an English mole in the KGB. From now on, no one could get me off that hook, except perhaps the Deputy Chairman of the KGB or Otto, who had given me my orders and sanctioned my acts: those few in Moscow who controlled Operation Traveller.

An hour flew by virtually unnoticed. Having arranged the next meet, and a fall-back one just in case, we parted ways in the doorway of the safe flat. I had about forty minutes until the rendezvous with the Austrian official. I was itching to make a phone call, but this was out of the question: knowing the SIS, there'd be somebody tailing me from the flat. Operational logic. So, calmly and without any tricks, I made my way to a small restaurant on the right bank and took a seat at a corner table, facing the entrance. The place was always nearly empty at this time.

Soon my 'cultivation object', to use the somewhat clumsy operational slang, our agent-to-be, Karl Gustav, entered and started to look around. I rose from my chair a bit; he noticed me and approached. His face was tense. There were beads of sweat on his forehead. He understood the danger – he could see where our games would lead him – yet played along. Yes, he was good agent material.

'Take your seat, Karl. And stop worrying, for God's sake!'

I commanded myself to forget about Stephenson and the events of the past few hours. It took a huge effort to put on a new mask: that of a Soviet intelligence officer; a friend and patron of my Austrian comrade; a man whom Karl Gustav could rely on, who would bring him cash in brown envelopes and look after his security and the wellbeing of his young family. All he asked in return was some confidential documents from the desk of the Austrian Chancellor and a little private gossip from his office. I caught myself wondering what was going to happen to Karl later on, when the British handed over the details of his double life to the Austrian counterintelligence. Stephenson had promised that he would simply be banned from jobs with access to secrets. However, this would not happen anytime soon: both the English and I needed him in order to camouflage our budding relationship.

Thanks to Dudley's promise, my conscience was clear.

'Don't worry, Dennis. Don't let it bother you. I give you my word. The Office does, indeed.' I chose to believe him and felt no qualms. Business is business. There's no room for morals; only expediency counts. However, it was customary to fulfil promises because, although success in our business was directly dependent on deception, treachery, manipulation, perfidy and cunning, there existed a number of unwritten rules and laws that were invariably adhered to by all players. A paradox: professional cheaters build their work on… trust. Within reason, of course.

Success in this line of work, you see, hugely depends on the personality of the operative, the field player, who often has to work alone, without any leader, in situations where it is physically impossible to control him. This is why reputation is of paramount importance. If a service is known to keep its word, people will be willing to deal with it. Nevertheless, one must never forget: always be alert to the exact formulation of any promises and beware of potential hidden interpretations. Implied terms, so to speak. In addition, be vigilant: no matter what the promises may be, the circumstances can always change; if you want to survive, it is advisable to stay ahead of the game.

Karl Gustav handed over an envelope containing copies of some Chancellery documents. We talked business, chatted about this and that. He relaxed a bit as we made our way through a bottle of red wine from the Wachau valley. I let him go and left a few minutes later.

It was about 6 p.m.; dusk and drizzle embraced me outside.

I caught a tram to Waehring, heading in the direction of home. On the way from the tram stop to my car, parked in a side lane, I nipped into a telephone booth that I had spotted and selected a while ago.

I dialled the Amsterdam number. Having heard the metallic voice of the answerphone, I cleared my throat. 'Hello, this is Ayden. I shall call again at four o'clock.'

The Traveller called for a rendezvous in Vienna, in two days' time.

Joseph, my courier from Moscow, brought instructions and best wishes from Otto / SV: nine seemingly blank pages, which I carefully swiped with a solution, also brought by my guest in an aftershave bottle. A pinkish text appeared on the pages. Having memorised everything important, I tore the papers into small pieces and flushed them down the toilet there, in Joseph's hotel room. In turn, I handed him a letter to Moscow – a similar collection of blank pages.

The paper was quite plain, by the way. However, it works as carbon-copy paper if you write on it with a specially prepared pen. An absolutely innocent pen, available in any stationer's, with a chemical agent added to the ink in our laboratory. So, if you write something with this pen and put a blank sheet on top of it, an invisible copy will be transferred to the top sheet, without any traces, such as the imprints, groove marks etc. that pencils or pens usually leave. The copied text can only be developed with a special solution. The formula is unique, it cannot be duplicated: if you do not have this particular solution, the blank paper that you hold will remain blank.

From now on, my courier (or live letterbox, as we call them) visited me once every two months. Once a month I had a rendezvous with Stephenson, and in between I kept my nose to the grindstone, working full time as a 'straight' diplomat in my embassy cover role, and as an operative for the KGB station, the *Rezidentura.* It is common for an intelligence operative to develop an alter ego as he plays the role of an ordinary diplomat, journalist or businessman, whatever his cover story demands. In my case, I developed three or four alter egos.

The embassy, the *Rezidentura*, the Traveller, the Brits. To say that living these triple, or quadruple, lives was tiring, would be an understatement. Often, I felt shattered, physically and mentally exhausted by the constant stress and role changes. Only with Elena and Max could I really relax, but time with my family was always in short supply. Moreover, what could I tell my wife? She knew about my KGB service in general terms, even attended special courses for officers' wives. Any details were, however, no-no. Out of the question. And about the other aspect of my work… she should never even suspect! Even if the notorious female intuition lead her to guess something, I must keep silent. My lips were sealed.

'Darling, will you be home for dinner?' The most usual of questions. To which I cannot give a straightforward answer.

'I don't know. Plenty of work today.' As I say this, I have to gesture to her not to ask any further questions: the flat is bugged, and no third parties must be aware of my movements.

'How was your day? Where have you been?' Normal questions like this could not possibly be answered frankly: there was always a cover story that she had to pretend to believe. Even when we went out for a walk, so we could talk freely, I could not make a clean breast of it. Secrecy was an absolute rule, no exceptions.

Not every woman could cope with this. It was not for nothing that the average divorce figures in the intelligence services at that time were around eighty per cent…

In the meantime, the old familiar world kept changing, the pace of changes becoming more rapid and erratic. Soon it was crumbling before my unbelieving eyes.

The Soviet Union was being torn apart by internal unrest, which had already led to violent conflicts on the country's periphery. The Baltic republics voiced their claims to independence ever more loudly, pressing for secession; their example was soon followed by the others. Our allies from the Warsaw Pact were also leaving, one after another – Hungary, Czechoslovakia, the German Democratic Republic and Poland, until the organisation itself passed away peacefully.

The Station head, our *Rezident*, gathered us one day and read out loud a directive from Moscow, which instructed all KGB officers to treat the former allies from the Pact as potential adversaries and, therefore, our targets. Shocked, we, the officers, gathered that night at the Sternwartestrasse house and drank ourselves silly. We said, or shouted, what we thought about all this, out loud; "fuck all" being the politest expression; we were outspoken and for once nobody cared if they were overheard. Where was this all going to end?

Then the Berlin Wall came down, and Germany headed full steam for reunion…

Moreover, the Soviet leader Gorbachev was not trying to stop the disintegration of the giant empire; on the contrary, he seemed to be simply presiding over the process. Indeed, about ten years later, he confessed as much with some perverted pride. 'I took charge of the

Communist regime in order to dismantle it,' he said. In reality, he let in chaos and destruction, and dismantled the whole nation, an elephant of a state, the largest surviving empire of the twentieth century. Salivating, impatient hyenas hungrily devoured the body of the elephant, still alive but already decomposing…

The instructions that the Vienna KGB Station received from Moscow grew ever more erratic. The KGB HQ seemed to be uncertain, not knowing what to do in the absence of clear policy and directives from the country's government and its supreme leader.

By contrast, the instructions that I received personally, those pertaining to Operation Traveller, were very clear, tough and demanding. These contained disinformation – or chickenfeed, as we call it informally – purported to be top-secret government and KGB directives, and designed to compromise Gorbachev and his team in the eyes of the West. Andrei / Joseph brought microfilms from Moscow and developed them at our safe flat in Vienna. I, in turn, photographed them there, as if I were in our KGB *Rezidentura,* and handed over my microfilm to the

Friends. Their appetite for secret documents divulging the 'true' state of affairs in our chaotic country grew with every passing day. Their requests, a euphemism for assignments, were polite, but insistent – just what I needed. My 'chickenfeed' was in high demand.

Whenever I had a rare moment to myself, I read books and attempted to make sense of the world. I needed to switch my mind to something completely different to stay sane, and maybe find some answers. I discovered Immanuel Kant and the ancient hermetics, the followers of the mysterious Hermes Trismegistus, the 'Thrice Great'. I was carried away by Carlos Castaneda.

I began to see things in a different light, as if a blindfold was taken from my eyes. I could observe my colleagues, my job and myself as if from a distance, a remote spectator. Life now seemed much more multi-faceted and immeasurably more interesting. And more comprehensible, once you understood that there are explanations that no one ever taught you at school or university…

I often caught myself thinking, analysing, drawing conclusions, even when playing with Max or sitting at the family dinner table; whether at the *Rezidentura* or meeting the SIS, my mind was busy in the background. There was no way I could share these thoughts with anyone; maybe with Elena, but carefully, in a censored way: I could not afford to alarm her. *Not now, I shall tell her later, when the time comes. But will it ever? Now I could only think to myself...*

We are so alike, even akin, the people of my profession; no matter what their country or nationality. We think the same thoughts, work mostly in the same patterns, act in a similar manner. We are guided not by law, but by lore, which equally applies to Russians, Brits or Americans.

This likeness sometimes borders on the laughable: you only have to compare the architecture of the Russian Ministry of Defence building with that of the British MOD in Whitehall; the Russian Intelligence Service HQ in Yasenevo with the CIA HQ in Langley; or the massive grey home of the Security Service, MI5, on Millbank, with the houses of their counterparts in Lubyanka,

Moscow. Just drive past them: you will see my point. No comment necessary. If they stood together they'd look alike as twin brothers.

Any thoughts to this effect are best left unsaid, just in case. The problem is that we report to different masters, our interests are often contradictory, not to say at loggerheads. However, we can be friends at times, circumstances permitting. Our political masters are far away and high above, and the political games change so swiftly. The players change; the rules do, too. The actors leave the stage, having played their part, no matter how plausible they looked. However, we are there, always, forever. Permanent, constant, guided by lore and capable of solving any issue. Covert, flawless, neat and slick, with no one to pass the buck to. Or else a scapegoat will be found, if needed, so that nobody will ever suspect foul play. Or will suspect, if expedient. But will only suspect what we want to be suspected.

It was Kate, my new London liaison, who brought assignments, or 'requests', from the Friends now: a charming, intelligent and extremely shrewd lady of about thirty-five. She also brought me the latest miniature camera, as well as (I was amused to find) several pens for copying documents using exactly the same method that we used in the KGB. I dutifully brought all the British instructions and 'shopping lists', as well as any special equipment, to the rendezvous with Joseph, to be copied, photographed and sent on to the Centre, the intelligence service HQ, for examination and analysis.

A word about the special equipment, by the way: the miniature camera that Kate brought me was a true masterpiece of technology. In those days, digital gadgets were still unknown, even in the world of spies. This analogue camera used a microfilm, and had to have a mechanism to wind it and draw it, but was small enough to be hidden in a packet of Marlboro, leaving enough space for cigarettes. Unlike the commercially available Minox, it was noiseless. This was an extremely important feature, since it allowed clandestine photography right under the enemy's nose. The tiny microfilm allowed for up to forty exposures. It only needed a normal desk lamp, no special lighting required. In order to focus the image, the required thirty centimetres to the document surface were measured by a thread and a needle as a weight, all fixed to the side of the camera by chewing gum. All set and ready to go!

Many times I had to copy documents covertly in the KGB Station cypher room, with the cypher clerk virtually breathing down my neck behind a thin partition… It tickles your nerves, makes your palms sweat. However, it works!

Of course, the KGB had comparable devices. It was a close contest.

Indeed, as above, so below; as without, so within. *Sapienti sat.* Enough for the wise.

Slowly, inconspicuously, unnoticed amid the daily routine and the momentous events, the year 1990 crawled to an end. As usual, on the 20th of December, KGB Day, our Head of Station, the *Rezident,* assembled the officers in a safe room and read out loud congratulatory telegrams from the Centre. He read a few citations – commendations and honours. A few medals were virtually pinned to a few jackets. Virtually, because the medals were handed out upon return to Moscow, never on posting abroad. I was the luckiest of all: for the recruitment of an especially valuable agent (if only Karl Gustav knew!) I was promoted from Captain, bypassing the rank of Major, straight to Lieutenant Colonel. `Now I can buy her that ring`, it occurred to me when I was smiling back at my applauding, somewhat tense brothers-in-arms.

The longed-for pause came at last. Cultivation objects, targets, agents, contacts: all left for their holidays. I could enjoy family life at last. Elena and I had dreamed of skiing in Tirol. It was high time for Max to try skiing, too. He was a good athlete; slalom should not be a problem.

Christmas, New Year's Eve, champagne and a couple of weeks of doing nothing serious – all this lay in wait.

And yet the palindrome year, 1991, the turncoat year, beckoned from the threshold. Premonitions and forebodings drowned in glasses of Veuve Clicquot only to resurface when it would be much too late to change anything at all…

Chapter 2. THE TRANSITION

On the first Thursday of February, on the way to the Embassy, I routinely glanced at the greyish wall of a house halfway to my destination. A vertical red line caught my eye: Joseph calling Ayden for a rendezvous. What had happened over there in Moscow? It was the first time in two years of Operation Traveller that I was summoned for a meet.

So much for the family outing on Sunday. Instead of taking ten-year-old Max to the Prater amusement park, I would have to solve spy riddles with my courier Andrei. I felt uneasy. An urgent meet was no joke; something serious must have happened. I made an effort to set aside my worries, but somewhere deep inside my mind a warning red light kept flashing. Or rather, an exclamation mark, as on a road sign, alerting you to an imminent, yet unspecified hazard.

On Sunday Elena, Max and I went out for a walk in Tuerkenschanz Park, not far from home. Stopping at a park café, I bought Max his favourite strawberry ice cream and coffee and apple strudel for Elena and myself. The night before I had whispered to her that I would have some business for an hour and a half, not more. She sighed, rolled over, turning her back to me, but in the end put up with it as usual. Actually, even if she wanted to argue, the flat was no place for it, as it was bugged – I'd checked immediately after we had arrived. Whether by our own, or by the other side, I couldn't tell. Perhaps both. When we first moved in, we were even too shy to make love, unable to shake the thought of somebody eagerly eavesdropping... They would turn you into unwilling exhibitionists, given half a chance.

We were strolling hand in hand down a quiet path while our son tirelessly circled on his brand-new bicycle. Elena said suddenly: 'When the posting is over, quit your work. Resign. Or we'll end up getting a divorce. I can't take more of this life.'

‘Honey, why? Don’t be like that!’ I wanted badly to hug her, hold her tight, but there was no bloody time. Besides, I had to concentrate before an important rendezvous and could not afford to go soft.

‘Listen, let’s do this: I’ll go and sort out this business now, return as soon as I can. Then we can leave Max to play with his friend Alex. I’m sure the neighbours won’t mind. And you and I will go out, sit and talk everything over. Deal?’

She clung to me, kissed me on the cheek, sobbed.

‘Let’s. I am so fed up with everything, Den.’ Her voice trembled, ‘Let’s do it. Please come back soon.’

Having left them in a café, I walked briskly down the alley, struggling with my inner turmoil. I turned right to the park exit and there he was, loitering by the newspaper kiosk. To my astonishment, I saw not Joseph, but SV himself! What a guest! But why?

Looking indifferent, he stepped away from the kiosk and made his way to a nearby lane, where an inconspicuous grey Opel Omega was parked. While SV was getting inside, I caught up with him and took the front passenger seat. The car started immediately. After a ten-minute drive in total silence, we parked in a quiet narrow street. About fifty metres down, there was an entrance leading to a block of flats; SV open a door on the first floor with his own key. I found myself in a small studio, apparently rented specifically for this clandestine meeting. I had not known about this safe flat before.

'Well now, hello Dennis!' He embraced me, and then shoved towards an armchair. 'Hey, relax. Sit down.'

'Hello Serg…' I began.

He cut me short. 'Otto. I am Otto here.' SV picked up a bottle of Black Label from a coffee table, poured the prescribed two fingers for both of us. 'Here is to your promotion, Lieutenant Colonel! A well-deserved one.'

We raised our glasses and sipped the whisky. I waited, tensely, for what would follow. Otto played with his glass, staring at me with his leaden grey eyes.

'Now to business. You are following the developments in the country and in the world. You see what is going on;

you are astute. We are coping fairly well with our mission; however, the Baldie (this was what he called Gorbachev) still enjoys serious support in the West, especially after the reunification of Germany. He is selling the country down the river, shopping everything to the Americans. We do not have much time. If we don't stop him, he and his clique will tear the country apart.'

'More trouble and tribulations forthcoming?' I put my glass on the coffee table. 'So where are we headed then?'

'Don't interrupt me. You will see soon enough. We shall recover, don't you worry. But now let us talk about you.'

SV/ Otto coughed to clear his throat: 'Now then. In July, the Baldie travels to London to beg for more money to support his reforms. He's invited himself to the Group Seven gathering, playing the poor relation. We must do our utmost to ensure that he leaves London empty-handed. Without a penny! His failure shall be a signal for us to act. And you will help us greatly in this matter.'

'But how? Well, I can pass on more chickenfeed to the Friends, but will that help? So far it doesn't seem to have seriously influenced them. Just look, they bit off one lump after another…'

'True, but they have solved the German question to their satisfaction, and now the Soviet Union is on the brink of falling apart. Exactly what our Western so-called partners need, fuck them. They are carried away; they have decided that the process had gone so far that it cannot be stopped or reversed. They will overplay their hand. Why give more money to Gorby when the rot has firmly set in? But they are still hesitant, they have doubts. So we shall help them to sweep those doubts away. You, Dennis, shall help them to cast away any doubts.'

'But how, damn it?' I was not following him.

'Let us drink some more.' Otto raised his glass. 'To you, old boy.'

'And to you, Otto.' I swallowed the whisky and looked questioningly at my visitor.

'We move on to Stage Two of the operation. In July.'

‘But how? It…’

He cut me short. ‘Don’t object. This is no longer a hypothesis; moreover, it is urgent.’ SV raised his hand to wave away my protest. ‘Something has happened. A coincidence; but all to the better.’

Stage Two of Operation Traveller had always been considered a remote possibility, never a probability. However, having heard what Otto had to tell me, I realised that bloody Stage Two had become not only a probability, but an inevitable certainty.

The matter was as follows.

The SIS, the British Secret Intelligence Service, was of course one of the best in the world. It was certainly the oldest and the most experienced one. However, after the Second World War, the Service gradually, step by step, began to descend to a place subordinate to its closest ally – the American CIA, or the Cousins, as they were known in the British Service, whose very creation and operations in the early years to a large extent drew from and relied upon the SIS’s formidable know-how, skills and history.

Nothing surprising here. The once mighty British Empire had become a junior partner of the United States of America.

Understandably, cooperation between the two services was the closest possible. Intelligence was exchanged routinely, on a regular basis. The junior partner was willing to ingratiate himself with the senior one, the rich Cousins from 'the other side of the pond'. They wanted to provide something particularly important, relevant, something that the Americans could not obtain on their own, and thus prove once again the junior's importance and irreplaceability. Well, and to justify an increase in the budget at the same time…

According to my controller, I just happened to be in the right place at the right time. Indeed, the world was experiencing monumental changes: the Soviet Empire was crumbling, we were on the brink of a global redistribution of influence, property and territory. The need for reliable intelligence from trustworthy sources was immense. And the English had me! A source inside the KGB Foreign Intelligence with serious connections to the Ministries of Defence and Foreign Affairs. To crown it all, a relative of a ranking official from the Communist Party Central Committee International Department (which was not true: we had prepared this lure for the Friends, so they would swallow the chickenfeed better).

Obviously, my intelligence was extremely valuable; the English shared it with the CIA promptly and regularly. Naturally, the source was never disclosed. However, the nature of the information and the way it is supplied can lead a professional analyst to figure out, roughly, the circle that it comes from. That's the starting point. The rest is a matter of time and skill. Narrowing the circle of suspects and tightening the noose are skills well mastered by counterintelligence folk both in Russia and across the ocean.

At that time, a certain Aldrich Ames worked on the CIA Counterintelligence Staff. He was head of the Soviet Section: a serious position with enviable access to top-secret information of various kinds. Simultaneously, he was a fully-fledged KGB agent, a mole, and for several years had unloaded onto his Moscow masters everything he could lay his hands on. And that was quite a lot. In the 1980s, about ten KGB and GRU (military intelligence service) officers who had been recruited to spy for the CIA had their cover blown by Ames, and were consequently arrested and shot. Even more were imprisoned. The damage he caused the CIA was irreparable.

His smug bespectacled face, sporting a fashionable moustache, became known worldwide after he himself was arrested by the FBI in 1994. But then, as early as 1991, SV could only inform me about the imminent danger, without going into details. I felt my skin crawl as I sat listening to his narrative, delivered in a deliberately monotonous manner. He told me about an important source that the KGB had inside the CIA.

This much I was aware of beforehand: this was exactly the reason why, earlier in Moscow, they had decided that the Traveller should come to the English and not the Americans.

However, this source in the CIA turned out to have had access to the very intelligence material that the British service shared with its senior partner from across the pond! The fact that the source of this intelligence – that is, me – was kept strictly secret even from the allies did not matter: the stream of information from the SIS to the CIA flowed for months, full, comprehensive and uninterrupted. Then it travelled even further, from the CIA to the KGB, courtesy of Ames. The boomerang effect! By analysing the intelligence as well as timing it – and the SIS started sharing it two years ago, which coincided with my arrival in Vienna – by doing this, sooner or later our KGB experts would make the correct conclusions and identify the correct culprit: me.

SV / Otto was specific and particular: 'Section Five of the Directorate K of your FCD is very busy looking for an English mole. Not in the KGB as a whole, but inside the intelligence service.' Section Five, or Five K as we referred to it, was the FCD internal counterintelligence service, our own security team. It was they who, in the 1980s, unmasked Oleg Gordievsky, who had worked for the British for many years. He had managed to escape, but they were unlikely to screw up like that again…

'Dennis, there is no reason to panic at the moment. I reckon you have at least half a year before all the pieces fall into their places and the puzzle is solved,' SV went on in the same monotonous voice, 'but we shall take the necessary steps now. Besides, the time is just right.'

He sipped his Black Label, paused to think for a minute, and scratched his chin. I kept silent, my gaze fixed on the coffee table.

'Well, the decision has been made: Stage Two is on. Please understand: if they grab you, we would be unable to help. We would not even try. There is too much at stake. The country's future. Careers of very important people. For the sake of our cause, in order for it to succeed, we shall not defend you or protect you. The very existence of Operation Traveller shall be denied. It is deniable, Dennis. You know the rules of the game. So you will have to go through hell before the time comes to get you off and out.

And nobody knows at the moment when that time might come. Please, do understand.'

I shook my head in disbelief. When the offer came to become the Traveller, I had consented of my own free will; no one had pressured me. Now I had to live up to Moscow's expectations. In for a penny, in for a pound.

SV leaned towards me. Now he spoke passionately, convincingly.

'Everything will change soon. In a year or eighteen months, the country will change beyond recognition. We will extricate you from England. You'll be a hero. We'll look after Elena and Max, take care of your parents, explain to them as far as possible… Do you hear me, Dennis?' He put his hand on my shoulder.

'Serg… Sorry, Otto.' I looked him straight in the eyes. They were so sincere that, if I had not known where this man came from, I would have trusted him.

'You've convinced me. It is true, I have no choice. And surely I shall be of more use among the English Friends than in Lefortovo prison?'

SV nodded approvingly.

'I am glad. Good for you. Now, let us go through all the details. The cover story for your English Friends, liaison, dates, the lot. Time flies, you shall need to be at home soon, before they start to worry…'

That night, having put Max to bed, Elena and I went out. We walked leisurely for half an hour to make sure that none of our attentive and caring Sternwartestrasse house neighbours were around.

Then we dived into a wonderful, cosy wine cellar, which I had spotted a while ago. We took a corner table; the waiter lit the candle and brought a carafe of red wine.

That evening I promised my wife to quit my work. However, first I had to complete my posting without any hiccups. Once we returned to Moscow, I would submit my resignation for health reasons. This happens in our line of business; a man can simply burn out. All done cleverly, there should be no aggravation and they would let me retire on full pension.

I am not sure whether Elena believed me or not. The odds that she did were eighty per cent. When I need to, I can sound very convincing. I felt disgusted with myself; it nauseated me to have to lie to her in the full knowledge of what she would have to go through before long. My disappearance, uncertainty, an KGB investigation. This investigation would seem genuine even to the investigators; before the time was right, no one, Elena included, must ever be aware that it wasn't genuine after all…

Would she ever forgive me? I felt a complete scoundrel. The only justification I could find for myself was duty. The notorious duty that has to be done no matter what, all doubt, guilt and remorse cast aside. I swore allegiance to my country and its government; never mind what I thought, I had to carry on regardless.

The last few weeks and days before the move I lived like a robot. The countdown was ticking in my head. I knew exactly what to do and when, and step by step was getting closer to my goal. I carried on with my work in both the *Rezidentura* and the Embassy as usual and was a loving husband and father at home. Very much loving – Elena and I made love every night, passionately, ecstatically, feverishly gorging on each other as if trying to make the most of it in the face of our forthcoming separation. Of course, I was the only one who knew about the separation, although sometimes I suspected that she sensed it too.

Andrei / Joseph came over from Moscow. He gave me a few documents for the British, which I photographed. Amongst them, there was a telegram that my KGB Station Head, the *Rezident,* purportedly received from the Centre. It said that my candidacy was on top of the list to fulfil the vacancy of Deputy *Rezident* for political intelligence (our Deputy's posting was over and he had returned to Moscow). I was wanted in Moscow for formal interviews to confirm me in the new position. In two weeks I was to go, alone, without my family, for three days.

On the surface, the telegram looked innocent; however, in the context of recent events it could not help but alarm the SIS. The issue was that, just a month ago, at our regular meeting, I had told Kate what my KGB colleague

Stas ostensibly leaked to me after he had returned from an annual holiday in Moscow. After a few drinks and in strictest confidence, he had supposedly told me that there was a serious mole hunt going on inside the First Chief Directorate. For an English mole, not a CIA one. He had allegedly heard the story from a chap serving in Directorate K, the FCD counterintelligence. They had been close friends and drinking partners for donkey's years.

The Friends were still smarting from the relatively recent Gordievsky episode. The man, the acting *Rezident* in London, had been working for the SIS for over ten years when he received a similar telegram: please come to Moscow to be confirmed as permanent *Rezident.* The telegram looked plausible; having weighed the odds with his English controllers, off he went. The day following his arrival in Moscow, he was cross-interrogated by two ranking KGB officers, the interrogation poorly camouflaged as an interview. He was told not to leave the capital and put under twenty-four-hour surveillance. An arrest could follow any minute. Gordievsky's legendary escape from the Soviet Union in 1985 was a miracle: somehow, the SIS managed to extricate him, whisking him out of the country right under the noses of the KGB watchers. Nobody is sure how they did it exactly: there are several theories, one more unlikely than the next. The truth is well hidden under lock and key. It is also unclear why the KGB didn't just arrest him upon arrival, instead of engaging in some indistinct cat-and-mouse game.

Be that as it may, the predictable unwillingness of the British Intelligence to risk another agent was extremely important to me and to the success of Operation Traveller. We bet strongly on this: that they would analyse the report about the English 'mole' that I had fed to Kate, and come to the conclusion that I could have come under suspicion because of the intelligence that the SIS shared with the Americans. Or for another reason all together. What if the KGB had penetrated the SIS? And this telegram… I was too young to be appointed Deputy *Rezident;* it was too early in my career. It looked exactly like a lure designed to bring me over to Moscow.

Thus, I had every reason to call an urgent rendezvous with the British. I made a telephone call from a booth in Central Vienna and left a message on Stephenson's pager. Four zeros. See me the day after tomorrow.

On that day there were two people waiting for me at the safe flat: beautiful Kate, who had travelled over from London, and Dudley Stephenson. Aha, they were worried! Excellent.

I handed over my miniature camera with about thirty exposures on the microfilm inside the tiny body. Then I told them in detail about the telegram that was on one of them, that they were to read later. As Kate and Dudley listened tensely to my comments, I kept my voice purposefully calm. Sure, the danger existed, but there was always danger in our line of business. Yes, the odds were fifty-fifty, but I was prepared to take the risk. What if I was really promoted? That would be such a big success for our cause, a true breakthrough…

'Dennis, don't try to be a hero. Above all, we need you alive and well. The Office needs to check everything out, to analyse things. That will take a few days. In the meantime…' Kate fixed her profound hazelnut eyes on me, 'in the meantime, go to work as usual and pretend to get ready for the trip to Moscow. Book airline tickets with Aeroflot.'

'And at the slightest sign of danger come to me immediately, or ring me directly. We shall pick you up from wherever you are,' Stephenson put in. He stood up and went to a chest of drawers across the room. On top of it was a camera with a big, semi-professional lens. An expensive Cannon.

'Come here. Stand against the wall.' He pointed to the white partition opposite the window. 'This is for your British passport. Just in case. I need photos of your wife and son, too.' He glanced at his diary. 'Bring them on Thursday. Suits you?'

I nodded. Apparently they had decided everything and were just waiting for approval from the top brass in London. I would bring the photos, of course. However, I couldn't tell them that my family would not be joining me in England. Elena and Max would be waiting for me in Moscow, looked after by my caring KGB colleagues. This decision was final. They wanted insurance. They were afraid that I might grow too fond of England…

Outside the June sun shone. Vienna looked fabulous, all dressed in fresh green, adorned with flowers. I felt nauseated, sick; the burden on my conscience was almost physical, making me stoop. There were four days to go until Thursday, today included. In four days, Stephenson would tell me the Friends' decision, tell me how long I would have before the big change of scene… What theatre, dammit. One could play until one died.

Our calculations proved to be correct: that Thursday Stephenson, this time unaccompanied by Kate, told me that the Office considered the danger genuine, and did not want to risk me. I was going to England.

The logistics were not complex at all. According to my cover story, or 'legend' in the KGB parlance, I was to catch a plane to Moscow the following Wednesday. Which meant that I would not be expected in the Embassy that morning. The previous night, Elena, Max and I would go out for a walk, and be picked up by a car in a certain place: that was all. Dudley would be in the car, along with our new British passports. In three hours we would reach Munich, and board a plane to London. Even if my colleagues in the Soviet living compound suspected something and started looking for us, they would have no time to do anything about it until it was too late. 'Don't worry, Dennis. Our chaps will be nearby to cover and protect you, just in case. And if you're followed, we will cut the tail off. There will be no surprises.'

I had to get used to hearing my name pronounced with the stress falling on the first syllable, English style, I thought suddenly. What an idiotic thought. Blast.

'Dudley, about my wife and son. As we agreed, I hinted to Elena about an eventual defection… I implied rather strongly, within limits… She is uncertain, a little volatile. I believe she might refuse at the last moment. To be frank with you, I am at my wit's end. What can I do? I cannot tell her openly about our plan. That's out of the question…' I let the unfinished sentence hang in the air.

‘That would be extremely dangerous. She could betray you by chance, inadvertently. Don’t say anything.’ Stephenson waved his hand as I attempted to say something, and sighed. ‘Women, eh?’ He leaned back in his armchair, took off his spectacles and started polishing the lenses.

‘Let us do what we can, Den. I know how much you love your wife and son. The Office guarantees the three of you monetary support, a house and a job, and private schooling for Max. This much I have already told you. This guarantee is for life. Even if they can’t join you now, we can always bring them across to you later. Not right away, certainly. But in six months, a year. The world is changing. It’s very feasible.’

Yes, but only if Elena still wanted to join me, after everything she would have to go through, I thought to myself. And only if my true bosses let her go. And they would never release her, not while they needed a guarantee of my returning to the fold. Besides, they were the only ones who knew and could prove that I was no traitor, no defector. Deputy Chairman of the KGB. SV /

Otto. Andrei, my liaison. Perhaps one or two more people that I wasn't aware of? I would become a traitor to my people at the FCD, and remain a traitor until those at the very top, my controllers in the KGB Central Headquarters, decided that the time had come to show their hand. Until that time, there would be no medals, only contempt and curses.

'All right, Dudley. Let us see what happens. I shall act accordingly. There is enough space for three passengers in your car; however, if I have to go alone, well, so be it. I trust the Office. I am sure they will help me to get my family across. May I?' I motioned towards the bottle of Glenfiddich on the table.

Dudley poured the whisky into two tumblers. 'Good luck on Tuesday!'

After we'd drunk the whisky, I went out into the bright summer day. I wanted to get drunk, completely pissed; to erase it all and start again, from scratch. Well, that would have to be postponed till London.

The few days until Tuesday were a torture. At work I could keep a straight face and stay on course; I met with my agent Karl Gustav and reported the intelligence received to the Centre; I had a meeting with the *Rezident* and we worked out a plan for the further development and exploitation of the source. Our *Rezident* was a good man; I felt badly about having to let him down. However, he too had to go through an ordeal for the sake of the success of a cause of which he knew nothing. Not yet, that is. Would he have agreed if he had known?

Well, in our business nobody asks for agreement. This is the Service. Nobody forces you to enter, but once inside, go ahead and work, forget your doubts, concerns and misgivings. Moral principles and virtues do not apply in our world. How can one apply such criteria to something that is essentially amoral to begin with and is only guided by expediency?

To recruit an agent means to tempt, or to force, a person to commit treason; to carry out a sting or false flag operation, to manipulate, to elicit information means to deceive and cheat in the everyday language that normal people use. That is how we work. Anything goes, as long as it serves a purpose. What purpose? Our leaders above know. As far as we are concerned, we protect and defend the realm and its interests by employing our special skills and methods. This is useful, necessary, important and selfless work. Observed from the outside, though, the little that can be seen of this iceberg looks rather dirty. That is why they invented the 'plausible deniability' principle. If we're caught red-handed, our political masters can always plausibly deny any knowledge of anything untoward: by God, honestly we know nothing, and could not possibly comment. All players know the rules of this game, so you'd better not get caught out.

Bad as it was at work, it was even more difficult at home. Unlike Special Services, women cannot be tricked by complicated mind games. A loving wife is always tuned in; she feels the state her husband is in, the movements of his soul. I could not conceal my inner tension, no matter how hard I tried to pretend to be all right. On Sunday, while we strolled in the magnificent gardens of the Shoenbrunn Palace, Elena demanded to know what was wrong with me. Max was not with us, his classmate had invited him to a birthday party, so there was nothing that I could distract her with, and the interrogation was a tough one. I put my behaviour down to being tired, to having serious problems at work.

'I cannot go into details, you understand… I am sorry, this is my bloody job… It happens, but August is near, we shall go on holiday, leave Max with your parents to stay in their countryside house and go to the Black Sea, the Pitsunda resort, just you and I, and forget everything for a month… And then, in a year, my posting will be over, I shall quit the bloody job and we shall start a new life.'

In fact, the new life started much earlier. The following Tuesday, around 6 p.m., I whispered to Elena that I had to go. I had warned her about my 'business trip' in advance; I told her that I was likely to be away for a day as I had a special assignment. There was no disputing that.

So I kissed my wife and son and left the house in Sternwartestrasse for the last time. I would never return, ever. There was a knot in my stomach. I felt sick. I had to switch my mind quickly to what lay ahead, or I would have broken down.

There was a chest of drawers in our bedroom; I left an envelope with a note and cash inside. *I love you. Do not trust anyone. It has to be like this. Soon we shall be together again. Please destroy this note after reading*. I left about two thousand US dollars' worth of money in Austrian Schillings: not much so as not to raise suspicions. Later, in Moscow, they would pay Elena everything that was due to me; she and Max would never have a rainy day, would not lack anything. Except a husband and a father.

I turned into Gregor-Mendelstrasse, then to Heizingerstrasse. A grey Mercedes 220 was parked ahead in the street. Dudley Stephenson was sitting behind the wheel. I opened the rear door and got in. A man appeared from around the corner on the opposite side of the street, crossed it quickly, pulled open the left rear door and jumped in next to me. The car started immediately. Having driven for five minutes, Dudley said: 'Dennis, meet Michael.'

We shook hands. Was he strong! One would never tell from his appearance.

'All is going to plan. We ought to be in Munich soon. Here, take this.' Over his shoulder, he shoved me a booklet in a black leather holder, embossed with a golden lion and unicorn. 'Your passport. Mr Dennis Bates, of Her Majesty`s Service. Don`t let the name bother you, we can always change it afterwards`.

'Drink?' Michael offered a hipflask.

The whisky went straight to my head, took the edge off my nerves. I felt the urge to talk, complain about having to leave Elena and Max behind, but this was out of the question. Bad form. I was a pro among pros.

'Don`t worry about your family, we will get them across, you will see,' Dudley said suddenly, as if he had read my mind. I did not believe this for a second, but still felt grateful.

'Thank you, Dudley. I trust you,' I croaked, my throat dry, and gulped more Scotch from the flask.

The rest of the journey went without a hitch. We raced to Munich airport to be met by another SIS officer – middle-aged, of medium height, and rather senior, judging by his demeanour. It was he who took over control from that moment on.

'Richard,' he said, shaking my hand quickly, a light aroma of a recently smoked expensive cigar around him. 'I shall be your travel companion to London.'

We said goodbye to Dudley, who had to drive back to Vienna, checked in at the VIP register and went straight to boarding. The British Airways Boeing was ready to take me on the final leg of my journey.

Two hours later we landed at Heathrow. New faces, new handshakes. Bypassing other passengers, we walked through deserted corridors directly to the waiting car; one more hour, and I was unloaded, at last, to a lovely small hotel in mock Tudor style, in an equally lovely small town with a church on top of the hill. Later I learned that it was called Farnham. Here I was to spend a few days, while a regular flat was being prepared for me. Michael occupied the room next door, just in case.

The English proved to be wonderful, genial hosts. They gave me a hearty welcome. So, here I was, among the people who were supposed to be the enemy; I had to become one of them to serve my true masters in Moscow, to do my bloody duty. And to harm my hosts if so ordered; unpleasant as it was, this was my job, nothing personal.

The next morning Richard and Kate dropped by, and we all had breakfast. Here, I was introduced for the first time to some of the many peculiarities of British life and etiquette. To my surprise, I discovered that you had to hold your fork with its tines facing down; even if you want to put mashed potatoes or salad on it, you should use the back side only, never turn it over to use as a spoon. You have to be really deft if you don't want the food to fall off. Very inconvenient, but very proper. Very English, too. Tea is poured in strict order: milk first, then tea. If you forget to tell the waiter that you want 'black tea', your tea will automatically be white. We laughed and joked a lot about all this; the breakfast was a jolly affair.

All the while, in my mind I was picturing the events in Vienna after my KGB colleagues discovered that I had disappeared. *Did Elena have time to read my letter before they came for her to our flat? Or to her surgery at the Embassy compound? I hope she did, and destroyed it, as I asked her. When will they evacuate her and Max to Moscow? Immediately, of course.* I kept telling myself that times were different now and Elena would be treated well. I had to convince myself that it was true and that Otto would keep an eye on my family as promised…

Michael left us after tea, and we sat down in the corner of a lounge that was empty save for a tough-looking young man in an armchair, sipping coffee and paging through the *Telegraph*. The time had come for me to learn what was going to happen next.

My controller, Otto, would be delighted: my hosts wasted no time. The following day I was to be received by C – the Chief of SIS, at Century House, the then Headquarters of the British Intelligence at 100, Westminster Bridge Road. It was a promising start. The day after tomorrow I'd have a question-and-answer conference with the top Foreign Office officials. The reason was obvious: July was nigh; that meant the G-7 summit, where President Gorbachev of the USSR would be a guest of honour. The issue of direct financial aid for the staggering 'Gorby' was to be addressed and decided upon; a lot was at stake. To give, or not to give, and let it all slide completely downhill? They needed time and resolve to prepare an answer that could have historic implications. And they had me, a fresh defector, a source from the KGB Intelligence! Clearly they must pick my brain.

Richard enlightened me as to what in particular would be of interest to my interlocutors. Well, I would take this into account, and feed them all the information – or rather, disinformation – that the Traveller brought over from inside the KGB and the Soviet government. That is what I came here for.

There was no question of attempting to contact Joseph. The instructions to Ayden – that is, me – had been explicit: not to even think of it for the first month, as I was likely to be under round-the-clock surveillance. Later on it might be possible, situation permitting; I was to employ my best judgement and remember that security was of paramount importance. I had to rely on my best tradecraft, always. (Tradecraft is professional slang for spycraft). It was a shame, as I wanted so badly to know what happened to my family... However, the powerful whirlpool of events sucked me in completely. I kept my nose to the grindstone, there was hardly any time left to reflect... Thank God for that: work was the straw that kept me afloat.

Beside the top-level meetings and various lunches and dinners, there were debriefings on the agenda, virtually every day. These took the form of friendly, informal-looking interrogations, where you were questioned about everything that you knew and could remember (and if you couldn't, they would help you remember it); experts from different fields examined you, tested your knowledge. The current issues of intelligence and counterintelligence, politics, education, childhood, family and relations, useful contacts, face recognition from blurry photographs, technical and military matters, modus operandi, psychological portraits, all of it over and over, endlessly iterated.

Simultaneously they probed, they studied you. One could be certain that any discrepancies and inconsistencies in your behaviour or delivery would be detected. You had to be alert and vigilant, always. Big Brother was watching.

C received me in his office on the tenth floor of a nondescript glass and concrete building with creaking lifts that turned out to be the legendary Century House.

The tall, lean Scotsman rose from behind his desk and motioned genially to me and Richard to enter, pointing to the coffee table. His dark eyes of indistinguishable colour contemplated me curiously from under bushy eyebrows.

'Sir Colin, may I introduce Dennis Antonov, also known as Dennis Bates' said Richard in a formal tone of voice.

'I have heard much about you, Dennis.'

C gave me his hand. I shook it, bowing my head slightly.

'Do have a seat. Make yourself at home. You are safe now, among friends, what?' He winked, 'Let me be mother. Coffee, tea?' C poured coffee for the three of us.

I have to say that this manner, friendly, easy and seemingly democratic, was a pleasant surprise to me. There was no self-importance, no pomposity, no haughtiness. Later I came to meet three more Cs, both former and active, and it must be said that this one was not an exception. However, this friendliness never led to familiarity or cronyism. It was rather respect shown to one's juniors' dignity while observing the nuances of subordination. The latter never translated into rudeness or impertinence of the superiors, or subservience of the subordinates. There was something for my KGB colleagues to learn here…

By the way, C is the only person in the SIS hierarchy who is addressed 'Sir' or 'Chief'. All the rest, no matter of what rank or age, are on first-name terms. Certainly that used to be the case; I do not know about nowadays. One's position on the Service ladder was revealed via intonation and other nuances so characteristic of English discourse.

It seems that I had made a good impression on C. 'It has been only two years, but what years, so eventful. It is impossible to overestimate your contribution.' These were his words. When he asked me what I wanted to do next, I did not hesitate. It would be a great honour if I were allowed to carry on working for the Service. My work had been interrupted because of an 'accident'; such was always the risk in our business. However, I wanted to continue to contribute in any way that I could.

C smiled, nodded towards Richard. 'I thought so. Richard shall see to the details.'

Later that night there was a friendly, informal dinner where I was introduced to several of the Service's directors and their deputies.

Later on, perhaps six months in, they might begin using me operationally. However, right now, before the July G-7 meeting that was almost upon us, there was a pile of analytical work to contribute to, reports and forecasts on the immediate and middle-term prospects of Gorbachev and the USSR based on everything that I knew on the topic, from all the sources that I had access to.

Three days later, I moved to a comfortable service flat half an hour's drive from London. The windows overlooked the Thames, all set in green meadows and leafy groves. There was plenty of fresh air, it was easy to breathe, think and work here. Every other day I went to the Office; at the same time, I was carefully selecting anti-surveillance routes and traps, as well as public telephones from where I could make a secure, undetected, overseas call.

The only news from 'the other side' so far was a report that Elena and Max had left for Moscow; my KGB colleagues saw them off at Schwechat Airport, Vienna. There were no formal enquiries yet from the Soviet Ministry of Foreign Affairs regarding my disappearance. Waiting, waiting, waiting… There was nothing worse than that.

From the fifteenth to the seventeenth of July, London hosted the Big Seven, or G-7, summit. The heads of the seven richest countries of the world gathered to discuss the most important events and trends, to work out common positions and to determine how to keep this world turning. Indeed, everything depended on these seven and their stance. The Soviet President Mikhail Gorbachev took part as a guest; he had virtually forced his way into the London summit. The Germans and the French supported his insistent requests; the Americans and the British reluctantly agreed. However, all his pleas for direct financial help to the USSR ended in assurances of friendship, of support for his reforms and other empty declarations. Nothing binding, nothing concrete. Group Seven offered him every support, short of real help. Gorbachev was pampered, cosseted and sent home empty-handed, to the country that he had bankrupted and left for his cronies to loot.

Indeed, why would they give him anything? The West believed that the disintegration of the Soviet Union had become irreversible. They had already started playing games, informally, behind their pet Gorbachev's back: with the Balkans, the Ukrainians, the Belorussians, the Azeris. A whisper here, a promise there…

Gorbachev became, quite obviously, used, soiled goods. A tired horse ready to be put out to grass. He had received his reward the previous month: the Nobel Peace Prize. What more could he expect? They patted him on the back, showed him a lot of affection, flattered him, plied him with champagne for the road and then sent home, none the wiser. He had done his job well: he had capitulated unconditionally before the West in the Cold War; liquidated the Soviet Empire and, as of that moment, had practically ruined the USSR itself, to all intents and purposes. What more could he do? Go and take a well-deserved rest.

He had achieved more than his so-called partners had dreamed about for decades; they would not have dared even think of it in earnest. And it had happened!

Now it was high time for new players to take the stage in Moscow: those who had been waiting behind the scenes for their hour to strike. Gorbachev had lost the ground under his feet, lost his position hopelessly. His authority was all but gone. The holiday season was near, which meant that the self-contented victors would not be so alert. The moment had come for resolute action: enough of casting stones; time to gather them! The country could still be rescued. This was it, the moment my controller Otto told me to look out for! I held my breath and waited, watching the TV news several times a day.

The weather in the beginning of August was fine; hot, even. There was much less work to do now that most people had gone away on holidays. I decided to spend a few days in Bournemouth, at the seaside: it had excellent sandy beaches and the water was warm enough to swim in. If only I could have a splash there with Max, with Elena watching us, laughing…

Richard cleared my little break and offered an escort (not a long-legged blonde, but a quiet, polite muscleman), which I politely rejected. He gave me a round-the-clock telephone number just in case, jotted down the name of my hotel and asked me to check in with him every evening. I did not suspect for a minute that I would be on my own in Bournemouth – someone would be asked to look after me – so I chose a good moment before leaving to make a phone call. Having checked carefully for surveillance, I dashed to a public phone inside the large John Lewis department store in Oxford Street and dialled the usual number. I was surprised to hear a live, female voice at the other end, in Madrid.

'*Si?*'

'Oh hello, this is Ayden. Can I speak with Joseph?'

'He is away now, on holiday,' the voice said, with a heavy Spanish accent. 'Call again in two weeks.'

Ring off, short beeps. Well, all right: contact in two weeks, and now off to the seaside. I felt good, at last.

I returned from Bournemouth ten days later, well-rested and tanned, and sat down to write an analytical report – a new assignment from the Friends, a 'request' from the SIS Director for Counterintelligence and Security himself. On the morning of the nineteenth of August, having done my morning exercises and taken a shower, I made some strong coffee and huddled in an armchair in front of my TV set.

I turned on the BBC News and was stunned, totally dumbfounded: their live report showed tanks in the streets of Central Moscow! I switched to the CNN. The same picture: crowded streets, tanks rolling past the shop windows, barely avoiding the angry, shouting civilians. The announcer kept repeating the breaking news: a state of emergency had been declared in Moscow; Gorbachev was removed from power and isolated in his holiday villa in Foros, the Crimea; the most prominent Soviet leaders had taken over the office and established the State Emergency Committee (SEC). They included my direct superior, the KGB Chairman Vladimir Kryuchkov! I had expected something of this kind to occur, but all the same, the news caught me by surprise. At last! These people would stop the country from sliding into the abyss. But the tanks…It was confusing.

I rang up the Office and spoke with my controller. He told me to be within reach; they would summon me if needed. Well, I stayed at home, glued to the screen, greedily watching the news. I would call my Moscow controller later; the two weeks had just expired.

The more I watched, the more my feelings overwhelmed me: at first hope, then amazement, followed by disbelief, bitterness, grief, desperation and hopelessness.

The bodies of the three protesters crushed by tanks; the huge tricolour, the white, red and blue flag of Imperial Russia, being carried by a multitude of Muscovites through the streets, towards the Kremlin; the shaking hands of the SEC Chairman Yanayev, the acting President of the USSR, as he spoke at a news conference. Boris Yeltsin, the President of its largest part, the Russian Federation, standing on a tank, addressing the cheering crowds.

The leaders of the SEC were the most powerful men in the Soviet Union. They held in their hands the armed forces, state security and the police, industry – everything: the Minister of Defence, the Chairman of the KGB, the Minister of Internal Affairs, the Minister of Heavy

Industry, the Vice President of the USSR, the majority of the all-powerful Central Committee of the ruling Communist Party. Yet in just three days, from the nineteenth to the twenty-first of August 1991, they somehow managed to fail miserably, and lose it all!

Really, power per se means nothing – not without the political will and the resolve to use it. And these misfits demonstrated a complete ineptness, an inability to act resolutely and independently. They kept turning to Gorbachev, the man that they themselves had deposed (unless it was just a game?) Whatever the truth of it, the results were the same: they lost the momentum, the initiative and, consequently, the power.

The power that had practically fallen out of Gorbachev's hands, and that the impotent SEC leaders proved to be miserably unable to recover, was picked up by the newly elected and ambitious Russian president, Boris Yeltsin. At the same time, on the outskirts of the empire, the local feudal lords became kings. The parts were destroying the whole.

Although the USSR had passed away de-facto, it would struggle on for another six months de-jure. A state that had become dysfunctional to all intents and purposes, still continued to exist on paper.

Its final death sentence was signed in December 1991 in a mansion in Belovezhsky Forest by the new leaders of Russia, Ukraine and Belarus, hungry for real and unrestricted power. The enormous state fell apart, having lost half its population and a quarter of its territory; Russia had inherited the rest. Indeed, it was a cataclysm of universal proportions.

What did it all mean to me, personally? The game has grown far more complicated. Now I faced a huge number of unknown factors and variables in the problem I had to solve.

The KGB Chairman Kryuchkov and his first Deputy Grushko were arrested and remanded in custody. I could not imagine what might have happened to my Deputy and the other leading KGB Headquarters officers. One thing was clear: the HQ was thoroughly purged; those who were not arrested or charged were lying low, trying to wait it out. The FCD Chief Shebarshin, the Head of Intelligence and my former direct boss, was fired and sent into retirement.

President Yeltsin appointed a new Chairman of the KGB, Vadim Bakhtin, his political crony. The sole purpose of this appointment was 'Getting rid of the KGB'; later Bakatin himself would publish a book with this very title. Dismantling, castrating, re-assigning. This involved downsizing, mass redundancies, structural changes and staffing chaos, with all the dreadful consequences for operational efficiency and effectiveness.

Thus, the country which I came from, and the organisation which I served, were now no more.

So, I faced the eternal Russian question: What to do? What the hell was I going to do?

First of all, I decided, I would try to get in touch with the controllers of Operation Traveller. If that proved impossible, I'd try to test the water with my own department, the FCD. However, since I was, to them, a defector, this route would most likely be a non-starter. Still, it was worth a try. The worst thing was that, in the circumstances, it was unclear who I could talk to, and, most importantly, who I could trust. Now it was every man for themselves, everyone was playing their own game… Moreover, it was extremely important not to blow my cover and betray myself to the English, or I would end up between a rock and a hard place.

Failing that… well, there would be no such thing as a Plan B if Plan A didn't work. And would it? I couldn't possibly know, couldn't even guess. I could only wait and see. Time would bring a decision; I needed reliable information for ideas to crystallise.

A week later I made my first post-coup contact attempt. I dry-cleaned thoroughly; this time I used a bicycle, which I had bought recently in order to keep in shape. An excellent tool of the trade, a bicycle is. It can get you where no car would ever go – woods, parks or one-way streets, for example – and no one can catch up with you on foot. And if they tried to run after you? You would spot the runner right away. Watchers can use bicycles or a motorcycle, too, but that is less effective, as a trained eye would easily detect a tail. All that is left to the watchers is to cover the probable directions and areas where you might be headed; this requires large resources, both human and monetary.

It was all clear. Having enjoyed my ride, I made a call from a pre-selected public phone to Madrid, then to Amsterdam – only to hear: 'The number you have dialled does not exist.' I rang the London emergency number that Otto gave me at out last meeting, just before my defection. The call was answered by a boorish man who snorted curtly, 'Wrong number, mate,' and hung up.

The following day, on Wednesday, I went to London. On the way to Century House, in a lane off Praed Street close to Paddington Station, I left a signal calling for an urgent meeting: the same old vertical red line on a wall. If, exactly seven days later, I saw it crossed by a horizontal line, the rendezvous would take place on the same day in a safe flat that was rented by a front company near Marble Arch.

The following Wednesday there was no cross on the wall. My 'exclamation mark' remained as was, standing out like a sore thumb.

This was not merely a hang up. This was a complete break up.

Meanwhile, the developments back in my mother country gained momentum, leaving me less and less room to manoeuvre. Newspapers and television, to say nothing of my British colleagues, reported a chain of odd suicides and car crashes, which took the lives of a number of top government officials, both civilian, military and from Special Services.

Immediately after the SEC disaster, General Pugo, the Minister of Internal Affairs, and the former Chief of General Staff, General Akhromeev, ended their own lives, apparently. They were followed by the Chief of the Central Committee Administrative Department and his deputy, who allegedly chose to jump out of their windows: these people, by a strange coincidence, were in charge of all the financial affairs of the ruling Communist Party, now suspended by Yeltsin.

There were a number of other deaths, accidental or voluntary, less conspicuous perhaps, but very significant and indicative to insiders… All those who knew too much, or who might be in a position to take over office, were being removed.

Looking on the bright side, the Soviet Ministry of Foreign Affairs had at last enquired with the British Foreign Office whether I, by any chance, happened to be in the United Kingdom. The answer was polite and affirmative: alive and well, and granted political asylum. If I were willing to contact the Soviet consul, there would be no obstacles as far as the British authorities were concerned.

Now it was official, at last I could ring my wife and parents!

Feeling overexcited and nervous, I called Elena first. My heart was pounding; my hands trembled as I dialled our Moscow number. For security reasons, I had to call from Century House, from the Friends: ostensibly to prevent my former KGB colleagues from figuring out my whereabouts. I understood that my British colleagues wanted to listen in. I didn't care: let them listen, and record it too, if it made them happy.

Elena was dry and concise. She told me in an even, calm tone that they were fine and didn't want for anything. She refused to call Max to the receiver: said that he was with our neighbours, playing with his friend. I could hear his voice though, shouting: 'Mama, Mama, who is it?'

I dialled the next number with a heavy heart. My father picked up the receiver. A cough, a short 'Hello?' He did not even sound surprised. His conversation was guarded, stilted; clearly he knew that the line was tapped. He called for my mother; there were tears in her trembling voice, but these were tears of joy. Yes, I am well, in good health, everything in order. I will call regularly now, I promised. I put down the receiver, shaking, my head dizzy.

Richard, from whose office I made the calls, looked at me with sympathy and poured a double Scotch. One for himself, too. We drank. Then I left for home, so that the next day, with a head slightly aching from a hangover, I could drown myself in work. Destiny itself had made the choice for me.

This was the end of an era. On 25th December 1991 the official flag of the Soviet Union that flew over the Kremlin was lowered for the last time and removed, forever. The symbolism was heavy: not only Christmas Day, but Western-style[3] Christmas Day. For me, the Sun set in the East that Christmas.

The way back East was forbidden for the Traveller. So, instead he wandered on to the West, where dawn was breaking.

---

[3] **Russian Orthodox Christmas Day is celebrated two weeks later, on the 7th of January.**

Chapter 3. THE TURKISH GAMBIT

Several months of debriefing flew by. It was interesting at first, but grew rather tiring after a while, the endless questions, all the ‘Please tell me…’ or ‘How did they…?’; ‘Look, do you recognise anyone in these photos?’; ‘Do you know this person?’; all the repetitions, specifications and clarifications asked for. Dull, bordering on boring.

Those who asked were not just the Friends, but also the Cousins, the Sisters (the Security Service, MI5), friends of the Friends – liaison services, both in England and on overseas trips. This routine was sweetened by the various social events, some excursions and sightseeing, and invariably lunches and dinners: generous, sometimes lavish, always liquid. That was all very well, but damaging to the liver.

One day I was invited to the Office to see my old acquaintance Kate. I have to say I was happy to see her after almost a year. When she told me that the debriefing had come to an end, I was even happier.

'Den, now the main question: what would you like to do next?'

'Holiday?' I grinned.

'That goes without saying. You deserve it. Her Majesty will be glad to pay for it. But I am asking you about something else: what do you want to do with your life? We are prepared to offer you a few jobs to try and begin a normal, civilian career. Of course, we will be there to help you and guide you when needed.'

I was looking at Kate, not listening, my mind somewhere else. Was she beautiful! Damn pretty! What I really needed now was a girl like her. All this time since my arrival in the UK I had had no private life at all, apart from a few sessions with prostitutes – but this sex for money was answering a purely physical urge; a man needs to stay healthy. Oh, to have a proper romance, with all the excitement, all the emotions. That would be so refreshing…

‘Den?’

She gave me a start. I suddenly realised that my gaze was glued to her deep cleavage.

‘Oh, uhm, certainly, Kate. I’ve given it a lot of thought, of course. I believe that the so-called normal life is a bit boring. If I could… I would prefer operational work for the Office. Is that possible, do you think?’

From the expression on her face I understood that the Friends had considered this option, too. She winked at me coyly: ‘Well, once a spy, always a spy, right? It does suck you in, true? I’ll report it to the boss. Let’s wait for an answer, and now – off you go. Holidays!’

She was spot on about once a spy, always a spy. Once you tasted operational work, in the field or in the cold, whatever you call it; once you tasted it, everything else seems boring and bland, flavourless.

Our work is gripping; it takes it out of you completely and has no mercy for failures. It requires a hundred per cent intellectual and nervous engagement, physical force and deftness, the ability to think and analyse on your feet, to shed your skin like a snake and to change your colour like a chameleon: quickly and unnoticed by those around you. You must adapt to changing circumstances and fit in seamlessly; become the best friend of an enemy in order to betray him and stab him in the back, when the time comes. You have to make decisions on which destinies and lives depend… and be ready to be sacrificed yourself in the name of higher interests, whatever they might happen to be.

What about this incomparable feeling of belonging to a secret brotherhood, the elite of elites, a tiny world sealed off from outsiders; the possession of a secret, to which only a handful of those initiated is privy… Indeed, even if you add together all the leading intelligence services on the planet, we are just a few thousand of the billions of people… Does all this make you feel exceptional, chosen?

Of course it does! This work is exciting, captivating; it gives you the utmost satisfaction and elation when you succeed and a deep sorrow and frustration when you fail. You want to experience the whole spectrum of feelings again and again. Truly, this is a narcotic. One cannot just refuse it.

And now that my old Master had vanished into thin air, I was free to serve the new one, the Master whom I found very worthy and wanted to be loyal to.

Upon my return from my holidays in Rome and Florence (I'd dreamed for a long time of exploring that great culture, the cradle of the European civilisation), I was invited to see Hugh. He was head of the SIS group in charge of non-proliferation of nuclear weapons and fissile materials.

After the disintegration of the USSR this group was busy twenty-four hours, seven days a week, and this is not an overstatement. The threat was real, tangible: nuclear warheads were being stolen from depots and sold to the highest bidder. Whereas in Russia proper they were kept relatively safely, the situation in the other post-Soviet republics was nightmarish.

However, this was only half the trouble: the Americans and the English could, more or less, effectively control the storage of warheads in the Ukraine and Kazakhstan (from where they were being transferred to Russia, according to an international agreement). What they absolutely could not control were the vast, practically unaccountable resources of fissile materials, including nuclear waste. These could provide material for 'dirty bombs', or simply be used, for example, to poison a water reservoir: a terrorist's dream. Explode a conventional bomb filled with depleted uranium in a city centre, and what happens? The inhabitants have to be evacuated, the streets and buildings thoroughly deactivated. Panic, chaos. The clean-up could easily take years. The city in the meantime turns into a desert.

Thus, we were focused on finding and wiping out the channels of illegal export of such materials from the former Soviet Union. They multiplied like the mythical Hydra's heads. Cut one off, two grew in its stead. Small wonder: the supply was there, the demand as well, and human greed is boundless.

Before becoming a spy, Hugh was a scientist, a physicist and chemist doing his research at Cambridge.

He could not possibly suspect just how useful his specialist knowledge would be in his next profession. They made an excellent spy of Hugh the scientist; the combination pre-determined his appointment as head of the non-proliferation group.

I heard on the grapevine that Hugh had proved himself a pro in the field: his deeds were rumoured to be impressive. Outwardly he looked like a geek, a bit slow, a bit clumsy: a typical academic; a nerd. You would never guess that he could hide a dagger under his lab coat.

'Alistair (one of SIS Directors, Deputy Chief) has assigned you to our little club, Dennis. So welcome on board, as they say!' Hugh said, wasting no time; simultaneously, he was busily rifling through stacks of paper on his desk. 'Bugger, where did I put it? Never mind. Come along. Let me introduce you to the team. We'll have a briefing on a new operation at the same time. You're lucky! Into the fire at once; no time to get bored.'

He had finally found a thin green folder on his desk, and we went one floor down, to my new workplace.

……

One week later, several completely ordinary tourists arrived at Istanbul Ataturk international airport from different countries.

A young couple travelled from London on a Thomas Cook budget charter plane.

Germany's Lufthansa delivered three men in their early forties, typical second-rate office workers who had escaped their wives and children for a few days to paint the town red.

Lastly, Czech Airlines from Prague unloaded a man of about thirty-five, athletic, dark haired, grey eyed, sporting a goatee beard and a scar on his right cheek. According to his passport, he was a citizen of Latvia. Judging by his clothes, a successful businessman. His name was Raimonds Peters, also known at the Office as Dennis. In other words, me.

All the arrivals checked in at different hotels in the central Sultanahmet district. The old streets of the historic borough made up a labyrinth, abounding in hotels of all sizes and classes, shops, restaurants, cafes, shisha bars, brothels and what not. It was a human anthill, buzzing with tourists from all parts of the world; sellers and peddlers of anything one could think of; onlookers, passers-by, pilgrims attracted by the famous Blue Mosque and the ancient Byzantine St. Sophia Cathedral. It was easy to get lost in the crowds. Just the ticket.

Having left their luggage in their hotels, the guests wandered about town and, by 5 p.m., somehow found themselves in room 201 of the Four Seasons hotel. This room was occupied by Jean-Claude, a tourist from Belgium, who had arrived the previous day. Actually, his name was Vincent, the half-French co-ordinator of the operation with whom I shared an office in London.

All the parts were learned by heart. Everyone knew exactly what he or she must do according to Plan A and Plan B (which meant failure). Tomorrow was Tuesday, the day reserved for reconnaissance, or reccie for short: each support group familiarised themselves with the scene, going carefully through every detail. The following day was our D-day. The launch of Operation Step – the 'sting' operation designed to flush them out and destroy them: the illegal arms dealers supplying terrorists.

I was to meet Murat, our old contact. By the way, when I say 'our', from now on I only mean the SIS and nothing more. I still tried to contact the Traveller's controllers, once every two months or so; but so far to no avail. This was more out of curiosity than out of sense of some residual loyalty to my former masters; I no longer doubted where my loyalties lay.

Murat was a former officer of the Turkish Gendarmerie who, fifteen years ago, offered his services to the British Vice Consul in Istanbul, who was in fact an undercover SIS man.

Murat was not entirely straightforward. Historically, since the Second World War, there have been no straightforward agents in Istanbul: they were all doubles or triples. You recruit a man, and he reports to you in exchange for money. However, he sells the same information to your competitors: the German Abwehr during the war, or the Russian KGB after (or the SVR, as the Russian Foreign Intelligence is now known). In principle, information was treated as marketable goods, to be sold to the highest bidder, including drug dealers and terrorists. This was business. Everyone knew it, but it was not something that was freely discussed. It was the local mentality; so what can you do?

Of course, some people observed the rules of the game. The rules, however, are unwritten and adaptable to circumstances. The greedy ones and the weirdos were from time to time removed – that is, physically eliminated. The Germans, the Russians, ourselves, we all did a bit of weeding. However, the majority of such assets were still used, with fingers crossed. Not least, in order to supply the competition with chickenfeed through these doubles and triples. But it gets tricky here – how do you tell if you are a supplier, rather than a receiver? The Turkish authorities, the police and counterintelligence were fully aware of these games, but let the play continue – unless someone crossed the line, and harmed their interests. As a matter of fact, they themselves used the same agents, too…

The Office did not inform their Turkish counterparts about Operation Step. They might be allies, but one never knows. The operation was fully deniable, albeit informally blessed by the Foreign Secretary himself, who also whispered a word in the Prime Minister's ear. A failure or a leak meant that all the participants of Operation Step became personally liable, as neither the Foreign Office nor the Service would step in for them (unless there were some benefits to be reaped by doing so). There was no official sanction, nobody cleared the operation formally; a silly, adventurous initiative by some rogue individuals; we will look into this, sort it out, the culprits will be punished…

Yet we believed we'd be successful!

Politics was a game, but the national interest mattered above all. A healthy sense of adventure, that necessary feature of operational work, called us forward, too. Besides, the Office, unlike the politicians, does not leave its own in dire straits; even unofficially, it will do its best to pull you through if you are in a mess. We all knew it well.

Now, back to our Turk. For several years, this Murat had been supplying the SIS with very valuable information about the illegal international arms trade. He was completely immersed in this topic and had become 'one of them', an irreplaceable go-between for the black-market arms dealers. Naturally, we did not know who else he provided with information. Although he was a sensible man, we decided that it was better to be safe than sorry.

Murat was to be used blindly. His task was to get in touch with Raimonds Peters, the Latvian arms dealer and a former officer of the Soviet army. Peters was ostensibly looking for a buyer. He had a consignment of some very interesting, hot, goods. Murat was not to know that Peters, that is I, was also an SIS man. The deal was promising, and the commission would be very good. We were curious to see what Murat would report to the SIS after the first rendezvous.

On Wednesday lunchtime I came to the restaurant at the Sura hotel. Our 'lovebirds' were already sitting at a table, chewing the delicious Adana kebab. At the same time, the couple was surreptitiously making video and sound recordings, using a special camera and microphone hidden in the girl's handbag.

I took a seat. About fifteen minutes later a man appeared in the doorway. Fortyish, sporty, lean. He looked around quickly, saw a white cap with SPQR logo on my table and approached, leisurely.

What followed was an exchange of code phrases. This wordplay is an all-important and instrumental part of the tradecraft: one must be a hundred per cent certain that one is speaking with the right person.

Question: 'Hello, is the wine here not too expensive?'

Answer: 'I recommend Efes beer, it is better and cheaper.'

If just one word, or the order of words, differs from the prearranged version, the balloon goes up: alarm, all cancelled, retreat.

Murat smiled broadly and sat down at my table.

He spoke fluent English; I deliberately emphasised the East European accent

‘I have a potential client for your kind of goods; he is here in Istanbul. However, before I introduce you, he wants to know more about the goods and the supplier.’

Murat was a charming man and nobody’s fool. He could say the most trivial or controversial or even tough things so that they sounded like compliments, just short of flattery. A true son of the Orient, of course.

‘Well, the goods are as follows: uranium 235, strontium 90 and Red Mercury. Plenty of everything. I and my partners are all military officers, some retired, some active. I cannot say more for obvious reasons. We have a reliable supply channel and could start deliveries tomorrow. I have samples for the client to examine. They are not free; you know the price surely.’

‘A thousand Dollars per gram of 235?’ Murat asked this question in Russian, testing me.

‘*Da* (Yes),’ I replied in Russian, too.

‘Enriched? To how many per cent?’

‘Ninety.’

‘This is too little for such a price. It will need to be upgraded, you know.’

I winked to Murat: ‘Depends on what you need it for. I will have a word with the buyer. There are options available.’

‘All right then, and what is this Red Mercury exactly? Does it actually exist? I heard that this is all a scam. Please understand, the buyer is VERY serious; my reputation is at stake.’

‘I am not sure about the rest, but in our case, it is just a term. A code, if you like. I am certain that your client will be VERY interested, if he is interested in such things as uranium. You won’t be out of pocket, don’t worry.’

Murat was studying my face. I, in turn, was inconspicuously checking his, hoping that my make-up artists (the same English lovebirds in the corner) had done a good job and that my features looked natural at close quarters. It seems that he was satisfied

‘Nevertheless? I need to know.’

‘Plutonium 239.’

Murat breathed in noisily. Just ten kilos of weapons-grade plutonium was enough to manufacture an atomic bomb. Small, compact, devastating.

‘You have samples of this?’

‘Yes, I brought them. Sufficient for testing. But they are not free, either, dear Murat.’

‘Oh, please. My client has been in business for a long time and knows the rules.’

The Turk bowed across the table. His black eyes were glimmering. He must have sensed a good commission coming his way, as well as a bonus from the SIS (I wondered if he would tell the SIS about the plutonium at all).

‘Mister Raimonds, I need to have a word with the client. I suggest we should meet again here, in…’ Murat looked at his gold Rolex. Don’t they love all that glitters, I thought; although I was equipped in a similar fashion: a

Patek Philippe watch and a heavy signet ring with a ruby solitaire. Part of the arms dealer's uniform.

'Let's meet at seven tonight. That will give me enough time. Please have your samples ready.'

'OK, 7 p.m. suits. Same place.'

He put on the table a piece of paper with a mobile number scribbled on it.

'This number is only for liaison between you and me, and only when you are in Istanbul. No one else must know it, just in case.'

'Of course. See you at seven.'

We rose from the table and shook hands.

Those three 'second-rate office workers' who arrived from Germany kept the situation around the hotel under control. They and the 'lovebirds' from England were my support team. They were all very experienced officers who had been through hell and back, literally. Special Boat Service (SBS) veterans, anti-surveillance experts, the jacks-of-all-trades of Her Majesty's Special Forces.

With them covering your back, there was no need to be afraid of fire, water or terrorists. On top of that, the girl was a smasher and a charmer: she could set up such a honey trap… One could never imagine that Marion, with her slim, elegant fingers, was quite capable of breaking the Adam's apple of a man twice her size and coolly checking her lipstick afterwards. However, *errare humanum est*. He is lifeless who is faultless. One cannot relax even with such a great team, not in our business.

Having taken a leisurely walk past St. Sophia to the Bosporus, I descended into the old town. Here, traversing one of the numerous cafés, I read a signal: all clear, no tail this time (one of the team was nursing a coffee cup at a pavement table). Well, now I could head straight to the Four Seasons, go once again through every detail with Vincent, collect the samples, say a prayer for luck and… go ahead.

I approached the Sura hotel at seven. My team took positions around it from 6 p.m., keeping careful watch over the surroundings. At the entrance to the hotel, I glanced quickly at a table near a small café across the narrow street. An elderly lady tourist with a creased face and grey curls was sipping tea there, her handbag next to her, on the table. A signal from Marion: Murat is not alone, he's brought company.

Just as we thought he would. We had foreseen that the client would want to make sure I was clean and send his watchers to prevent me from bringing a tail to the rendezvous. This is why my team positioned themselves in advance, keeping under control the four potential directions in which I could be moving from the hotel. Plus, we had Marion in reserve.

Murat was waiting for me in the lobby, sprawled in a deep armchair. He noticed me and rose towards me, smiling broadly:

'My dear Raimonds, I am so glad to see you again. Let's not waste time. We are expected. The samples are with you?'

Silently, I lifted slightly a souvenir plastic bag with some advert printed on it. There was a small, hermetically sealed container inside.

‘In case you have a mobile phone or a pager, it is best to leave it for safekeeping with the concierge. Jasheet-bei does not like surprises.’

Jasheet-bei? Wow. I had read his SIS file in the Office. He was also known as Nazim and Tariq Ben Salah; however, we were not hundred per cent sure that these names went with one and the same man. His photo was unavailable, so we had to make do with descriptions. Well, this was going to be an interesting excursion…

A thought flashed across my mind: it was lucky that, just before leaving London on this mission, I had been to the SIS’s trusted solicitor and there, in his Gray’s Inn office, signed a will and a life insurance policy. There was a special form for the latter: I, so and so, am going on Her Majesty’s business, the nature of which is confidential… etc. No public insurance company would ever underwrite or issue such a policy – who wants to lose money when the odds are 50/50? I put down Elena and Max as beneficiaries. The Friends assured me that they would get the money, in case of a claim. This was a soothing thought. A few hundred thousand pounds would not go amiss. My son needed a good education. But I would still prefer to hand him the money personally, albeit not as much and a bit later. When he joined me in England.

I handed over my pager to Murat. He passed it on to the porter, said something in Turkish.

'Fantastic. And now, let me be your guide.' Murat made an inviting gesture and moved towards the exit.

We found ourselves in a crowded street, walked along for a hundred yards or so, and turned into a narrow lane. It was completely deserted, save for an elderly Turk at the end, who was busy sorting out his equally elderly scooter. We went past. The man, his face hardly visible for black and grey stubble, did not give us a second look. Well, who was he, a mere nobody; that is, if you did not know that this 'Turk' was in fact Steve from Tunbridge Wells, Kent.

Murat tugged my sleeve and we dived into another lane. There was a whole labyrinth of them here. One more sharp turn, and we were across the street from a small antiques shop; we walked briskly towards it and entered through a glass door with white curtains. A young man was sitting at the counter: he barely looked at us, said nothing and went back to paging through some books. We crossed the small shop floor, suspect 'antiques' scattered everywhere. Murat opened a service door and let me go in first. We climbed one flight of stairs and stopped at a solid carved wooden door. He knocked: three single knocks, two double. The door opened and Murat and I found ourselves in a big, semi-dark entrance hall. Facing us, there stood a broad-shouldered man in a business suit. Another one shut the door behind us: I saw his bulky figure out of the corner of my eye.

'Jasheet-bei will see you in minute. In the meantime, please excuse me.' He approached me with a hand-held metal detector, checked I was clean, then repeated the procedure on Murat. I could not place the man's accent. The appearance was North Caucasus. A Chechen? A Dagestani?

'Please sit down. Place the bag here.' He checked it first with the detector, then with a Geiger radiation gauge, and nodded in satisfaction. 'Please give me your documents.'

I put my Latvian passport in his open palm. A genuine one, the Office had assured me.

'Just a minute, please.' The man disappeared behind a heavy curtain that concealed another door.

While we were waiting, I tried to figure out if my team would manage to locate the meeting site without betraying themselves to the opposition. It seemed unlikely. Jasheet's people had followed me and Murat; this meant that my team had to keep a discreet distance to avoid being spotted. They could only work out the approximate site location and approach it cautiously, quietly taking the area under control. Knowing this, I realised that I could not rely on them too much, not at the moment. I was on my own in Jasheet's lair.

The curtain moved and the same bodyguard emerged. He stopped, holding it open. A dark silhouette appeared in the opening, and a man entered the room. He was below medium height, stocky, round-faced, with jet-black hair and a well-groomed short beard with grey strands in it. He crossed the floor and sat himself in an armchair facing me.

Black business suit, a black shirt with a stand-up collar, Iranian style. He gazed at me with dark brown eyes; bejewelled golden rings glimmered on his short, hairy fingers. There were two on his left hand and a massive signet on his right.

'Good evening and welcome, Mr Peters. Allow me to introduce myself: Jasheet-bei. Or simply Jasheet to my friends, in case we become friends,' said the man in a pleasant, velvety voice.

He said it in Russian! With an Oriental accent, but absolutely correctly. He must have studied in the Soviet Union, we trained a lot of them… He is testing me, obviously. I replied in Russian, but with a slight Baltic lilt:

'I am very glad to meet you, esteemed Jasheet-bei, and I hope that we shall have a mutually beneficial partnership.'

'While we talk, eh – tea?'

I nodded in agreement.

‘So, while we talk, my expert next door will have a look at the samples, a preliminary examination, so to speak,’ Jasheet-bei continued in English. His aide came up with three glasses of Turkish tea on a silver tray, picked up my plastic bag and vanished behind the curtain. The second one stood at the door, staring at me and Murat.

‘My dear Murat, now I must ask you to wait downstairs, please. With respect.’

Having heard this, Murat bowed slightly and left us.

The following thirty minutes or so we discussed the volumes and supply channels and prices, of course. The first consignment was to be twenty kilos of plutonium 239, the weapons-grade stuff, or ‘Red Mercury’ as we agreed to call it from then on, for security and convenience. Jasheet liked this code name: in the early 1990s Red Mercury was a hot item. Everyone on the black and grey market had heard of it, and some claimed to trade it. In fact, no one knew for certain what it really was. Some said that this agent could augment a bomb’s explosive power, many times over. Others were convinced that it was a super-powerful toxic agent. There was even a theory that Red Mercury could turn metals into gold, but that smacked of medieval alchemy.

The realists believed it to be a scam, 1990s style. Why not? The black-market demand for explosives and poisons of all kinds was huge, and the smoking ruins of the USSR could throw up absolutely anything.

The aide emerged noiselessly from behind the curtains, bent over Jasheet and whispered something into his ear. He nodded, content.

'Well, dear Mr Peters. The preliminary test was positive. The samples will be conveyed to my lab for further, proper examination. And now we can finalise the terms and conditions of the deal, can't we?'

'Certainly. Esteemed Jasheet-bei, I would like to get money for the samples. I trust you completely, but rules are rules…'

'Oh, of course.' He waved to his man, who left for a moment and returned with a brown envelope and my passport.

‘Thirty thousand dollars, correct?’

‘Indeed, esteemed Jasheet-bei,’ I carelessly stuck the envelope and the passport in my jacket pocket. ‘Now to business.’

Twenty kilos of weapons-grade plutonium were to be handed over to Jasheet-bei’s people in exactly one month, near Chop railway station, where Ukraine borders on Hungary and Slovakia. They had everything under control there, there would be no problem with the ‘window’. In return, I would receive thirty-five million US dollars, cash. Actually, plutonium was far more expensive than that, three and a half to four thousand per gram, but that was only if sold officially. One did not bargain too hard on the black market those days; you just snatched what fell from the back of the lorry and sold it quickly. I may be exaggerating a bit, but so it was, in general. The deal was very profitable for Jasheet, and Peters the arms dealer was not spoiled for choice: who would buy goods of this kind for this amount in cash, no strings attached?

We shook on the deal. All agreed.

I went down the stairs where Murat was chatting with the 'sales attendant'.

'Well, let's move on. Take me back to the hotel. There is no way I can find it on my own.'

We came out into the darkening narrow street. I answered reassuringly Murat's silent question:

'You will get your commission in a month's time, if all goes well. How do they say it around here? Inshallah?'

'Inshallah, Raimonds.'

On the way back, Murat and I discussed arrangements; soon we said goodbyes at the entrance to the Sura. I collected my pager from the porter and went to my hotel nearby, the Hagia Sophia.

The following morning, I had a flight to Prague. I also had a ticket for a Prague–Moscow flight, one day later. I left both tickets in my jacket pocket, hanging in the wardrobe in my hotel room, for the curious to see. In fact, from Prague I was to catch a train to Vienna, then a plane to London.

I was dying to know whether my team had managed to locate the meeting site and put Jasheet and his minions under surveillance. At the end of the day, the whole idea of this operation, at least at this stage, was to finally get a fix on this many-faced dealer and his channels. But that would have to wait. I'd find out once I have made it safely back to the Office.

As for now, strictly no contact. As a ruse, I placed a couple of telephone calls: to Riga, to Moscow. What else does an arms dealer do, having closed a big deal? Right, he goes to a restaurant and, after a lavish dinner, on to the girls. This was exactly what I intended to do; there was a good choice of suchlike in Prague, of excellent quality and inexpensive. One had to live up to one's cover story, after all. Never mind, it would not be a heavy burden for the British taxpayer, considering…

Afterwards, I downed a double Scotch and slept like a log.

Three days later, in Hugh's office, I found out everything that I wanted, and needed, to know. The 'need-to-know' principle is law: everyone is allowed to know only what is absolutely necessary for him to carry out his duty and do his work effectively. And not a bit more. Every serious intelligence service of the world stuck to this principle, invariably and at all levels of hierarchy. Breaches of the need-to-know rule inevitably led to appalling scandals, fiascos and the most unpleasant consequences for those involved…

So, Jasheet-bei's watchers tailed me all the way from the Sura to the rendezvous, and afterwards, from the site back to the Sura and further, to my hotel. While I was having breakfast downstairs, my room was searched; this meant they found the airline tickets to Prague and Moscow. Excellent. I had savoured my breakfast slowly, suspecting they would want to do that. Clearly it had worked.

Most importantly, our team managed to follow Jasheet-bei himself. After the meeting, he left by the back door leading to another street, and got into his car, accompanied by one of his aides. However, our 'Turk' was there with his scooter, watching. So, our boys followed Jasheet right to his lair. One of his lairs, to be exact. The other minion was followed, too, and his address established.

Now we could be sure at last that Jasheet-bei, Nazim and Tariq Ben Salah were one and the same person. Our team, the devils, somehow took a few snapshots as he was exiting the antiques shop. Experts compared the pictures and descriptions from several sources and drew their conclusions. There was no doubting it. What an active man this Jasheet-Nazim was! He had a very long form, his fingers in many pots.

'Den, now we must prepare for the finale, the endgame.' Hugh breathed out on his glasses and cleaned the foggy lenses. 'We must reduce the demand for this junk by force, and shut down the delivery channels.'

'And what about the supply?'

'While Eastern Europe is in turmoil, the supply will be there all right, driven by corruption and disorder. This is a matter of five more years, not longer, I believe. So, at the moment, we have to strike out the demand. Briefing tomorrow at ten, my office. That is all. Join the group downstairs. Oh, one more thing… Since you are the first violin in our little orchestra, I will tell you this: C has approved everything, but he does not want to know the details officially. Understood?'

Of course I understood; I was no starry-eyed freshman. All being well, you were a hero; but nobody would cover your backside in case of a failure or a scandal. Then they would be looking for a scapegoat. It was the same story everywhere. The plausible deniability was firmly in place. However, what worried me was the fact that this concept, so convenient to cover the backsides of the political masters, was ever more often used at lower levels of power. Those field players like me, the nuts and bolts of the profession, were not unduly troubled. Still, work is work. Terrorists and international criminals multiplied like rats. The fact that, at the top, they started calling our former enemies partners did not change the essence of our cause at all. Somebody had to sort out this pile of shit.

In my office, a few days later, I read a report from Murat. He described, rather eloquently, how, having cleared many hurdles, and having employed his unique resources, he managed to fulfil the Office's assignment and introduce Raimonds Peters to Jasheet-bei himself.

There was not a word about the nature of the goods, the samples, and nothing about what he knew of the business meeting that took place. Understandably, he was very interested in the success of this deal. One per cent commission of thirty-five million USD is a very serious reward. A note was attached to the report, stating that Murat was paid ten thousand pounds for the job. Truly, this chap would never be out of pocket. We would continue using him with care. Avarice is the strongest motive but it is also a double-edged sword. You have to watch it all the time, it's too easy to cut yourself…

Meanwhile, the preparation for the deal was in full swing. Peters' people were in touch with Jasheet-Nazim's people. Soon there was to be another meeting in Istanbul to finalise the details of the goods-for-cash exchange.

We tried to foresee the smallest of nuances, the unlikeliest of options. The trouble was that Jasheet could be anywhere at the time of the handover: Hungary, Slovakia, Ukraine.

Notifying the local services of our sting operation was out of the question for security reasons. The local authorities were so corrupt that any attempt to liaise, notify or coordinate would be practically a guarantee of a failure. There was not a shadow of doubt that an officer, or an official, having sniffed up such information, would immediately sell it to Jasheet. Money talked down there.

I visited Istanbul once more, this time with my 'partner'. We had a rendezvous in the same antiques store; by then, the samples had been thoroughly tested in a lab somewhere, the results were highly satisfactory and the trust between the parties increased. We were still carefully frisked with a metal detector. Nothing personal, just business.

According to the plan, the seller had to bring the goods to a site near Chop. From there, my people and Jasheet's representatives, each protected by their own guard, would follow to a rented garage, where the goods would be tested again on special equipment. Simultaneously, Jasheet's people and my representatives would be counting the cash in a barn near the village of Velke Trakany in Slovakia. As soon as both teams across the border were finished with their checks, they would communicate by satellite phone and confirm that all was clear. Jasheet's people would collect their goods, we would pick up our cash and all would go their own way.

Each side was responsible for their own security and for the safety of the goods and the money, respectively. It was agreed that during the deal, each party, both in Chop and in Velke Trakany, was allowed to have up to five armed people, including guards. Neither Jasheet nor I were supposed to be present during the handover. We were to communicate via satellite phone as required.

Jasheet was our prize trophy. But how to seize him? My whole group racked their brains over it. Most likely, he would be somewhere nearby; but 'nearby' could mean any of the three nearby countries, with all the complications that involved. Also, he could easily oversee the deal from somewhere else: Jordan, for example.

Then it dawned on us: the bodyguard! We'd managed to follow one of the two heavies from the rendezvous site to his flat in Istanbul. After that, he was put under very tight surveillance. We even had to bring in reinforcements from London. His three mobile telephone numbers were established. One was on permanently: most probably a link to his boss. The two others were used from time to time. The Government Communications Headquarters (GCHQ) in Cheltenham, our electronic wizards, were capable of watching the bodyguard's movements and fixing his location to ten yards' accuracy – provided that the phone was turned on. The odds that this fellow would be by Jasheet's side on the day of the deal were 70:30. This was, effectively, our only chance, in the absence of other leads.

From then on, all three telephone numbers were spied on around the clock. One of them, supposedly the work number, moved about Europe and the Middle East tirelessly. Three days in Marseilles, two in Rome, two more in Tripoli; then Doha and, finally, Amman. Hugh concluded that we were right and that the bodyguard was at Jasheet's side. We could only pray that he'd keep the same number until the date of the deal.

Hugh prepared a team of action men, all ex-Special Forces seconded to the Office, officially known as 'increment'. We decided to place the team in Vienna, whence, if needed, they could reach any place in Eastern Europe within a few hours, in case Jasheet showed up there. We still believed that he would prefer to be close to the goods and the money on such an important day.

There were a lot of presumptions, assumptions and speculations in Operation Step. This was not something unusual or exceptional – almost anything an intelligence service does contains plenty of unknown factors, unexpected occurrences and surprises. One always tries to eliminate them; nearly always such attempts are futile. What if he remained somewhere in the Middle East? We would have to start all over again…

Three days before the handover, the increment and I relocated to Vienna. We set up base near the Schwechat Airport, just to the east of the city, by the motorway. This allowed us to move quickly to wherever our target was. We chartered a light Alouette helicopter that waited in a hangar in the private area, in case we needed more speed.

Our goods containers were, of course, imitation. Who was going to risk real weapons-grade plutonium? We had them prepared in Ukraine, to avoid crossing borders unnecessarily. Four silver-grey cylinders, hermetically sealed, completely insulated and radiation-proof. Plutonium is so toxic that even the smallest leak could be deadly. Never mind that the contents were very different this time; the packaging should be kosher and arouse no suspicions.

The seller's team consisted of my 'business partner' Vladimir – in fact it was Scotsman Ken, who spoke Russian like a native – and four escorts, with the containers in two suitcases. Exactly as agreed with Jasheet at the last meeting, they were all armed.

The team that was to receive the cash in Slovakia consisted of five men, also armed, led by a Bulgarian called Zhivko. Well, this SIS officer did have a Bulgarian mother who emigrated to England after the war.

On the morning of the handover, on Monday, both teams set off to the arranged meeting points.

The increment and I were loitering at our Vienna base, killing time and getting nervous. The previous day, on the eve of the operation, the telephone signal from Jasheet's bodyguard had disappeared. The last time it was intercepted was in Amman. After that, the signal went dead. Nothing at all for nearly twenty-four hours. Would we miss the trophy, the ultimate prize? According to the plan, all Jasheet's men were to be apprehended at the sites, if possible. Plan B stipulated the elimination of all targets: killing them, in plain language… The Treasury could use the thirty-five million dollars, and the 'plutonium' containers were designed to self-destruct. It would all be written off as another gangster war. Such feuds were quite common in those parts, and no one would be any the wiser. This was all very well, but where would we find Jasheet then? The leader of the gang would lie low, and God knows where and when he would resurface. And what further mischief he would plot. He was an extremely dangerous type, not someone we could simply let go.

The air at the base was so electrified with tension that I was afraid the fuses would blow up. The boys pretended to be calm, but you could see they all had ants in their pants. Stumpy, Mike and Greg tried to play cards; by the way they were swearing, I could tell that it wasn`t much of a game. Stanley kept his cool, but when I suggested a game of chess, he shook his head, and lit a cigarette. His eleventh in the past hour. I kept pacing from one wall to another, drawing irritated side glances from my team.

They were itching for action. And, suddenly – bingo! Two and a half hours before the exchange a message came through from the Office: they had just got a fix on the bodyguard's mobile. Not the main one that he always used, but the second one. He was in Central Budapest. The Kempinski Hotel.

The whole team breathed out with relief. This had to be it! Jasheet had decided to be close to where the action was. There was not a minute to waste. Scramble!

By motorway, it was possible to drive from Schwechat to the Hungarian capital in just over two hours. You had to cross the border, though: in those days the border checkpoints were still in place. However, the Hungarian border guards never stopped anyone who entered their country, and their Austrian colleagues could not care less who left theirs. The hardware, our guns and radios, were very well hidden, no cursory check would discover them.

Nonetheless I kept my fingers crossed when our silver metallic Toyota Landcruiser with Austrian number plates approached the checkpoint. Out of the corner of my eye I could see that my fellow travellers, save for the driver, did the same. Typical superstitious spies.

We got through all right. The Toyota accelerated smartly and tore on, towards the unknown.

To use the military term, the time was H minus 25 when we parked the Landcruiser two blocks away from the Kempinski. That is to say, twenty-five minutes to the H hour, the time of the handover. London was constantly on the line, feeding us the latest fixes on the position of the signal. They weren't changing: the client was stationary. Apparently, he had set up his control centre in the hotel room. One by one we filtered through the main entrance into the hotel. Armed with a walkie-talkie and a satellite phone, I took up my position in the bar, which was empty at the time, save for a lonely hooker sitting at the counter.

Fighting and shooting at people is not my style, unless they start it first. In this instance, I thought it would be a turkey shoot, if it went that far. There is hardly anyone who could out-fight or out-shoot Special Forces chaps.

But where was his room exactly? It had to be a suite or a junior suite, which meant the third or the fourth floor. The bearing we received from the Office confirmed this. *Ten metres accuracy? I hope you're right, you wizards*, I thought. H minus 8 minutes. We were combing through the floors, eavesdropping at every door. H plus one. The handover started in Ukraine and Slovakia; both parties had met and were now moving to the garage lab with the goods and to the barn with the money.

H plus 15 minutes. Nothing yet, two guys were working on each floor…

H plus 21. Excited voices could be heard through a door to a suite on the fourth floor, shouting in Arabic – this was it! Stanley cracked the door open with one mighty kick. He and Greg rushed inside, pistols with silencers poised. Mike and Stumpy were running up from the third floor to join them.

Inside the suite, one bodyguard was standing with his back towards the door, facing Jasheet. The dealer was shouting into the satellite phone receiver. The guard turned around, simultaneously drawing his Glock pistol from the belt. Too late: he dropped to the floor with a hole in his head. His Glock, now harmless, flew to the corner. Jasheet ran towards the other room, from which the second bodyguard was coming, his Glock ready. They collided head-on, he lost his balance and the bullet went astray, missing Greg's head by two feet…

Stanley squeezed the trigger twice to finish him off, the bullets ripping the bodyguard's chest open. Jasheet dropped to his knees, horror in his eyes; his phone continued shouting abuse in Arabic from the floor. Mike and Stumpy arrived on the scene: now was the time to take the client safely downstairs. At that moment, police sirens screamed outside. The porter had heard the bodyguard's shot and called the cops. Hard luck.

'Plan B, all retreat. Plan B, over.' This was me, on my walkie-talkie from the bar.

'Sorry, mate.' Mike put two bullets through Jasheet's heart, one more through his head just to make sure. He was thrown back like a rag doll, his blood flowing all over the expensive Tabriz rug. Stumpy picked up his briefcase on the way out, Greg took the phone, which had at last gone quiet. Everyone left the room and silently dispersed. By the time the police were blocking all the exits, the team was already far away already. H plus 38. From there, everyone had to make their own way back to base under their own steam.

Stumpy, Jasheet's crocodile skin briefcase in hand, took a leisurely walk to the British Embassy, where he handed it to the SIS head of station. The briefcase, complete with his walkie-talkie and Walther, went to London sealed in the diplomatic mailbag. Stumpy himself caught an evening British Airways flight.

While the police were busy encircling the hotel, Greg and Stanley were already leaving the car park in our Toyota, a five-minute walk from the scene, enjoying the accompaniment of the wailing sirens. They drove off to Vienna, two innocent tourists on a jolly. To add to their image of men who went to Budapest on a couple of days' break, sightseeing, whoring and shopping at cut prices, they loaded the boot with a few cartons of Tokai wine and a few bags full of some rubbish they'd bought in a supermarket on the way. British passports (albeit operational ones, with aliases) were treated by the customs officers and border guards with respect. They were simply waved through. The customs official just wondered meekly if they were bringing large quantities of cigarettes. They were the first to make it to the base.

Mike left the hotel through the kitchen. While passing some rubbish bins, he disposed of his pistol and the radio, then walked on for a while and found a Marks and Spencer store. Here he bought a business suit and changed in the public toilets, got rid of his wig, put on glasses and proceeded to the railway station. He boarded a train to Vienna.

I was sitting in the coach next to his, on the same train. Having left the bar at the Kempinski, I gave way to half a dozen policemen, running across the lobby towards the staircase, their clattering boots making a godawful noise. Without waiting for their colleagues to arrive, I left through the main exit and strode towards the Danube embankment. I got rid of the walkie-talkie and the satellite phone here – threw them, underarm, across the parapet into the grey-blue waters. I was not carrying a gun. In terms of other potential evidence, I had a Latvian passport in the name of Raimonds Peters. It had become useless anyway; so, torn to small pieces, the passport was flushed down the toilet in a nearby café. Now I only had one travel document left, the British operational one: Chris Williams. A journalist from the UK. I flagged down a taxi and rode to the railway station. Behind the window, police sirens were going hysterical; a few ambulances zoomed past, hurrying to the Kempinski.

That evening, the whole increment team, except Stumpy, gathered at the Schwechat base. The next day we presented ourselves at the Office, where we learned what had happened to our two other teams.

In Slovakia, all went smoothly. Jasheet's thugs were neatly disarmed, dropped on the floor and tied. One, the toughest of them all, had to be roughed up a bit. Not a shot was fired. Having collected two briefcases with thirty-five million US in cash, our team vanished into thin air. At the same time, they made an anonymous call to their colleagues from the Slovak security service: the SIS had an excellent working relationship with them, and our participation in the interrogations to follow was guaranteed. It would be exciting to see the feedback. The team made it home via the Czech Republic and Austria. The heavily loaded briefcases went to England via the diplomatic bag from Bratislava.

The Ukrainian part was more difficult: the buyer's team there turned out to be tougher, and quicker, so there was no avoiding a shootout. Four of theirs were shot dead; we had one casualty, a gun wound to the left side. Among those killed we discovered the body of a Ukrainian Security Service (SBU) officer. Apparently, he had been bought by Jasheet to augment the security of the handover. Unlucky. We took prisoner the leader of the client team, though. Two of our boys drove him, packed in the boot of their Niva crossover, towards Odessa. They wanted, ideally, to try and ship him home by sea from this port city on the Black Sea. The port authorities were notoriously corrupt, which should have made it possible. If not, he was to be questioned on the way (they were experts at that, too) and, once completely drained, liquidated. This is what actually happened, because the local security forces went crazy, having lost a colonel of the SBU in the gunplay. It was too risky, so the thug's luck ended right there, in a cove by the road leading south. Just another weight on one's conscience…

The remnants of the ‘plutonium’ containers rested safely on the bottom of the river Tisa.

Our wounded chap was brought to Kiev by his teammate. He was all right, just lost a lot of blood. He spent two weeks resting in a rented flat, watching TV news about the special operation against the dangerous bandits and smugglers near Chop, brilliantly planned and executed by the security forces. A gallant colonel of the SBU, Taras Melnik, was killed in action, while fearlessly trying to take the bandits alive.

Later he simply went to Borispol airport, caught a flight to Berlin and from there to London.

Well, Jasheet and his people were annihilated (‘demand reduction’, according to Hugh). One of the channels of contraband of dangerous fissile materials was shut forever. On top of that, we had obtained valuable intelligence about Jasheet’s colleagues in crime, his clients and suppliers. The price: eight killed, all enemy. We had no losses, thank God. Besides, the operation turned out to be lucrative: the thirty-five million not only covered the expenses, but also paid nice bonuses to all the participants.

The Chief summoned Hugh and me. Words of appreciation, gratitude, a glass of champagne. Such a rare pleasure in our business.

But what about Murat? He had lost his commission, of course. He did not attempt to contact us; neither did he respond to our attempts to contact him. He seemed to have gone underground. Was he alive at all? Perhaps his 'colleagues' suspected the rat and removed him?

Two years later an officer of our Ankara station was travelling in Northern Turkey. He visited Trabzon, a city by the Black Sea, and stayed at a small family hotel just outside. Mustaf, the hotel owner, was Murat's copy. The likeness was amazing. The officer reported this to the Office. They checked it out, and came to the conclusion that this was none other but our vanished agent. After some consideration, it was decided to leave Mustaf / Murat alone. This would be safer for both parties. Let him live a quiet life, bring up children and earn an honest buck for a change. He deserved as much.

But no cigar.

Chapter 4. CARTE BLANCHE

The Manila International airport was large and spacious, but looked shabby and rundown, like a giant garden shed neglected by its owners. I passed through the passport control quickly; for ten US Dollars, they slapped a visa stamp valid for a month. Having squeezed through the humming human beehive, consisting of endless crowds and queues across the tiled floor, I dived outside at last, into the fresh air. Here though, fresh air was just a figure of speech: it was cloudy, stuffy and very humid.

It was my first time in South-East Asia, to say nothing of the Philippines. Manila was vast, about 15 million people at the time, not counting the suburbs. I found it striking: the colours, the smells, the sounds, the motley crowds – I greedily absorbed it all through an open taxi window (the air conditioning was not working). These strange, brightly painted long-base Jeep mini coaches, with the wheel bases extended by hand on the wartime vehicles, packed with an incredible number of passengers: they affectionately call them 'Jippee'… At the crossroads, there were military vehicles with mounted heavy machine guns. The driver explained that they expected another coup d'état attempt. People here were used to it and such trivialities did not affect everyday life. They kept smiling and carried on, minding their own business.

Thirty minutes later we reached my hotel, the Pan Pacific in the Malate district. An excellent four-and-a-half-star affair, and relatively inexpensive. It was located conveniently, for my purposes. I had no idea how long I would have to stay here; so, I checked in for two weeks, to start with.

There was a metal detector frame at the hotel entrance, flanked with guards armed with submachine guns. They treated security seriously here; on the one hand, this was encouraging but on the other, did this mean that the threat to security was so serious, it demanded no less than a submachine gun to counter it?

I made myself comfortable in a large room on the tenth floor and went through my plan, once again.

So, what did I have at my disposal? Client's name and photo (surely the name would be different now, perhaps his appearance, too); the name and the address of his supposed company, this was to be checked. I had a detailed psychological profile; I knew his ways, what he liked and disliked, his habits, his potential connections. Not bad. I looked out of the huge window, but saw nothing noteworthy except the skyscrapers of the Makati business district in the haze, far away.

I knew exactly how to set about this mission. And then… see which way the cat jumps: follow the developments, act accordingly. The Chief, C, had given me carte blanche.

And now, to bed. I needed to catch up on my sleep. Thanks to the eight-hour time difference, my jetlag was severe: my head was woollen, eyelids leaden. I would sleep on it. The morning will bring another day; my mind would be sharp as a razor blade, again. I did not know, however, when exactly this morning would have to be, my body clock being completely messed up.

Gordon Lee was a Eurasian: his father Chinese, his mother English. His daddy emigrated to England from Hong Kong in the early sixties; little Gordon was born a year and a half after his father, having received the leave to remain, opened the Lucky Dragon restaurant in Amersham, a north-western London suburb. His mother was middle class, a typical English rose, with milky white skin, fair hair, nice manners, low voice and a character of steel. They lived in a three-bedroom house with a small garden, saved money for Gordon's public school education and dreamed of how rich and famous their son would be.

Gordon lived up to his parents' expectations, and more. This wonder boy became famous, albeit in very narrow circles. He made good money, too, by illegal insider trading on the stock exchange, but could not use the spoils freely. With time, he grew bored of this situation and began to look for a way out of the idiotic dead end, as he saw it.

This was exactly what worried the Service: if a man as talented as Gordon finds the wrong path, the results may be disastrous. Well, very unpleasant, at least. Not only for the Service, but also for our friends and allies, and even for the human race, as a biological species. And Gordon the *Wunderkind* had already chosen a path that was incorrect, errant, not to say iniquitous.

This is why, officially, Gordon had to be offered a compromise that would be acceptable to him and the Office as well. In case he was to reject these terms or, in case it would be, for any reason, *not expedient to make the offer* (my controller stressed the last bit, looking me straight in the eye), I was to rely on my own judgement and act as circumstances dictated. One could easily guess what was meant. However, C, who saw me off in his office, did not go into details in his parting words. All was clear for the wise. *Sapienti sat.*

This was what the business was about.

Gordon graduated from Oxford with distinction and became a microbiologist. While still a student, six months before his final exams, he was discussing his thesis with his tutor. The latter asked him to stay for a cup of tea afterwards; a third man was to join them. He worked for the government and wished to have a word with Gordon about his future career. The intrigued student agreed. The tutor left them alone after the first cup of tea, and the guest, elegant, dressed in a smart business suit, easy-going but very serious, made Gordon an offer that he could not refuse.

Later on, it was routine: while Gordon was busy with his thesis and studies, the Office conducted positive vetting of him and all his relations and friends, close, near and remote. Although the rules said that, to be on the staff in the SIS, both parents of the candidate must be born British, they needed Gordon so much that an exception was made in his case, the rules slightly bent. It was taken into account that Gordon's father came from the Crown Colony, from a family that had been in the Crown's service for generations: the police force, the military – all served the Empire. His grandfather was even a ranking official in the Hong Kong colonial administration.

Gordon was invited for an interview at the SIS reception house in Carlton Gardens, off Pall Mall, opposite St James's Park. There he was informed that he had been admitted to Her Majesty's Secret Service. He signed the Official Secrets Act and, having celebrated his graduation from Oxford with a series of parties, and received his first-class diploma and a Batchelor of Sciences in October, moved to the South Coast. There he joined the new entry course of the SIS training establishment near Portsmouth. For the next six months he was busy exploring the intricacies of spy tradecraft.

One has to say that a talented young scientist, fully trained as an operative, ambitious and with an outstanding business acumen, could be an explosive mixture should something go wrong. Should he go off his rocker and should his masters lose control. In Gordon's case, there were no warning light at first. He was an excellent, disciplined worker, an officer making a good career.

Within three years he was put in charge of the bacteriological weapons group.

When the Soviet Union fell apart, Gordon's workload increased considerably. The threat of uncontrolled and unchecked dissemination of deadly bacteria and viruses became a real nightmare. The laboratories of the once powerful country that had turned into a pauper in a flash were now on the frontline of terrorism. This scare was even worse than the underground nuclear weapons trade. After all, it was much easier to hide and transport a vial or a sealed tube with spores, cultures or viruses, and the effect was beyond description. Cities with their infrastructure intact, devoid of population; poisoned water reservoirs; air that was no longer breathable; silent, invisible and disgusting death everywhere…

It was Gordon who was assigned to debrief the leading Soviet, now Russian, expert of a top-secret laboratory that developed bacteriological weapons. It was called 'Biopreparat'; for outsiders, it was just another pharmaceutical lab producing medications. The Russian defector was a well of knowledge and expertise, but not on medicine: his cup of tea was biological weapons.

Gordon Lee's dossier did not shed any light on the precise moment of, or the reasons for, his going bad. It simply said that he had disappeared, location unknown. It also featured a note addressed to C, which Gordon had written by hand. In it he asked to be left alone and advised against trying to find him. In the same note, he offered a deal: he wanted to sell several vacuum-packed containers with anthrax spores (a terrible contagious disease, death rate around 90 per cent). The asking price was one million pounds sterling. He also guaranteed that, in case of acceptance, he would never be heard of again. If the Office declined, Gordon intended to sell the goods to 'other interested clients'. The Office, that is the few at the top who knew, was appalled. Shocked. It was obvious that Gordon would not stop here. One could only imagine his connections among scientists and experts from the disintegrated Soviet Empire, all starved for money, which he had accumulated during his SIS career. Clearly, he was quite capable of setting up his own laboratory and producing the various deadly goods to sell to the highest bidder. A blood-chilling prospect. And he dared to blackmail the Service! This meant that his ingenious head had a screw loose. He was mad and unpredictable.

To be brief, our rising star Gordon had realised that a man of his position, with his talent, skills and connections, did not have to run errands for others. He concluded that he possessed real power, the know-how and the goods that all opened the way to serious wealth. All he needed was some starting capital, which he hoped to squeeze out of the Service. He had decided to take his destiny in his own hands.

To deal with the Office, Gordon needed a secure means of communications. In his note, he left an e-mail address. It was registered in Mexico. The contact was made through several proxy servers, the electronic letterboxes that ought to cut off the real location of the addressee. This was where he made a mistake.

To begin with, the Service dragged him into detailed negotiations about the terms and conditions of the deal, in order to give our GCHQ computer magicians an opportunity to figure out Gordon's true location. They also involved the American National Security Agency with its truly unlimited resources.

It became clear soon, that the connection to the Internet was made from several addresses in Manila, in the Philippines. The local SIS Station found out what these addresses were, exactly. Three out of five were hotels; all in Malate district. Interestingly, one of them was the Pan Pacific, where I decided to stay. One more address belonged to a big business centre in Makati, the district that consisted of company offices and serviced centres. There were a couple of dozen firms that rented offices at this particular one: a dead end.

However, the fifth address looked promising: a building approximately two kilometres from the Pan Pacific; here, there were offices of a unit of the Ministry of Labour, which dealt with Filipino émigré workers, as well as a big recruitment agency called the Pacific Partnership. The latter recruited crews for merchant ships and qualified workers and engineers for construction industries around the world. The agency was owned by two partners, both Chinese.

Although there are plenty of Chinese and Eurasians in Manila, one of these two could potentially be Gordon. There were some implications: the agency had changed hands about a year ago, when the present owners bought the business. This coincided with the time that Gordon had disappeared. Such a company could also be an excellent cover for his plot: officially, it had to deal with the selection and relocation of personnel, which meant good working relations (with a drop of corruption) with local authorities, the police, customs, immigration officials. In theory, this would allow him to bring into the Philippines specialists and equipment, all the ingredients to, for instance, put together a bacteriological lab, without any problems at all…

Basically, at the moment, everything pointed to the recruitment agency, so that was where I began my search. At the same time, London carried on negotiations with Gordon, to distract his attention and to keep him unaware: the date and time of the deal, the terms of money transfer, guarantees and the like, everything was discussed at length.

Pacific Partnership was a reputable firm. One came across its adverts in business magazines and directories. That was why it looked quite innocent when a Russian fishing company from the Far East contacted it. Having exchanged some letters, the parties agreed that Mr Sergei Nikonov, the director of Vostokryba Ltd together with his assistant, would visit Manila in order to negotiate with Pacific Partnership the recruitment of crews for its trawlers and, should all go well, to establish a long-term business relationship.

Vostokryba Ltd was indeed registered in Russia as a fishing company; it was traceable. However, it was dormant; its bubbling activity and developing business were the brainchild of the SIS. The 'head office' of the company was set up in London, well equipped with Vladivostok telephone numbers and a Russian web site and email addresses. Our technical wizards did a good job. But even they could not yet change time zones, so the 'secretary' and the 'staff' had to take turns to work at night because of the huge time difference: the start of the working day in the Russian Far East is late night in London…

The Service excelled in false flag operations of this kind; they have always been its stock in trade. A false flag operation meant that we chose an innocent third party – sometimes neutral, sometimes hostile; the main criterion was that it should be plausible. Then we acted as if we were them. Properly organised, the visit of the Russian businessman should not arouse Gordon's suspicions: it is a long way from England to Russia, to say nothing of the Far East.

I played the part of the Vostokryba director, Sergei Nikonov; my assistant was Scotsman Ken, who, as I mentioned, spoke incredibly good Russian, with a slight regional accent from Ryazan, a city to the East of Moscow.

On the day of our supposed arrival in Manila (where in fact we had been for two weeks already, doing reconnaissance, or 'reccie' as we call it, and preparing the logistics), Ken and I came to the airport half an hour before the Aeroflot flight from Moscow landed. All the visas and immigration stamps in our Russian passports were in place and looked impeccable. Now all we needed to do was to exit neatly, having mixed in among the passengers from Moscow, straight towards the representative of Pacific Partnership to be met and greeted. Our colleagues from the British Embassy helped with passes to the security zone, so that was not a problem.

Having blended into the crowd that was leaving the customs area, and carrying cabin luggage with Aeroflot labels attached, we paused to study the notice boards and cardboard signs held by those meeting the arrivals. We looked appropriately tired, disorientated and slow, as if we'd just stepped off a long-haul flight.

A manager of the firm met us and took us to the Heritage Hotel in a company Lexus. After a rest, we were to meet with Mr Zhou, one of the directors and a co-owner of Pacific Partnership.

'He will come to your hotel so you can go through the programme for tomorrow. Later in the evening, he and Mr Jiang invite you to dine with them, with some local specialities.' The manager smiled mysteriously. 'Well, Mr Zhou will tell you himself, and I will leave you in peace.'

The manager bowed himself out.

So, tonight it would be clear whether we had found Gordon or not. There was a fifty per cent chance that he was one of the two partners, either Zhou or Jiang. There was no chance that he would recognise either of us: we were not acquainted, and the Office had checked thoroughly every point at which our paths might have crossed: and found nothing.

When Zhou arrived, our chances of seeing Gordon decreased – or increased – twofold, for Zhou was certainly not him. This polite, smiling Chinese had not a drop of European blood in his veins, and did not look even remotely like our runaway. Of course, he could have teamed up with Gordon, and be well aware of his partner's shenanigans, but we could deal with that possibility later. At the moment, we just had to wait for the evening. At 7 p.m. a car was to collect Ken and me from the hotel and take us to the business dinner with Zhou and Jiang. Then we would see...

Both Ken and I had tiny beacons installed in our mobile phones. Our support team, two Special Forces chaps from the increment, would be constantly tracing our every move. If needed, I could signal them to capture Gordon. One of the boys, by the way, was an ethnic Filipino; he was to work at close quarters, visible as required.

If Jiang turned out to be Gordon, it was important to follow him covertly to his home; or, if we got the chance, to hijack him, quietly, on the way. We had no time to waste: every extra day increased the likelihood of us being uncovered.

The Pacific Partnership Lexus collected us from the hotel at seven sharp. A few minutes later, the doorman was welcoming us to the fashionable El Circulo restaurant. The manager, melting with hospitality, led us to a corner table; two smiling Chinese gentlemen rose to greet us. One was Zhou, and the other one… Gordon Lee! This was real luck. *Now*, I told myself, *be alert and focused. And do not give yourself away with good English.*

The dinner was a success, the atmosphere excellent, business-like but warm and friendly. On paper, Vostokryba had twenty-eight ships, and our Filipino-Chinese partners were hoping to find crews for them all. Besides, there were other opportunities hinted at: contraband of almost anything, for example. The opportunities were practically endless. Ken (alias Igor) and I implied that we were ready for dialogue and open-minded enough to discuss any possibilities.

The Chinese were congeniality personified. I did not doubt for a minute that the hotel management handed over to them photocopies of our Russian passports, with all the stamps and visas. It looked like we had passed this test. While we were savouring our second courses, Ken excused himself from the table and headed over to the washrooms. Passing by the bar, he smoothed the handkerchief in his breast pocket. The signal was duly noted by a Filipino sipping his cocktail at the counter, who remained as he was for another twenty minutes after Ken had returned to the table. Then he left the restaurant.

It was well past ten in the evening when our long dinner reached the digestive stage.

'And now, my dear friends, I want to introduce you to some purely Filipino delights. You will see that man's paradise is, quite possible, here on Earth!' Gordon, aka Jiang, announced ceremonially.

He paid the bill, and a taxi took us to the Asian Flower Club.

Jiang-Gordon was right. He knew what he was talking about. I was sprawled on a sofa, sipping at my cocktail and contemplating the local beauties, wriggling in an erotic dance. Simultaneously, light but strong fingers were massaging my neck and shoulders. Under the table, similar fingers took my shoes off and worked on my soles. It was so pleasant that it was a pity that I was on duty. Out of the corner of my eye I could see Ken; judging by the happy smile on his face, we shared the same thoughts.

Zhou excused himself: he was newly married and his wife waited for him at home. But Gordon let his hair down, he was enjoying himself, indulging himself totally. Nothing surprizing: his Office dossier noted his sexual promiscuity as a matter of fact. He called a few girls at a time to our table to choose from; stroked them, turned them around, touched them…The girls giggled, sensing a rich client. He explained that you could take one, two or several to the hotel – the price was ridiculously cheap by the European standards, eighty dollars per head per night. The ladies were petite, but very pretty, with voluptuous figures and cheerful smiles.

It was almost time for us to make our choice, pick up the girls and go. Inconspicuously, I pressed a button on my mobile and held it for five seconds. Our Special Forces increment, waiting in a car near the club, received my signal: *capture the client in the street now, we will not have a better chance.*

With the girls in tow, we came out of the Asian Flower. Ken and I warmly said our goodbyes to Gordon / Jiang; we agreed to meet in his office the following day, not too early. We took a taxi, the girls packed in the rear seat; Gordon and his ladies of choice got into the next one.

His taxi was following ours when, a few minutes later, an old, shabby Honda of indistinct colour caught up with it. When the cars reached a poorly lit, desolate road, the Honda accelerated suddenly, overtook Gordon's taxi, and braked abruptly, causing it to stop at the roadside. At the same moment, I stopped our driver; the Filipino prostitutes, startled, cried out excitedly. I threw a hundred-dollar bill on the passenger seat to shut them up. Ken and I rushed out and ran towards the Honda, into whose boot two tough blokes were packing Gordon. His taxi driver was clearly shocked. The girls in the rear seat were screaming. Ken looked inside the car and drew his open palm across his throat, as if he was cutting through it. The screaming stopped; he showed them two fifty dollar bills and dropped them on the floor. This would hopefully make them less willing to go to the police. We certainly did not want to hurt anyone, not unless it was absolutely necessary.

Our Honda zoomed off towards Malate, where the boys had rented a basement flat two days ago, near the slum area, especially for such an occasion. Gordon was quiet in the boot; he'd received a shot of tranquiliser in his neck and was looking dazed. We had to drag him into the flat, arms around his shoulders, as if he was heavily drunk. The street was dark and empty; no one seemed to notice us. The 'Filipino' drove the Honda away from the area and left it in a side street. It was unlikely that it would attract attention anytime soon. The girls and the taxi drivers, even if they reported the incident to the local cops, could hardly have memorised the number plates: everything happened so quickly.

In the meantime, the boys put Gordon on a mattress on the floor and prepared for an interrogation.

About ten minutes passed. Gordon, tied hand and foot, tried to get up, failed and mumbled something through the Scotch plaster on his mouth.

'Hello there, Gordon. Greetings from your colleagues in London. You left us so suddenly that you forgot to throw a farewell party. Look, we had to come to you ourselves.' I bent and tore off the plaster. 'Behave yourself, be good and quiet, and all shall be well.'

'Who the hell are you?' he croaked.

'Do you not get it? C was missing you and sent us over here. If you answer all my questions honestly and return what you have stolen, we shall leave you alone and in one piece.'

'Guarantees?' Gordon's brain was gradually turning on.

'You must make do with my word. C authorised me, personally. And if you don't cooperate, look here,' I pointed at Ken, who readily produced a syringe filled with yellowish liquid.

'You are an educated man; you know what it is. This chemical will loosen your tongue. Whether you like it or not, you'll tell us everything. But you might remain a vegetable for the rest of your life. Nasty, eh?'

'You'll really let me go?'

'Promise.' Always leave them some hope, a straw to clutch at. 'Now, to business. We are short of time. First question: what did you steal exactly, from where, and where do you keep your stash?'

As I was listening to Gordon's narrative, I felt my hair stand on end. From an Oxford laboratory that stored samples of pathogenic agents, cultures of the most dangerous bacteria and viruses, he stole vials of anthrax, bubonic plague and Dengue fever. He had access to the lab as he worked closely with it. It was his area of expertise and responsibility at the Office. All he had to do to avoid being caught red-handed was to swap the vials for identical containers, with identical labels, filled with tap water and sealed. Nobody took any notice. And why should they? He was Gordon Lee, a very important man from the Service. A government man.

He kept these 'goods', capable of causing an epidemic on a whole continent… in his flat! In a small lock-up fridge. The key was on the ring that we took from him.

While I carried on with the interrogation, Stan, one of the boys, rode his motorcycle to Gordon's address. He returned an hour later. In his hands, he was holding, very carefully, a plastic container that looked like a cool-box.

'Is that it?' During the hour that Stan was away, I had learned a lot about Gordon and his deeds, plans and intentions. He was scum, and I wanted to crush him like a scorpion.

'Yes. It is all here. See, I told you the truth!' I could hear hope in the bastard's trembling voice.

But he had buried himself already. I was not going to leave him alive. It was too dangerous; and it was impossible to extract him from here and bring him safely back to England. And, well, the Chief had given me carte blanche. I made a decision on the spot.

'The truth? That's something we are going to check now.' I beckoned to Ken and his syringe.

'Nooooo! Doooon't!' Gordon screamed, terrified; he was so loud that we had to hold him and put a plaster over his mouth again. Ken stuck the needle in his sinewy neck. The truth drug started working almost straight away.

Nobody could resist it. Well, perhaps there exist super agents, who have special mantras implanted in their heads. Apparently, even under chemical interrogation they reply to all questions with these mantras. Until they die. I've seen them in spy movies, but never in real life. Gordon was no super-agent; he answered all my questions in a changed, strangely pitched voice.

When he worked with the Soviet defector, a biological weapons expert, he obtained data on other specialists of the Biopreparat laboratory. He managed to establish a working relationship with two of them. They were starved for money and not burdened by moral principles. Besides them, Gordon contacted one scientist in Pakistan and one female specialist from the Tropical Disease Center in the USA.

They were all going to join him in Manila and set up a small private lab. Their products could be used to blackmail governments, or else sold on to terrorists. He felt no qualms. The lab equipment was already ordered in different countries, and the experts were just waiting for Gordon's signal to buy airline tickets to Manila.

We had arrived just in time. One more month and it would have been too late.

Now we had all the data on the scientists; Gordon told us all about their liaison system. We were in the position to carry out an elegant operational game; or else simply shop his colleagues to our partners from friendly services, to deal with as they pleased. We could think that over later…

He knew nothing more of interest. Zhou, his partner, was not in on the plot; his only sin was a bit of smuggling. Thank God, one death less. The lab was not built yet, and we had seized all the bacteria. He could not have kept anything from me during this chemical interrogation.

Gordon's eyes rolled; he was losing consciousness. Let him; I did not need him anymore. I could not feel anything but disgust for this scum. No human emotions. His greed and ambitions had eaten away his humanity.

Our 'Filipino' fished another syringe out of his rucksack. He quickly prepared a heroin dose large enough to kill a horse and looked at me, waiting.

'Go ahead,' I nodded.

Death by heroin overdose is commonplace in these slums. One more would excite no one, if they even bothered to find the body in this filthy lair…

While Ken and I were waiting for Gordon to descend to hell as he deserved, the boys went out to a nearby rubbish dump. There, they carefully poured petrol over each vial and container from Gordon's 'cool-box'. Once done, they moved away to a safe distance and set fire to it.

Gordon Lee died at the same time as his cherished bacteria perished, failing to bring him the wealth and fame of an evil genius.

Afterwards, our foursome split: everyone followed the rules, each making his own way back to base. I did not specify their routes; I didn't need to know. Besides, they knew what they were doing. I simply went to Pan Pacific, where I was known as Mr Prior, another one of my aliases. There was just one more matter I had to attend to, before leaving the Philippines. For when would I visit these parts again, if at all?

There were almost twenty-four hours to kill before my flight to London. I sent a coded message to the Office by email: mission completed, success. Having finished with my duties, I whispered a few words in the ear of the concierge; a twenty dollar note discreetly disappeared in his ready palm. An hour later, I heard a soft knock on my door… The rest of the time I dedicated to thorough research and exploration of the design and behaviour of native females.

Breakfast and lunch for three were brought in by room service; I only left my suite to get into the waiting taxi, and head straight for the airport.

I shall remain silent about the results of my research, for decency's sake. And to keep them off the record, of course. Why make those deskbound colleagues envious?

Chapter 5. THE WATERSHED

One bright May morning of 1995, Alan invited me to see him in his office. He was the newly appointed head of Economic Intelligence.

'Here, look through it carefully.' He shoved towards me a rather voluminous file. 'It contains personal data on some interesting individuals. Possible targets. You may find someone you recognise from before. Come back at the end of the day. Let's pick each other's brains.'

'Yes, it is a small world. Perhaps I will recognise a mug or two. I'll be off then. See you later.'

An interesting chap, this Alan. Around forty, he held, until recently, a secondary position in counterintelligence; however, when the new Chief moved in, his fortune changed and he skyrocketed up the ladder. No surprise at all: they had worked side by side in Latin America, then in the Middle East. The new C trusted him; they fit together well. Alan was friendly. Too friendly, even. But not to be messed with: the Office rumour had it that he was jealous and vengeful. If you crossed him, he was quite capable of stabbing you in the back. He was a man to have as a friend, not as an enemy. Workwise, he was crafty, inventive, innovative, even talented; always loyal to his team members, as long as it did not harm his interests.

Once in my office, I poured a cup of black coffee, made myself comfortable at the desk, and opened the file. Inside, there were resumes of some prominent Russian businessmen and politicians. To begin with, I browsed through the documents, page by page; one dossier, another, one more… The fourth file sent shivers down my spine. *Impossible!*

The familiar face stared at me, point blank, from a high-resolution photo. The features slightly less sharp, less defined; apparently he had gained some weight with age. 'Sergei Vladimirovich Lapin' said the caption above the photo. *Alias Otto*, I muttered to myself. *Well, hello there. What an interesting turn of events. And I did not even know your real surname. Auld Lang Syne, my friend, how long has it been? Where have you been hiding yourself, while I was looking for you, making all these risky, futile, frustrating attempts to contact you?*

Suddenly, I felt deeply relieved that I had not opened this file in front of Alan. I could imagine the expression on my face: as if I had seen a ghost.

Well, Otto, life has treated you well... So, you left the KGB in 1992, during the purges. Understandable, a lot of people resigned then, or were forced to resign. But where did you get all the money from? Good luck? The Chairman of Kominvestbank, the fifth largest commercial bank in Russia. Running for the State Duma, the Russian Parliament. It would appear that the dough came from the Communist Party Central Committee, now non-existent. From 1990 onwards, until the collapse in December 1991, it was very busy transferring and hiding the funds overseas; billions flowed across the border to end up in offshore bank accounts belonging to front firms and organisations, as well as natural persons, normally fake personalities. Later some of it was re-invested in the new Russia to set up private banks, or to buy oilfields, factories and plants, for peanuts.

The International and the Administrative Departments of the Central Committee oversaw this massive theft. But the ones who actually carried it out were, of course, the KGB people: from the First Chief Directorate (external intelligence) and from Central HQ. Vladimir Kryuchkov, the KGB Chairman, seconded his experts and operatives to these departments, by order of Mikhail Gorbachev himself. No one will ever know how much money and how many national treasures disappeared abroad, without a trace. No one will ever know, as no loose ends were left by the KGB. Remember all these strange accidental deaths and suicides in the early nineties? The most indicative ones were the 'suicides' of the head of the Administrative Department and his deputy, who followed his boss's suit just a few days after he jumped out of his window – they knew all the ropes, to their misfortune. Colonel Veselovsky of the FCD was in charge of a special team seconded to the Central Committee; when it was over, he himself moved to Canada and vanished without a trace.

So, Otto, you dealt with the 'Party gold', too. I understood now, why you lost interest in the Traveller. That was it. The era ended, Communism was buried, and the future promised great deals and super profits. Dennis / Ayden had no place in your new world; he would make it somehow, over there in England. The fact that I was deprived of my family, my country, and my good name, was of no importance or consequence. The new times brought new values to new Russia: money, money, money.

In December 1991, when I realised that I was left on my own, I made a decision: from now on Britain was my country, the place where I would live and work. The country where I came from was no more, its superstructure, the state itself, had dissolved like sugar. What remained was something very different, I could not grasp it. But the people, the officials and Party people who loyally served the old system, remained in place, for the most part; they went to offices which had different names but retained the same addresses. They just had different official portraits hanging above their desks. This troubled me a great deal. The country was ruined, but its supposed protectors and defenders were alive and well, having changed colour en masse and virtually overnight. The ones who did not soon found themselves out in the street, or worse.

Nonetheless, both in 1992 and 1993, and even once in 1995, I attempted to make contact using the Traveller rules. Mostly out of curiosity; but hope was also there, deep inside, I must confess. All the attempts were futile. I was also waiting to be contacted through Elena, my now ex-wife, or through my father. This would have been easy, if there had been a will to do so. Although Elena and I divorced, which was her initiative (on advice from my KGB colleagues), we kept in touch. Besides, I saw my parents once a year, they visited me in England. Clearly, they did not know what my real job was; but surely they could pass on a message?

My futile attempts were almost a tribute to the past, nostalgia. Deep down I knew that I was no longer tied to the Russian state. I did not belong there. In those early years, it was ugly, sordid, miserable and scary at the same time. And it was governed by a gang of kleptomaniacs. All in all, it was the Russian state that refused me and made me an outcast; not the other way around. The notions of a country and a state shouldn't be mixed up: I became Her Majesty's subject, loyal to my sovereign; at the same time, I had a Russian soul and my heart was bleeding for Russia. I did not see a contradiction there. However, sometimes I felt that it was tearing me apart.

Years passed, and nothing happened on the Traveller front. I thought that perhaps my controllers and those who knew about the operation had died, or been dismissed from the Service, perhaps arrested for supporting the State of Emergency Committee. I thought first and foremost of the Deputy Chairman of the KGB and Otto. Something must have happened to them in the turmoil that followed 1991. This is how I explained it to myself. They could not, physically could not, liaise with me. What other explanation could there be? We do not just abandon our own, do we?

But what if we do? In 1991, the leaders abandoned millions of compatriots to their fate, leaving them unsupported and unprotected in the newly independent ex-Soviet states. So, what waited for me in Russia, should I return to this new country, living by new rules, but under similarly unscrupulous leaders; those who rose to the top from the second league and were not bound by any of the promises or principles of their predecessors? Most probably I would be arrested and charged with high treason, since the SVR, as the Russian Foreign Intelligence Service was now known, knew nothing about the Traveller. Only my liaison, Andrei, was aware: but he only knew what he was allowed to know, and needed to know. He was a professional, but a mere pawn; not much help, even if I managed to track him down.

I had not in my worst nightmares imagined that they could simply forget me. Just like that! As a child forgets his toy once he grows bored with it and is attracted by something new. I am an even-tempered man, I hardly ever lose control over my emotions, but now I was enraged. Cold rage, the most dangerous kind, engulfed me totally.

It was extremely important now that I didn't betray myself. My SIS colleagues must not suspect anything.

Yes, dear Otto, the Office will play a game with you. Not the game it thinks it will be playing. It is going to play my game, a game with no name. Enjoy your life for now, and I will get ready. Without hurry, carefully, thoroughly, so that there will be no chance for you to wriggle out of the trap. Look forward to seeing you again, my dear Controller.

I could not think of anything else for a long time. Offense, bitterness, utter disappointment: no matter how hard I tried to quell these feelings, they prevailed. Outwardly, my inner turmoil did not show. I started drinking more, but on weekends only. My Office colleagues did not notice, and I did not have a wife or a girlfriend to take me to task. At that time, I dated a couple of ladies, but carefully controlled the relationships, never allowing them to develop to the move-in stage. I preferred to go out with them, not to stay in. To be emotionally involved was not something I was prepared for, not then. Wine, dine, sex, relax, enjoy, see you the next time, whenever.

I was so preoccupied with concocting a plot that, slowly, quietly, the thirst for revenge overwhelmed me, vengeance became my *idee fixe*, my obsession. There was nobody to share my burden with, as usual. This is normal in our business. You carry your own weight, silently. Of course, one could talk to a Service-provided psychologist, but one would have to be an idiot to do so. These shrinks skilfully allow you to relieve your soul, to discharge all the black, negative energy; stroke your head, give you a shoulder to cry on; but that would be the end of your career. You spill the beans; they pay for your treatment and put you out to grass. Or, in the worst case, into the Great Void, depending on what you told them in a moment of weakness and uncontrolled sincerity…

I have always known that revenge is a dish best served cold. However, as it turned out, I had completely forgotten another piece of ancient wisdom: before you embark on a journey of revenge, dig two graves: one for your enemy, another for yourself.

So, I started plotting. I needed a tool to help me achieve my goal: Alan looked like a convenient one. The background for what I had in mind was complex, but highly suitable.

In those exciting times, the nineties, Russia was awash with black and grey money. De-facto, the country was ruled by a gang of oligarchs. They threated Russia as an industrial area, simply to be exploited: fortunes were made there, everything was for sale or to be stolen; the cash flowed abroad like a mighty river, tens of billions a month found a home in offshore jurisdictions, or such reputable countries as the United Kingdom, Switzerland, Canada and the USA.

The recipients mostly turned a blind eye to it: how can one refuse such megabucks! For appearance's sake, from time to time and selectively, governments unleashed their law enforcement agencies to crack down on those 'businessmen' who went too far (and were not too important), accusing them of laundering criminal money. Thus, they could avoid losing face and look vigilant before the public, the voters. And inside the Russian industrial area, the main task of the big players was to stay in office, that is to keep in government the President

Yeltsin clique that they had bought wholesale; by any means. There were no holds barred for the oligarchs, and they enjoyed a complete licence as long as the clique could be propped up.

Objectively, this coincided with the West's interests, on the condition that the West, namely the USA and major European powers, could ultimately control the situation. The ruling Russian elite had willingly delegated this control to the West and happily carried on selling out the nation's natural reserves; meanwhile, just a few years after 1991, the country was moving to the brink of another, this time probably terminal, disintegration.

Thus, everyone who was lucky to have their fingers in the Russian honeypot was terribly pleased. However, they were troubled by the coming general elections to the State Duma, closely followed by the presidential elections of 1996. President Yeltsin's support was down to nil. The voters who had been tramped upon, shamelessly cheated and looted for five years could easily vote for the opposition, the Communists. The lavish party would be over for good, then.

At one of his briefings for the team, Alan , looking suitably important, put it this way: `Gentlemen… eh, and ladies (having glanced in the room corner), the task that we face is twofold: on the one hand, to do our best to help the ‘correct’ people to win the Russian elections, and, on the other hand, to keep the cash flow from Russia under control, so as not to endanger our own elections. This meant that we should keep propping up the so-called democracy in the ‘industrial area’, and at the same time, should appear to be firm in our fight against money laundering and crooked foreigners here in the West. We could cooperate with the good foreigners and even support them over here, to an extent and for a while. Allow them to ship their cash in by the wagonload: we could use it, at the appropriate juncture. Let us see which way the wind blows`.

Otto’s Kominvestbank was expanding rapidly and aggressively, especially in the merchant banking and portfolio investment sectors. I read in his file that the bank intended to apply to the Bank of England for a licence to carry our operations in the UK. The procedure stipulated stringent vetting, involving police and security services checks. This gave ground for a preliminary evaluation of Kominvestbank and its Chairman, Otto, as potential SIS targets.

How exactly this evaluation would be carried out; how deeply we would dig and in what direction would largely depend on my assessment and how I reported back to Alan.

So, from the thick folder that Alan gave me that morning, I selected several suitable dossiers, Otto's among them. Later that afternoon, I came to his office to share a few ideas.

Alan listened to me with interest. I was hoping that, having digested all the information and ideas for a couple of days, he would report it to the top brass, with some modifications and additions, as his own proposal.

Well, all I could do now was wait. So, I, a typical commuter, went back home. First, by tube to Paddington Station; then by train to Slough, another twenty minutes; my car was waiting in the car park. Fifteen minutes more, and the asphalt grey BMW 535 brought me to Old Windsor.

Some time ago I had bought a flat here, in a small eight-unit apartment block, a cosy private development. I had used my savings, the bonuses I had received for several operations, and had taken out a small mortgage that was nearly paid off by now. A flat is more convenient than a house if you live alone. Fewer things to look after, and if you leave, you can just lock the door. I loved my flat and the area. Windsor Great Park, Saville Gardens, the Thames, gastropubs, the lakes. May and June were especially enjoyable. Fabulous air, lush greenery, nightingales singing… A world apart from the huge megapolis fifteen minutes' drive away. A complete change of scene, so restful for the mind and soul.

I did not have to wait long. Friday morning Alan and I came across each other in the ground floor lobby, right in front of the glass security doors in the Office's entrance hall, facing the Albert Embankment.

I forgot to say that shortly before these events, we had moved into a new, modern and comfortable building by Vauxhall Bridge. From the outside, this edifice looked like a Babylonian zikkurat temple – a rectangular, tiered and terraced structure. It was rather fitting. No one would ever know what gods they prayed to, what sacrifices were made, and to whom, in this temple on the Thames.

'Hello Den. See you at 10.30 in my office.' Alan disappeared in the direction of the lifts.

Yes, he was capable of broad thinking and producing far-reaching ideas. I suggested to him that we should cultivate several potential recruits, Otto among them, and substantiated my proposals with solid arguments. He developed my proposals, added his own and, ultimately, managed to convince our top brass to allocate very substantial resources to this project, which from now on received a codename: Operation Fatcat. Less than imaginative, but to the point.

Being a native Russian speaker with good local knowledge, that is to say I knew Russian affairs, circumstances and personalities, so I was appointed deputy controller of the operation and its coordinator. Alan was in overall charge. We could draft in any experts as required: operatives, technical support, economists, tax and financial consultants and lawyers. A special corporate consultancy was formed. We registered it in Geneva, with branches in London and Road Town (Tortola, British Virgin Islands). It was called Global Capital Management S.A., a name that should attract clients by implication.

The company was a cover for our operation and a magnet for our targets, both immediate and potential. According to our plan, I was to head up the Geneva office – of course, under a different name and with a new set of cover documents: Donald Bruce, the offspring of an old Scottish family, whose ancestors served Russian Tsars from the times of Peter the Great. This explained, plausibly, both my knowledge of the Russian language and culture, as well as my particular interest in Russians (and their money, naturally).

The plan was good; I was quite happy with it. The only possible fly in the ointment was that, theoretically, I could chance to meet Otto face to face. This was to be avoided at all costs. Initially, I planned to have the Service cultivate Otto until we'd acquired hard evidence of him spying for Britain and other compromising material. Then, I would shop him to the Russian Federal Security Service as a traitor, a foreign spy, thus depriving Otto of his business, his career and his liberty.

Any personal contact with him was clearly out of the question as the consequences were so unpredictable. How would Otto react? What would he do? I was too dangerous for him; likewise, he would be far too dangerous for me, were I suddenly to surface from the oblivion where he had consigned me five years ago. Should the English learn about Operation Traveller, I would be in deep trouble. There would be no return to my previous life.

Destiny gave me a unique chance to get even with my former boss; one more twist of fate would be highly unlikely. I was in a position to supervise and to a large extent control, on a day-to-day basis, the developments of Operation Fatcat. This meant that I should be able to prevent an undesirable turn of events. In particular, running into Otto.

However, there is always an element of chance and unpredictability in the intelligence business. Here we have Fortune, or luck, to factor in, whether we like it or not. When you have everything worked out to the minute, every move calculated, everything foreseen – although it is beyond humans to foresee everything – then, a whim of Fortune can send the most brilliant operational plan crashing down. It could ruin the best, perfectly winnable chess game. And it did so, many times. Most spies are superstitious; they believe in luck.

I firmly believed in mine. I also believed that I was justified in what I was planning to do. What self-confidence… It never crossed my mind that the game that I had started might put me in conflict with the Service, with duty, the national interest, even common sense. My mind was clouded by the thirst for revenge. Those whom the gods wish to destroy, they first make mad…

Much later, trying to analyse what had happened, I remembered one episode which occurred during the preparation for Operation Fatcat. This was an episode that stirred up a very powerful feeling of foreboding…

I'd never experienced something like it before. At the time, I just made a huge effort and swept aside this irrational feeling, no matter how difficult it was. But really it was a warning, a sign: a vivid, compelling stop sign. Why is it that the we most often see the light retrospectively, when it is too late?

The episode per se was minor, negligible. I landed at Geneva airport, collected my car from Avis and drove to the Beau Rivage Hotel. I came here to choose offices for the Geneva office of Global Capital Management, S.A. On the way, I stopped at traffic lights at the junction leading to Quai du Mont-Blanc, the Mont Blanc Embankment.

Suddenly, my car was pushed forward. Nudged, rather. I turned around and saw that a biker had hit my rear bumper. He, in turn, was thrown forward by a Ford Escort with two girls in the front. They were probably chattering and not paying attention to the road. Now they were sitting in their car, looking guilty. I got out of my Mercedes: on the rear bumper, there was a black mark left by the bike's wheel. The biker, a young fellow, stood nearby, his head in his hands: his new Kawasaki was damaged. The lights were broken; the back was dented. We exchanged insurance details and moved on. A trifle. Nothing worth remembering.

So why then, when I was leaving the site of the accident, did I feel a sudden chill inside, as if caught in a blast of Arctic wind? The world around me turned grey, all colours gone in just a flicker, as if turned off abruptly; I felt sick in my stomach; something disgusting, slimy, wobbled about inside. My inner voice was not whispering, but shouting: *turn around, fly home, lock yourself in your flat!*

Beads of sweat dropped from my forehead. I felt miserable. I struggled to overcome the weakness in my arms and legs and drove on to the hotel. Once in my room,

I took a cool shower, poured a double Scotch, and tried to analyse my strange reaction to this smallest of accidents.

There was no rational explanation for such inadequacy. Moreover, the shower and the twenty-years-old Glenmorangie took the edge off the most unpleasant sensations and quelled the panic. The colours returned to my world; however, the aftertaste lingered. As well as the premonition. Why?

At the time, I did not believe in intuition, signs and suchlike. So, I found an explanation: fatigue and nervous stress, commonplace in our business. Never mind, I knew how to cope with that: relaxation techniques and a change of scene. When I was finished here, I would take a week off and go somewhere nice.

It was not until much later, after I'd survived some shattering ordeals and blows, that I learned to treat life and all its developments consciously, to notice and read the signs, which something or somebody sends to guide us, from time to time. This entity has many names, but the real one, and its nature and essence are forever obscured;

it is a *noumenon*, a thing-in-itself, as Kant called it. Something beyond human understanding; yet to be reckoned with. Then I learned to regard sudden insights and flashes of intuition with attention and take them into account. The path towards such perception was long and painful, full of obstacles and trials. Apparently, this was the path that I was meant to walk.

But for now I was too snowed under to think deeply. In Geneva, I had countless business meetings with partners, lawyers, experts in offshore business and banking, investment fund managers. Besides, I needed to find a respectable office for Global Capital in the city centre; somewhere we could receive serious clients.

Time flew by, and the incident was forgotten amidst the daily grind. I barely remembered it until future events reminded me – brutally – of that sense of foreboding.

Having launched the Geneva office, I returned to England two weeks later.

Global Capital Management, or GCM for short, started an aggressive public relations campaign to attract clients.

We advertised both in the English language media, including *Newsweek* and the *Economist*, and in Russia, using respectable glossy business magazines such as *Dengi* (Money) and *Expert*. We needed a big client pool, in order to conceal the true nature of the company. Clearly, we were not averse to making some money, either.

The response was beyond expectations. The Swiss and UK branches were firmly in business, full time. The Service was happy. Alan and I were plotting: we were working out plausible ways to bring home our listed targets, Kominvestbank among them, using our fast-growing consultancy business. A fashionable trend provided a solution: an international business conference on offshore investment, complete with leading experts in the field, top-notch participants, potentially lucrative connections, all washed down at lavish cocktail receptions and formal dinners.

At that time, similar events were taking place in London a few times a month, aimed at the countries of the former USSR, organised by all sorts of providers, some reputable, some just rip-off artists. The Russians loved to attend conferences and seminars abroad and paid good money, since it was all tax-deductible as training and education expenses. Besides, capital export from Russia, as well as tax avoidance (or evasion), had become a national sport. Everyone who made money did their best to find proper contacts and channels, and to obtain schemes in order to do it covertly, safely and, where possible, not too illegally.

Well, the Office could offer first-rate expertise and experience in these areas! We had plenty of that, plus resources. We could provide prominent speakers and participants for our conference. Our relations with the City had always been excellent; and some ranking civil servants from the Bank of England and the Treasury would not refuse our offer to speak before the audience, to add to the event's respectability.

Thus, Global Capital Management became the organiser of an international conference called 'Investments 1996' under the auspices of the European Bank for Reconstruction and Development (EBRD), the

International Monetary Fund and the Russian-British Chamber of Commerce.

Our speakers list boasted directors of leading UK and European banks, chiefs from top-ten law and accountancy firms and blue chip corporations, and a couple of retired but well-known politicians as the icing on the cake. The conference was opened jointly by the British minister for trade and the head of the EBRD. There were over a hundred guests from Russia and the former Soviet republics.

While we were at the final stages of preparation, I sent out personal invitations to the heads of twenty leading Russian corporations, six of whom were on our target list. It goes without saying that Sergei Vladimirovich Lapin, aka Otto, received one of these letters, printed on gilt-edged Conqueror prestige paper.

Wily Alan had mobilised for GCM a trusted SIS agent, Anna. A luxurious, well-bred woman of thirty-five (I only knew her age because I had access to her personal file), Anna possessed incredible sexual magnetism. When she turned it on, no male could possibly resist her. Add to this a razor-sharp mind and a fearless nature, and you had a formidable weapon. As an SIS agent, she specialised in honey traps, naturally. I do not think it necessary to explain what this term means.

It is amusing that the English term for this spy method, the honey trap, coincides literally, one hundred per cent, with the Russian analogue, *medovaya lovushka*. Such is life. Flies are always attracted by honey, wherever they are, London or Moscow. And men usually play the role of flies in this case. .But not always so. Male honey traps were also extremely successful against ladies: PAs and secretaries for high government officials, for example; there were gay honey traps, too… Any weakness, any hidden passion, that could be discovered in a target, may be deemed useful and exploited. This is what human intelligence is about. This is why the Service studied very thoroughly any potential target, before making a move.

This was how Anna became, temporarily, one of the directors of Global Capital, responsible for clients from the former USSR. And I took care to make Otto one of her targets. He was on the list of participants as head of the Kominvestbank delegation of three people. Just let him come to London; from then on, it would just be a matter of time. Nobody had ever escaped Anna's charm; a former KGB officer would be no exception, no matter how shrewd or important he was.

The venue for the conference was the Barbican. A whole week of speeches, lectures, seminars, negotiations and other formal and informal events. At first, Otto had me worried; his colleagues arrived in London without him. However, he joined them on day three of the conference. It seems that he was waiting for his subordinates to report to him first, to let him know whether the conference was worth attending. Having learned that it was, he flew to London.

We had to take into account the fact that he was a former professional spy. There was no physical surveillance put on him as he was likely to detect it. However, his two-bedroom suite at Claridges was bugged throughout: we could hear his every word and see his every move.

Anna approached him the same evening, at a reception in the medieval Guildhall. At the beginning of the conference, she met with his Kominvestbank colleagues (the chaps happily salivating over our lady director). So, everything looked quite natural and smooth – Otto's own deputy introduced Anna to his boss, as a representative of the organiser.

They started with a bit of small talk, a bit about business, this and that…

I did not attend the conference in person, scared I would run into somebody who might recognise me. Alan agreed with this argument. Instead I watched and coordinated it from a distance. It was so amusing, so much fun to direct this spectacle.

Scene two of the play was promising: during the reception, Otto was constantly looking for excuses to return to Anna and engage her in another chat. In the end, he invited her to dinner the following day. She blushed a little, her eyes sparkling, and said that she herself would choose a good restaurant – was it not Sergei's first visit to

London? `Ah, you had been here twice before, but only briefly, on business? That doesn`t count, you could hardly see anything`, Anna smiled coyly, `I would be happy to show you around a little, play the hostess.`

The dialogue itself was trivial. But it was not about what was said, but how it was said. It was so sensual; I could almost feel the surrounding air charged with electricity. So what that Otto was married and, as far as we knew, had two children? The male in him had conquered both the husband and the spy.

The following night Anna took Otto to the Square. This restaurant is located just off Berkeley Square, a green jewel in the crown of Mayfair, the most elegant part of London. The restaurant is stylish, comfortable and very delicious, a place for serious connoisseurs of fine food and wine. It was not awarded two Michelin stars for nothing. Just a few minutes' walk from here, across Berkeley Square, was Annabel's, an exclusive and elegant club frequented by VIPs and minor royals. Only members and their guests were allowed in. The dress code was strict: gentlemen must wear suits and ties. Once, as an experiment, the management allowed men to relax a bit and go tieless. The experiment did not last long: the management could not tolerate such frivolous attire and returned to the previous dress code two months later. This conservative streak had a purely English charm that I found quaint and endearing.

The Office had provided its agent with a membership about ten years previously. The membership fee had not been a waste of money: Anna's visits to Annabel's always bore fruit.

Having finished dinner at the Square, the couple, snug and warm after the lavish and sophisticated dishes and wines, walked to Annabel's, hand in hand. They stayed there, dancing until three in the morning; then Anna, all blushes and quick glances and tiny smiles, succumbed to Otto's insistent invitations to have a glass of champagne at his hotel. A nightcap, no more.

I shall not describe all I saw on the video the following morning. If only they had an erotic film contest at Cannes Film Festival, our recording would have taken the Palme d'Or, no doubt. The partners were worthy of each other. Our beauty was an ace in the course of duty; but, viewing Otto's exploits, I felt a surge of pride for my former Service, the KGB.

This material could only be compromising stuff in the eye of Otto's wife, surely; otherwise, pornography would not harm him; not even his parliamentary career. Different times, different rules: during the Soviet regime, it would have cost him his job.

However, our aim was not to blackmail him – this method is mostly counterproductive and so is rarely used by the Service. Instead we wanted to draw Otto, gradually, into cooperation with the SIS, by creating motivation for such cooperation. An amorous relationship with Anna which could, hopefully, lead to love, was just one way to develop his motivation. The video was a by-product, something for the records. Still, it would not go amiss: it might be useful in the future, as an argument, for educational purposes. Things happen.

Meanwhile, the relationship was flourishing: in the three days that were left of the conference, the sweethearts spent every spare moment together. Now they spent their nights at Anna's flat in a beautiful Victorian house in Chancery Lane. This was actually a service flat that belonged to the Office. Anna had it converted into a love nest, with all the attributes of the profession, such as bugs, cameras and telephone taps.

Anna learned that Otto liked classical music, so she treated him to 'Le Nozze di Figaro' at Glyndebourne. One could hardly find something more English than this private opera not far from Brighton. Together, he and Anna picnicked on the grass in the lush gardens, surrounded by revellers in dinners jackets and evening dresses, all warming up before the Mozart began; he was delighted.

Smitten as he was, Otto did not forget about business. With Anna's help, he established contacts with useful people and consulted GCM specialists. He was serious about creating a scheme for discretely transferring assets from his bank to overseas companies that he himself would be behind. Discretely. Global Capital was for him an irreplaceable tool. We began to build an offshore empire for Otto, which could absorb, without a trace, tens and hundreds of millions of dollars. It was still 1996, full two years before the Russian default and financial crash, and Otto was preparing himself already. What foresight!

Information, intellect and intuition. The three 'I's. The recipe for success.

I felt successful, too: the lure had been taken; Otto was eating out of my hand, unwittingly. Hiding big money is much more serious than having love affairs on the side. Colleagues, partners and authorities never forgive something like this. One must share!

The London conference plus the PR campaign bore fruit: Global Capital now had a considerable pool of clients, and more were coming, from different countries. We sieved them through our filter, choosing those who had access to intelligence of various nature, of interest to the SIS. The rest we watched carefully, in order to detect different grey and black schemes and machinations; money laundering, mostly.

When the time came – that is, when there were some political benefits to reap, or when the clients crossed the line and had to be stopped – we simply shopped them to the police, discreetly, confidentially slipping them the evidence.

We were behind several well-publicised money laundering court cases across the world. There was one hiccup, though: in the Cayman Islands. Here, the prosecution tried too hard, and inadvertently exposed the Service's role in this case: it had clandestinely introduced damning evidence against the accused. Unfortunately, the act lacked our usual technical sophistication: the defence could prove that some 'evidence' was planted into the computers of those sitting in the dock. They even managed to show that the trail was linked to the Office. The judge was indignant; an old-school fellow, he could not tolerate such flagrant abuse of process and threw the case out of the court. He even published a lengthy statement blaming the prosecution and the Office.

The case gained worldwide media coverage; however, the interest soon died away and in England the whole affair was successfully hushed up. The accused bankers were released; however, their dodgy bank was closed for business, and many millions in illicit proceeds blocked, and later confiscated. A result, notwithstanding. In general, Operation Fatcat was an unqualified success. Alan was a happy man. Rumour had it that he had been shortlisted for yet another promotion.

The following year Otto visited London once a month on average, always staying in Anna's flat. He was really head over heels in love. He had lost his mind – so much for the cool head of the *Checkist*, much praised by the founder of the Soviet secret police, Felix Dzerzhinsky.

There is no ice that hot female caresses would not melt. Our charmer was now sporting a Cartier watch inlaid with diamonds; a Chopard necklace around her slender, sensual neck. Apart from love, she gave Otto valuable advice and interesting business solutions – she was a GKM director after all. Money flowed from Otto's bank and from those of his partners, finding a home in the intricate network of offshore banks and companies, under our supervision and control.

It was through Anna that we introduced him to John, our most experienced agent recruiter, when the time was ripe for it, in Alan's judgement. John was tall, suave, with aristocratic manners; actually, he was a viscount from a family that boasted a thousand years' pedigree. John quickly gained Otto's trust. The latter was flattered by the new doors that such a friendship could open: races in the Royal Enclosure at Ascot; lunches at the Athenaeum in Pall Mall; dinners in John's ancestral pile in Berkshire, where he rubbed shoulders with barons, marquises and earls.

I was sure that Otto was conscious, as a former intelligence officer, of being entangled – or seduced, rather – into cooperation with the SIS. It seemed that he was not really against it: on the one hand, he was charmed by good old England, and on the other, deeply in love with Anna. And of course, he had more mundane, pragmatic motives…

Soon it was time for John to show his hand and have a serious chat with his target, really get to the point. Otto's political career was brilliant, just as glittering as his business one, so his access to confidential and top-secret information was gradually increasing and so was, in parallel, our desire to recruit him as a full-blooded agent.

Otto ran for the State Duma, the Russian parliament, in 1995 and was re-elected. He managed not only to keep his seat, but to become a member of the Duma International Affairs and Security committee, with very good prospects of being promoted to its head in due course.

In the 1996 presidential elections, Boris Yeltsin and his team barely retained office, prompted by the concerted effort of the Russian oligarchs, Western election experts and pollsters, and the news media, who had been bought wholesale. This boosted Otto's career and, with his background as a ranking KGB officer, the prospects for our potential new asset were excellent.

As I read in the very detailed accounts of the meeting in the case files later, including the tapes transcripts, John invited Otto to the Athenaeum, where he introduced him to a high-up official from the Foreign and Commonwealth Office: Montgomery, the latter called himself. After dinner, they retired to the library and sank into comfortable, deep Bordeaux leather armchairs around a coffee table, equipped with glasses of very fine cognac and cigars. This club treated privacy very seriously, so the distance between the tables was such that it precluded conversations being overheard. Discretion above all; the Athenaeum's list of members included some of the most powerful people in the country, both retired and active: politicians, civil servants, business elite and aristocracy.

'Sergei, we appreciate your friendship. Both on a personal and business level. You realise, of course, just how important it is for us in England to understand and judge correctly what is going on in your turbulent country, with its young, fledgling democracy.' Montgomery let out a puff of cigar smoke and sipped on his cognac, before continuing.

'I am very grateful to John for having introduced us to each other. Today's conversation was a revelation for me,' carried on the Foreign Office mandarin, 'and I would so much like to be able to turn to you in the future, should I need an expert explanation of one issue or other; for consultations of a private, confidential nature. You would not mind that, I hope?'

Otto looked first at Montgomery, then at John. He himself had many times held conversations like this, some friendly, some less so. His job as an operative of the KGB was exactly that – recruiting agents. So, he must have recognised the garden path up which the Englishman was leading him. The moment of truth had come.

A rejected proposal would mean a real threat to both his business and his private life. Accepting it would mean working against his country – treason, to be brief. He was cynical enough not to be swayed by such pathetic high notions as 'the motherland' or 'the national interest'. The country for him meant hardly more than an industrial area where he made or stole his money. Where was his personal interest? What was the risk? Otto had answered these questions for himself a long time ago, as he had expected such a turn of events.

So, he decided to play along in the exciting game that he was invited to join. A game so familiar from his, not too distant, KGB past.

'Montgomery, I have become very fond of this country. I have fallen in love with it. I can see, clearly, that I have genuine friends here.' Otto emphasised the word 'friends', which caused Montgomery and John to smile and nod in appreciation. After all, 'the Friends' was how the SIS people liked to refer to themselves.

'I certainly will do my best to help you,' Otto was gazing at Montgomery, looking him straight in the eyes, 'not least because here in England, I have enjoyed excellent business relationships, support and assistance' (A hint: not for free. He would ask for services in exchange, John told me afterwards).

'Well, why don't we drink to this real, strong partnership?' Montgomery raised his glass. They drank the toast.

'Now, my *friends* (he stressed it, too, Otto noticed), I have to be on my way; need to be back at my department.

Please discuss all the necessary details in my absence.' He stood up and shook hands with Otto, sealing the deal; then nodded to John and was gone.

John and Otto agreed to meet in person once a month, circumstances permitting. Otto was a busy man and held a prominent position, he was often in the spotlight; thus, London was not ideal. They could meet anywhere outside Russia, when Otto went on business trips. Geneva, for example. Or at a resort, when the Russian was on holiday. Discreetly, without attracting unwelcome attention.

John could always be contacted through Anna; they were old friends. 'Oh no, not in this sense, Sergei. She is not one of us; just a friend,' he hurried to answer the question that was about to be asked. John did not lie, exactly; Anna was not on the staff, only an agent. That is, not a career officer. 'Just tell her when and where, and I shall come over. I will leave messages for you with her, you are in regular touch, correct? Or ring me up whenever you need me, but never from Russia. Well, you are a professional, you know better than that.'

Otto's first assignment (or rather, 'request' – such a high-level source is always asked politely, never told) was to find out whether Russia was prepared to follow NATO's lead on Yugoslavia. Civil war was raging there and Western pressure on President Milosevic was increasing. In case of NATO's military intervention, would Russia support NATO or Milosevic, or stay neutral?

Otto readily agreed. He was now a proper agent, an SIS asset, a source codenamed Derby.

As I had initiated the cultivation that led to his recruitment, and supervised it at all times, Alan decided to keep me as a controller of Otto's case. Security wise, this precluded new people learning about Derby, thus restricting the already tight circle of those who knew. John worked with Derby in the field, he was his liaison and went to all the rendezvous. I analysed the intelligence (it was always top-rate material) and produced shopping lists, that is new requests; I was in charge of the logistics and the budget of the operation. Quite a considerable one, by the way. This source did not need us to pay him, he could afford to fund the Service easily himself, with his fortune. However, he had expensive tastes, corresponding to his elevated position; and a bottle of Chateau Petrus at a clandestine business dinner with him cost us from three to five thousand pounds… Noblesse oblige. But it was worth it.

Before long I had accumulated so much damning evidence against Otto that, if he were to be grabbed by the Russian Federal Security Service (FSB), no connections and no bribes, however large, would save him. He would go down as a spy, lucky to get a ten-year prison sentence and his assets confiscated.

It was important now to work out the way to realise this evidence; how to plant it on the Russian counterintelligence in such a way that my cover would not blown with the FSB or the SIS?

Up to this point, the meetings with Otto had been relatively brief. There was no time for John to dig for gold in his KGB past: there were simply too many pressing, current issues that we urgently needed intelligence on.

And to blow such a source by too frequent or lengthy rendezvous was out of question.

Yes, at this stage the SIS had no time for the past, because of Yugoslavia, Chechnya, Iran, oil, the financial affairs of the Russian elite… But sooner or later, it would come to that.

Then, Otto would tell the story of a certain Dennis Antonov, whom he himself set up as a double for the British Intelligence back in 1989. I could not let that happen; so, I had to hurry to prepare a package of evidence for the Russian FSB and figure out a plausible channel for its handover.

Everything was ready by the summer of 1998; I was waiting for the right moment, and soon it came.

Otto had an office in Geneva, which traded in oil products and managed part of his assets. A couple of months previously, he had allowed the Russian Federal Security Service to send their man to work there under cover. The FSB by that time was authorised to carry out operations abroad, ostensibly to augment the SVR, the

Russian Intelligence. So, they approached Otto and asked him for a cover slot in his office. To refuse would be silly; far better to have the FSB on your side. Besides, it was safer to have your potential enemy close and know his face and movements. Not to let him guess that he is, really, your adversary. Makes sense. Otto discussed this with John, who supported the idea.

Recently the FSB bloke had been posted to Geneva. I now had an opportunity to slip the damning material into Otto's office, in such a way that the spy would certainly find it, 'by chance'. It was not too difficult a task. All I needed to do was to wait for Otto's next trip to Geneva, so that everything looked natural: he brought the staff and left it in the office, where it was discovered.

At the end of July, John told me that Derby was in London and brought a package and a microfilm containing more secret documents. The material was sent to the translators, with one copy forwarded to me: Alan was impatient to know the contents and I was privy to the operation and a Russian speaker.

John also told me the most important thing: the next meet with Derby was arranged for the end of September in Geneva. This was it! In two months' time, I would get even with Otto, Derby, Sergei Vladimirovich. I could book a ticket to Geneva. My trip there would look innocent to the SIS: after all, I was head of the Geneva office of Global Capital Management.

And these documents that Otto had supplied, plus some material that I had prepared specially, would be found by the FSB undercover officer in Otto's office. One can imagine what would follow. I was full of anticipation.

A month later, in late August 1998, Alan gathered our group in his room for a briefing. Having finished with instructions, he dismissed the officers. I was on the way to the door when I heard him say: 'Den, could you hold on a minute?'

I returned to the conference table, sat down, and looked at my boss inquisitively.

'I am all ears, Al.'

Alan took a thin 'In' folder, opened it and fished out a document: an urgent incoming call record.

'So, Den. Your charge and protégé, Sergei Lapin aka Derby, asked us for political asylum.'

'What???'

I could hardly keep my face straight; inside, I had the same disgusting, sticky, cold feeling as three years ago in Geneva. Suddenly, I had a flashback – the foreboding hit me with full force. Alan's office turned grey, just as the world did that time in Geneva…

'Where is he? What happened? Did he give a reason? Did he blow his cover? What shall we do, Alan?' I managed to ask, my voice turned hoarse; I coughed a few times convincingly. 'Sorry, bloody allergies.'

He poured a glass of water and shoved it towards me.

'Derby is a very successful case of ours, of course; your case, actually. Over the past year, he's supplied top-grade intelligence. It's a shame to lose such a source. I don't know myself yet, what happened to him in Moscow.

Obviously, he's in danger. This man is too serious to play the fool. But he came like a bolt from the clear sky. Flew in last night from Germany, and called John, his liaison. He is in our safe flat in Chelsea now. John is babysitting him. I am going over there right now. Any thoughts for the first questioning session?'

'Let me see… Aha. He was about to be confirmed as member of the National Security Council, as last week he became Chair of the State Duma Committee on International Affairs. His defection would be a huge scandal. Do we need that right now?

'We appear to be friends with President Yeltsin; a scandal would not be appreciated above…' Alan wiped his forehead, staring at me.

I struggled to keep my voice calm. 'The reason, at first glance, seems to be his conflict with his oligarch friends: our Sergei became too politically important, a heavyweight figure, and somebody felt threatened, their interests infringed. Most likely, he crossed someone; his financial machinations were tracked by someone close to him; and this someone sold him down the river. The authorities, thieves themselves, do not like when somebody steals from them. Do you know how much money he transferred from Kominvestbank to himself? Well, to those companies which he personally controls?'

'Around two hundred million?' Alan raised his brow.

'If you count all the assets that he controls through the scheme which we assisted him to set up, four hundred and fifty. Not dollars. Pounds sterling.'

Alan sucked in air noisily, then exclaimed: 'Crickey! Are GCM's arses well covered?'

'Yes, legally, Global Capital is as clean as a whistle. There is hardly anything we do not know about his scheme; we created it ourselves. And we can kill it any moment; he must understand this. Now look: there is an economic crisis in Russia, the country has defaulted. Private businesses have monumental problems. Kominvest is no exception. Politics over there is a jungle. Our boy was not KGB for nothing, he…'

‘Forestalled?’ Alan poured a glass of water for himself and drank.

‘Precisely. He’s decided to save his arse and assets, using Her Majesty’s protection. I am sure he will tell you how he was framed by his oligarch colleagues, how a criminal investigation was launched into his affairs, etc. And it will be the truth, but not the whole truth, of course. Fair enough, such developments are doubly dangerous for him as he is our agent. The investigators may well sniff him out, and that means the end of him, guaranteed. So, he did the right thing, from his point of view.’

‘OK, we shall play it quietly, try to keep everything under wraps. No public statements. If it comes to asylum, we shall grant it, but not on political grounds; on humanitarian grounds. Nothing precipitate, nothing official.’ Alan frowned, looking frustrated at having to lose a top-level infiltration agent. He sighed, clearly resigned to the thought, and wiped his balding head with a silk handkerchief.

‘As for this moment: he came over here on business and decided to stay on for a while. Health reasons. And he has a lover here, after all. His debriefing will show what to do next: Derby has a lot to tell us, what with his background and connections. We have plenty of time for that now, unlike when he was in the cold.’

I felt my stomach quiver.

Alan stood up. ‘Right, off I go. High time. `

We left Alan’s office together. He went to Chelsea, just across the Thames, and I to my desk.

What an appalling mess I was in! Otto’s debriefing meant total disaster for me. Up until now, I could control all the material received from Derby and edit it, should it become necessary. His intelligence was current; we were not interested in the past, as there was no time for it. Now I had lost control completely.

At this point I had accumulated so much damning evidence against Otto, that the Russian FSB would certainly pack him in. *But the bastard pre-empted me!*

Now he was safe and sound; there was plenty of time, our chaps would work with him slowly, methodically, and, sooner or later, every detail of Operation Traveller would be divulged to the SIS. My plan had backfired on me. The poacher had turned into game. Now I had to think, and quickly, how to escape the tsunami looming relentlessly on the horizon.

My head buzzed with conflicting thoughts and ideas.

Shall I run? I had some savings to live on, a passport in a different name. This would keep me afloat for a while. But where to? Certainly, not to Russia; soon enough, the West would become dangerous, too. The Office and the CIA 'cousins' would be looking for me. Should I go to ground somewhere in Latin America or Asia? They would find me all the same; it would just be a matter of time. So what, live the rest of my life in hiding? My head was about to split.

I went home, to Old Windsor.

Dazed, I was sitting with a pint of Old Speckled Hen in my local pub garden, on the riverbank, trying to work out all the possible scenarios. There was only one positive thing about the whole story: the Office would definitely want to keep the Operation Traveller business hushed up. A leak would be damaging to both our bosses, and those on the political level.

Most likely, they would bleed me white at interrogations, and throw me out on the street, bound by a secrecy agreement and blacklisted. Live as you like, but we will be watching. My colleagues know full well that I had no one to turn to. *But they could simply whack me, couldn't they? Sorry, 'eliminate' me?*

Oh, well, what the hell. It was all the same to me now. I felt strangely remote, indifferent, sitting there gazing at the Thames' quiet waters, as if they could help me make up my mind. The barman, as though he was tuned in to my thoughts, put on 'Stairway to Heaven' by Led Zeppelin:

'There is a sign on the wall, but she wants to be sure,

'Cause you know sometimes words have two meanings...'

A mere coincidence? The lyrics echoed my feelings. A sign on the wall… Oh yes, there was a writing on the wall, in huge bloody letters. And the words may have different meanings, two or more. Depends on *how* you read them. But I knew that in my case, there was only one.

Oh, well, I still had a little time. They cannot move that quickly. I would sleep on it and decide tomorrow, and now…

One more pint! *I am about to face interesting times now*... I thought, playing with the ancient Chinese curse: 'May you live in interesting times!' They were coming closer and closer, obscuring Old Windsor, the cosy pub, the river, the pint of beer on the table, turning my present reality into a mirage…

Chapter 6. INTERESTING TIMES

Tempus Fugit

The following day I went to work as if nothing had happened. Everything was quiet, nobody summoned me anywhere, no one looked at me askance. Maybe I would get away with it? I fought off the idiotic thought. There was simply no such thing as getting away with it; the machine was already grinding and would not stop until it was done. A matter of time, nothing more.

By the way, I apologise for using Latin frequently in my text, in case the reader finds it annoying. This language, albeit dead, is so precise and laconic that it can hardly be compared with any modern one. It is sometimes best to define the essence of the intended meaning in Latin. '*Tempus fugit*' is often translated as 'time flies'; but *fugit* actually means escapes, flees, runs away, as a fugitive...

I made up my mind: I was flying to Geneva as planned, on Global Capital business. Operation Fatcat was still running and I was still in charge. It was best to be away from the Office when all hell broke loose… With a spare set of documents, just in case.

My secretary reserved a ticket in the name of Donald Bruce, my alias, for the following day. I collected Donald's passport, driving licence and credit cards from my safe and went home to pack: it was a morning flight. On the way, I popped in the Coutts Bank branch in the Strand. There, in a deposit box, I had a Greek passport and twenty thousand pounds in cash. The Office was unaware of it; at least, I had taken all the precautions and rented the safe deposit box in the name of Gerhard Schmidt. This German passport was a fake, but good enough for the bankers.

The Greek one was genuine, one hundred per cent. It could pass any checks with flying colours. Janis Sokratos, its former owner, had been dead for three years now. Unofficially dead, so to speak. He had no relations, no attachments, and was a free spirit, a vagabond to be exact;

no one would ever miss him. Disappeared; oh well. How had I obtained his passport and driving licence? That is a different story, one of those accidental occurrences, a coincidence that was hardly a coincidence at all. The important thing was that we were roughly of the same age, and the face on the passport photo looked like mine. The shape, the nose, the ears, the eyes; the short dark hair: basically, all the features that the professional, trained eye of a policeman or a border guard would spot.

In those days, digital and biometric passports were still a thing of the future. Back then it was not so difficult to create correct documents to support a cover story; and nobody took your fingerprints at every turn, unless you were arrested. Why did I bother to have fall-back documents? Did I foresee something? Or was I planning something naughty? No, neither of these. It is just common for people of my profession to keep such stashes for a rainy day. Life is life; one never knows. Best to be prepared. It's a matter of survival.

The following morning, my British Airways Airbus took off, headed for Geneva. I relaxed in the comfortable

Club class seat and closed my eyes. Aeroplanes always calmed me down; it was easier to concentrate and think. The world with its hassle, its constant irritations, was far below, in a different dimension. There was nothing to distract me... I had nearly two hours to replay the scenario that I had worked out.

Well, how long did I have, until Otto, aka Derby, told the Office about a certain double, a set up called the Traveller, who had worked successfully for SIS for many years, at the same time reporting to Moscow? Bloody embarrassing. A trusted man, popular with the bosses, having access to top secret information. Shocking.

It was not the first time something like that had happened, of course. After Philby and Blake, the Service could hardly be surprised by any sort of treason. Add to this the rogue Richard Tomlinson, recently fired from the SIS, who was now running from country to country, threatening damaging revelations. The Office knew plenty about damage limitation; they had learned it from their own bitter experience. I was in deep trouble.

It seemed that I had very little time. Otto was likely to make a deal with the Office first: he needed guarantees, clear terms and conditions; a legal ground for the continued relationship. Not that his bargaining position was good: he needed the SIS to protect him; still, they would negotiate a deal. That would take one or two days. And then he would start pulling rabbits out of his hat. I had no way of knowing how many aces he had up his sleeve: surely, quite a few. He used to be a Colonel of the KGB and had served at the Central Headquarters for years. What I knew for sure was that every special service puts its own security above all else. Thus, any lead, any information pointing to an alleged penetration of a service, would be top priority! Always marked urgent. Otto knew this full well. So, the Traveller would be among the first pearls offered to the Office. Which meant that I could be grabbed at any moment.

Moreover, the Office would know that I knew that they knew about me. It was Alan himself who had told me the day before yesterday that Otto had asked for asylum in England…

On the one hand, I could go to Alan and tell all, fully and frankly. And hope for mercy. A fault confessed is half redressed, is it not so? However, this old saying was hardly applicable to modern times, times devoid of honour and the sense of good and bad. Another one came to my mind, a much more relevant one: a little sincerity is a dangerous thing, and a great deal of it is absolutely fatal. Oscar Wilde was an expert; he was an immoral chap, all right. So, I had to find a different way.

What was the worst-case scenario? Isolation at our safe unit in Kent; months of rough interrogations, possibly chemical, with the truth drug; certainly on the polygraph, the lie detector. Later, most probably, a release under supervision and without a penny. Maybe with a small severance payment, if they were happy with the interrogation results. No friends, as I did not have any who were not the Office. No chance to find a worthwhile job, and, in all likelihood, no passport. The national police database would have my name flagged: should it come up for any reason, be it a minor car accident or an application for a travel document, it'd be reported immediately by telephone number so-and-so.

In the best-case scenario, I faced interrogation all the same, but not as rough a treatment; a bit friendlier, so to speak. At the end of the procedures, same as above, but with a small pension. In my native country, I would survive that. Relatives, friends, I would have a lot of support. But in England? I was all alone, all by myself. This would mean a slow, but steady degradation, going slowly under, becoming a vagrant in real life.

Thus, the choice was between the plague and cholera. I could hardly avoid becoming Janis the Greek and leaving the hospitable Albion for good, before it strangled me in its embrace.

So, was it not best to carry out the metamorphosis, without waiting for the inevitable trouble to catch up with me? I had my answer. With Otto out of my reach and not removable, it seemed to be the only one.

By the time the Airbus landed in Geneva, my mind was made up. It was a shame to have to part with my colleagues, my work and the country that I sincerely loved; however, I could see no other way out, at least not for the time being.

I took a taxi and went straight to the GCM offices, without stopping at the Bristol hotel, where my secretary had booked a room for me. I needed to collect something from the safe in my room: several folders containing dossiers. I needed details of various offshore companies and banks, our laundromats for dirty money. The ones we helped our clients to set up and run. I could use this ammo in the eventual future negotiations with The Office.

The GCM offices were located in a small street behind the fashionable Des Bergues hotel. We had four staff: two Englishmen, one of them a fluent Arabic speaker, the other spoke Russian and was also SIS; there was one Swiss lawyer and a charming Italian lady, the office manager. The time was almost half past eleven when I entered; they were all drinking coffee.

'Hello everybody!'

They rose from the sofas and the armchairs; Jean-Claude came up and shook my hand, Leticia, all smiles, presented her beautiful dimpled cheeks to be kissed; Clive and Neil bowed their heads slightly. Neil, the Russian speaker, looked a bit tense. *Was that it? Was it happening already? Had Otto laid his cards on the table? The son of a bitch. So quickly?*

I was lucky to have been in the air at the time. But Neil was clearly warned and had been put on alert. This meant that our special action team was on the way here. I knew very well what they could do and how they would do it.

I announced an office conference at three in the afternoon and added that, right now, I had an important client meeting. Then I entered the director's room, and put my hold-all on the floor. I stuffed my briefcase with dossiers from the safe and cash from the bag; the Janis Sokratos passport went into my breast pocket. The mobile phone I locked inside the safe, having turned off the sound and the vibrator. Let it stay online, for those who wanted to check I was in my office. The Donald Bruce documents I took along with me. They could be used in talks with the

Office, if such talks ever materialised. At this moment, there was a knock on the door and young Neil came in.

'Boss, I wanted your advice on one client. This is urgent. The Office is waiting for a report.'

His eyes were shifty. Clearly, he had been told to delay me until the tough boys arrived.

'Look, Neil, I have a meeting in fifteen minutes. This will take roughly half an hour. Let us do this: as soon as I finish, I shall return, without even going to my hotel.' I deliberately pushed my hold-all bag towards the desk, for him to see. 'Then I am all yours.'

'Sure, Boss,' Neil relaxed visibly, having bought my ruse. He did not know that I knew, that the Office already knew, that I knew. He was not supposed to know it: on this occasion, the 'need to know' principle had worked for me.

I walked out into the street. It was raining: a good sign for the road. There was a cash machine on the corner; I inserted Bruce's credit card: had they blocked it already? Not yet: the machine spat out five hundred franks. Great, let them think that I had no other money. I broke the card in two and threw it into a rubbish bin. Credit cards and mobile phones are your worst traitors: they allow others to follow your moves to the minute.

I flagged down a taxi around the corner and went to Annemasse, a small town ten minutes' drive from central Geneva. The important thing was, that it was in France. That is, in a different country, in a different jurisdiction. Donald Bruce did not enter it. A certain Janis Sokratos did.

The taxi slowed down as it approached the customs checkpoint: the Swiss officer waved me through, the French one saw the Greek passport and followed suit. The French customs are only strict with the French and the Russians: they always check them for illicit cash. They pay little attention to other Europeans. Fantastic, here the trail goes cold. Nobody bothered to read my documents, so the Sokratos name was not marked at the border crossing. Well, and Donald Bruce flew to Switzerland and just got lost there.

From Annemasse I caught a train to Lyon; then from there, having changed a few trains, to Rome. The border checks had been abolished a while ago: thank God for the European Union.

The Eternal City was an excellent place for a temporary hideout; huge, a little chaotic; the inhabitants relaxed and easy-going; the system slightly corrupt. Everyone minded their own business; everyone, police included, lived and let live. If one did not stick out and draw attention, it was hardly a problem to disappear. With my new cover story, supported by genuine documents, no special services would track me down for a long time.

And I needed time to catch my breath, to reflect on what had happened, to analyse and plan the next steps – not forgetting to enjoy and admire the incredible delights and the unique atmosphere this amazing place had to offer. I felt like a traveller in time, visiting the Ancient World.

I moved into a family pension a stone's throw away from the Octavian August mausoleum. Living next door to the remains of the greatest and wisest Roman Emperor gave me hope that all would be well in the end and that I would find the way out of this mess…

Knowing our kitchen, its procedures and recipes quite well, I could vividly imagine what was going through the minds of my colleagues and superiors, in the corridors of invisible power that I had left behind. Some of it I surmised; most of it, however, was confirmed at some stage or other by people who I cannot possible name.

So, in the meantime, in his office on the bank of the faraway Thames, C was listening to reports from my now ex-boss Alan and the SIS Director in charge of security and counterintelligence, Richard.

'Well, there we have it, gentlemen. First, we need to evaluate the damage that Antonov has caused. Or could have caused. Both before he defected to England, and after. Alan, let us set aside your idea that he could have worked for us honestly.'

Alan started: 'But Chief, he took part in three serious, dangerous and successful operations. He risked his life!'

C raised his hand, impatiently. ‘I know. We shall give him credit for that, but now’s not the time. Right now, we proceed from the worst-case scenario. I agree with Richard about this. It is about the Service’s security, after all. Where shall we look for him? Any thoughts? Perhaps he’s with the Russians already? `

Richard shook his head. ‘Hardly. Derby is absolutely certain that all documents pertaining to Operation Traveller, as the KGB called it, were destroyed back in 1991. All but his own memo to the Deputy Chairman of the KGB; a progress report on the op. He later retrieved it, kept it, and brought it over here. You have the translation.’

‘Any witnesses? Who else in the KGB knew of the operation?’

‘The Deputy Chair was fired and arrested after the August 1991 coup attempt. He died of a heart attack in 1993. Apart from Derby, there was the courier, the liaison man. But his knowledge was strictly limited as his functions were purely technical. He resigned from the

FCD in 1991 and left Moscow, destination unknown. Also, the Deputy's aide. He shot himself after his boss was arrested. This is all, officially.'

Richard breathed out, feeling uneasy under C's steady gaze.

'This means that, on the surface, it is dangerous for him to flee to Russia. Officially he is branded a traitor there and he cannot prove otherwise, correct?'

'Yes, Chief, ninety-five per cent correct. I would leave five in case there is someone Derby does not know about. And in case Antonov has been playing a double game all these years.'

Then Alan intervened: 'But Antonov has worked for us a long time, without attempting to flee to the Russians. Indeed, his work caused damage to Russia. He was sure that he had no support over there.'

'What if he simply carried on serving Moscow all this time? An infiltration agent who was authorised to cause limited damage to his own? And what if Derby is not omniscient?' Richard looked C in the eyes, his expression eagerly obliging, ‘You are right, Chief; we must proceed from the worst-case scenario. However, in the case of a double game, he would be in Moscow already. This is what we have to find out as quickly as possible.’

‘Very well, so we are decided. You know what to do. Use all our assets in Russia that you may require. Richard, report to me daily, please.’ C nodded his head, dismissing the officers.

This meeting occurred on the second day after my disappearance. All allied and friendly services in Europe and across the Pond were advised and requested to assist. Interpol received a notice from the Office with all my real and operational names, aliases and details known to the Friends. Clearly, the notice said that I was wanted for large-scale money laundering on behalf of organised crime. The police and the media must not be enlightened as to what and who I really was…

What a wonderful stroke of luck that I had met a Greek fellow some time ago, whose passport I was now using.

This name was not on the wanted list; but a detailed description of my appearance and my photo was there, all right. Naturally, I had no way of knowing all this, but it was not so difficult to figure it out; we worked along the same patterns. Those, who did not, were called geniuses. Or fools.

So, I started with my appearance. To begin with, I bought spectacles with plain glass instead of lenses. This simple device together with a moustache (artificial at first, before the real one grew) changes your facial lines and proportions. Then the hair: I had always worn my dark wavy hair short. Now I was sporting a wig: long, straight and light brown. Later, when my own hair had grown enough, I would dye it and straighten it, instead.

I also began to learn Greek by Berlitz do-it-yourself course. I had to live up to my cover story, know enough Greek not to blow that cover right away, in case of a chance encounter. It would never work in Greece, naturally, but hopefully I could pass the test before Germans, French, Italians or Anglo-Americans. All I needed was a few words, a few phrases, in order not to betray myself.

There were still two vital issues left to address: to find a source of income and to determine a permanent dwelling place. My passport was valid for four more years and I could have it extended or changed without a problem. Within Europe, I could move freely, without leaving a trace, provided I was reasonably careful. However, I only had twenty thousand pounds in cash: not enough to live on for any considerable length of time, not in Europe.

I did have a flat in the UK, of course; worth around three hundred thousand pounds at the time. A car, another twenty. About fifty thousand in my savings account at the Royal Bank of Scotland. But how could I reach all these assets? Even if they weren't blocked and frozen, they would surely be watched.

Could I use my solicitor, Jeremy? He did some conveyancing for me some time ago when I was buying the flat; he also dealt with my family affairs. He handled the divorce with Elena. Responsible, trustworthy, meticulous and pedantic, in the best sense of this word, he was a chap who could not be leaned upon or pressured. He was unlikely to help my SIS colleagues against me, his client.

Be that as it may, they would watch his every step in the hope that he would lead them to me. They would follow all his contacts with me, any monetary transactions…

Which meant, first of all, that I needed a reliable, safe means of communication that would cut off my hideout completely. Secondly, I needed a couple of bank accounts in countries where the Office and its allies do not feel at home.

Or, should I simply ring up Alan, arrange a meeting and tell him everything? Put an end to this delirium; live a normal life? Would they allow that?

No, I was not ready for that yet. And no, they would not allow it, not yet. When I was prepared, when I felt strong enough to make my colleagues understand that I was not a miserable runaway who was losing ground and about to reach his breaking point: then we could have a productive conversation. Then we could discuss the terms of our future relationship, as equals.

And for now, I would call Jeremy. The Office would intercept the call, of course, which was fine. They would understand that I had not escaped to Russia. This would cool down some hot tempers and quell the urgency to catch the running fox. Then we could talk.

Fully aware of being on the wanted list, I travelled to Belgium to make my phone calls. The country was convenient: far from Rome, squeezed between France, Germany and Holland (forget about the tiny Luxembourg), which meant that after the calls, three avenues of approach and retreat would be open.

In Brussels, I bought three SIM cards in three different kiosks, and a couple of the simplest Nokia handsets, to use as burner phones. I made myself comfortable in a café not far from the railway station and dialled my solicitor's mobile number. Jeremy answered the call right away, as if he was waiting for it. His voice sounded a little stifled, checked. Presumably my colleagues had spoken to him already. I was positive that he did not doubt that I realised this.

‘Hi Jeremy, I am away on a lengthy business trip. Won’t be back anytime soon.’ I said this deliberately, in order not to set him up for those who were eagerly eavesdropping on his phone. ‘Please can you put my flat and car up for sale? I have sent you the keys and a special Power of Attorney, in case you need it; you have a general P of A that is valid, don’t you? The same to control my RBS account. Your commission is five per cent, OK?’

‘Den., How are you? How can I contact you? This number you are calling from?’

‘I am all right, travelling on company business, you know. I would rather get in touch myself or, if you need me urgently,’ I emphasised the ‘urgently’, ‘you can leave a message on my answerphone.’ I dictated a telephone number in Holland, which belonged to an answering service that I subscribed to.

This was a great service, very advanced for the time. Rather expensive; but it made it practically impossible to detect the location of the subscriber, provided he used mobile phones with caution. You could call your dedicated subscriber number from anywhere in the world, dial the PIN number, enter your mailbox, and retrieve messages. Then get rid of your SIM card. Sure, the messages could be heard by third parties, but if you were aware of this, what did it matter? You could just speak in code. I never used my laptop for communication, to be on the safe side; and smartphones were unheard of then.

The Power of Attorney, as well as the keys to the flat and the car, had gone off to Jeremy by registered mail from Brussels, before I made my telephone call.

I did not go to the railway station; out of the question. The used SIM card I pulled out of the handset and threw into a rubbish bin near the café. Let them check the CCTV cameras in and around the terminal, trying to find my likeness.

In a car park, a few blocks away, a very used black Ford Sierra with Roman number plates was waiting for me. I'd rented it for cash for a week from a semi-dodgy small rent-a-car firm called, rather fittingly, Palermo Cars, under a logo featuring Don Corleone from *The Godfather* movie. Good thing they did not call it Mafia Cars. No matter: they accepted cash with minimum paperwork and did not ask questions. I drove my Sierra leisurely back home, through Germany and France. On the way, I bought a few more burner phones and SIM cards.

As usual on the road, I felt shielded from the outside hassle; calm; my body alert to the world around me, but my inner gaze defocalised, allowing my subconscious to take over, freeing my mind. Memories were replaced by ideas, thoughts crystallised and plans emerged.

As I presumed, my telephone call to Jeremy was intercepted and the transcript put on Richard's desk an hour later. He summoned his deputy and gave him some orders. The Dutch phone number was checked and taken under control. The Belgian one was forgotten about:

clearly it was a one-off. Just in case, the Office informed their colleagues in Brussels of my visit.

However, the fact of the telephone call was eloquent enough: it proved that Dennis Antonov was not in Russia. The site from where the call was placed was located through the local call operator, accurately to a hundred metres: everything pointed to the café near the railway station.

So, if he had not fled to Russia by this point, there could be only one conclusion: Dennis had not worked for the Russians after his defection to England, and he could not possibly go there, it was a forbidden land for him. This confirmed the information received from Derby / Otto. What a relief that was…

But what to do with him now?

First: all the details of Operation Traveller must be squeezed out of him, in order to determine how much damage had been done. Second: although not formally on the staff, he was an SIS man, the bearer of many secrets, which could be extremely damaging if he leaked them to others. His disappearance per se was embarrassing and damaging, too. The Service couldn't afford to have him on the loose, wandering uncontrollably from country to country, doing God knows what. Who knew what was in his head? These fugitives often go off the rocker… And this was a specially trained one.

Richard thought for another five minutes, then dialled C on his direct number.

I could more or less imagine what would follow my telephone call to Jeremy.

The Office would realise that I was not a double; however, not everyone concerned would. There were some chaps there who were paranoid enough to see a ploy by the Russian Intelligence to deceive the SIS. Bob, one of Richard's deputies, was like that; he could see conspiracies and plots everywhere. Penetration agents, doubles, triples: the late James Jesus Angleton, the notorious spy catcher who virtually paralysed the CIA, could move over. Perhaps that is why Bob's wife left him. I recalled Lisa, the eccentric blonde, and could not help smiling. She and I had that chemistry; we were definitely attracted to each other. A pity it did not come to an affair; although I was against having affairs with colleagues' wives, Bob surely deserved it.

Most likely, they would try to get in touch with me. They had the Dutch cut-off telephone number; give it a few days, then I'd check the incoming messages. They would attempt to calm me down, to talk me into returning to England. They would offer guarantees…

Which certainly could not be trusted. The moment I arrived back in the UK, my life would be at the Service's discretion.

So, what shall I do? To begin with, I had to keep on my toes. I couldn't afford to relax. The best option for the Office would be to catch me: then they would not have to offer any guarantees at all. Clearly, I would remain on the Interpol wanted list until we reached an agreement – or until I was arrested. Yes, I need to contact them, but on my terms. I had to find a safe meeting site, in a neutral territory somewhere. Let Jeremy get on with selling my flat and car; the Office would not thwart him while we were having a dialogue. When he had sold the assets, the Service could have them frozen, in case our dialogue failed to bear fruit. Although, they must realise that such a measure could force me to start selling secret information… I knew quite a lot; besides, I'd snatched some documents from the GCM Geneva office, to strengthen my hand. They were well aware of this.

It was important for me to do a deal with the Service. A life on the run may look romantic and interesting, but only to cinema-goers. In real life, it exhausts you, wears you down, ruins your nerves. It sucks you dry, destroys your soul. In many cases, successful fugitives who could not be caught, end up breaking down and giving themselves up to the authorities.

I could offer the Office a full and frank account of Operation Traveller, provide all the details known to me; in exchange, I would want an end to the pursuit and my removal from all the wanted lists. I could return the Global Capital documents and sign a pledge never to disclose the fact or the nature of my work for the Service. I would demand written guarantees from the SIS in return, of course. I would have the right to choose where to live, and I would promise to keep the Office informed of my whereabouts. Naturally, I would stay in regular contact and would be at their service if and when required… That was roughly how I pictured my future life.

But first things first. The rendezvous site… All NATO and EU countries were excluded, as well as some others, like Australia, with whom the Office and the Cousins closely cooperated. In any of them, I would be captured on the spot, before I could blink an eye; after that no courts and no lawyers would help me. Argentina or Brazil might work, but they were so remote…

Lebanon! The civil war there had ended at last; the country was firmly under the influence of neighbouring Syria, which was hardly a fan of Great Britain or the USA. Its capital, Beirut, was an excellent place for such operations. It was easy to get in and easy to get lost in. Besides, the city had a sentimental value: it was in Beirut in 1963 that Nicholas Elliott, one of the SIS Directors, made his friend and colleague Kim Philby confess to being a Soviet spy, a traitor; it was here that the great spy Philby handed over to Elliott his written confession, admitting having worked for the Soviets for years, before fleeing to Moscow. I could not do the latter, though: for good or for bad, I was not sure.

Without drawing historical parallels, Beirut seemed to be ideal from my point of view. As for the Office, I hoped that my proposed rendezvous site would not cause an allergic reaction. We were pragmatists above all; what happened here forty years ago was history. The place was convenient, that's all.

In the process of thinking all this through, I barely noticed that the parasol pines along the road grew taller and closer to edges, and the traffic heavier and even more chaotic; I made it to Rome. By the time I entered the rental company car park to hand in my Sierra, I knew exactly what to do and when. In a week, I would call the answering service in Holland: messages from Jeremy and from the Friends will be there for certain. In the meantime, I would study Beirut. I had to select a secure meeting site, figure out approach and retreat routes, check and prepare all the logistics.

Straight from Palermo Cars, I walked to a travel shop and bought a few sets of maps and brochures. Beirut, the Lebanon, Syria. These, plus the Internet resources, by then quite reliable, should suffice for the preliminary planning. As soon as I had made arrangements with the Office, I would go to the site to do a reccie.

A week later, I picked up two messages from my Dutch answering service. The first one was from Jeremy: 'I received your letter. Keep on working on it. You have an offer: 270 thousand. The car is in a garage now, up for sale. You will get eighteen thousand when completed. Please call when you can.' Not bad, all things considered. Good man, my solicitor, very efficient. Well, and the five per cent commission is a good stimulus, too.

The second message was from Alan. A slightly muffled voice, the words clearly pronounced, crisp and to the point:

'Den, this is Alan. Do not disappear. Please contact me as a matter of urgency. It is very important. My telephone number is 07575617877, any time. I repeat… I look forward to your call. Your friends say hello.'

Now I could ring him up and arrange the rendezvous that everyone wanted.

I flew to Beirut from Frankfurt am Main three days later. Before that, I called Alan from Milan, using one of my numerous burner phones. He was clearly pleased. Alan did not try to stall, he agreed to Beirut without a second thought, and we selected a suitable date. On the day, I was supposed to call a mobile number provided by Alan and tell an SIS representative (Alan promised that it would be someone I knew) where to come for a chat.

I insisted on being removed from the wanted list immediately, as a pre-condition for our meeting (let them think that I had problems with my documents). ``Listen Al, since we are friends again, strike me off that damn wanted list, we don`t want the bells ringing all around while we meet and talk`.

Alan said OK, within two days my details would be removed from all the computers.

`Sure old boy, let me handle it`. I pretended to believe him. We said goodbyes almost warmly; after that, I discarded my handset and the Sim card, and boarded a train to Germany.

I wanted to be in Beirut at least two days prior to the meeting, in order to check all my findings once again: the carefully selected hotels, the cafés, the dry-cleaning routes. I had never been here before, and such important decisions could be made only after a thorough reconnaissance, on the ground: a map, even the most accurate and detailed, would not be enough. When personal security is at stake, no precaution can be spared.

My Greek passport did not attract any special attention at the Beirut airport. A policeman stamped in, off-handedly, a tourist visa, muttering 'Welcome.' A taxi driven by a cheerful and talkative driver was taking me along the sunny ancient streets, all still scarred by the civil war. Eight years had passed since it ended, but the devastation it left was so awful that it would take another eight to rebuild the ruins of the once prosperous Phoenician city with a history of many thousand years. Bullet-ridden walls, ruins still protruding from the ground here and there, children playing in the rubble next to rising new skyscrapers…

However, they were building everywhere. There was a construction boom in Beirut; the city strove to return to the fame and glory of being the 'Paris of the Mediterranean'. Another ten minutes, and we arrived at the newly opened Albergo hotel. Stylish, high class – just right for a Greek businessman and civil engineer, who had come to examine the potential for developing the urban infrastructure. This was my cover story for the trip.

For the rendezvous with the Friends, I have chosen a different place: the old, shabby Private Hotel, where I reserved a suite with a balcony offering a sea view and, more importantly, a view of the two adjacent streets, both one way. Thus, I could feel more in control of the situation. In case I had to escape, I could use the balcony to enter the room next door. But all this smacked more of spy movies; it hardly ever worked like this in real life.

In two days, a certain Gerhardt Schmidt, a German tourist, would check in here. Before that, I planned to walk around the city at length, past the British Embassy; from where my vis-a-vis was likely to go to the meet. This was a half an hour walk from the Private. Before Schmidt checked in, I wanted to be satisfied with the accidents of terrain, so to speak. If I were dissatisfied, the hotel would be changed.

I was very tempted to pop in to Joe's Bar, just off my route. It was here that Kim Philby could regularly be found propping up the bar before his flight to Moscow. However, such a visit was too risky: it was too close to the embassy, and too popular with the English, both diplomats and journalists. I could run into someone I knew. Not this time, I told myself; maybe later.

On the day, at about two in the afternoon, I checked in to the Private Hotel. For the very last time, I was to be Schmidt, the German: after the rendezvous, I would need to destroy his passport. His identity would have played its role and could be dangerous in the future.

The suite was large, the sitting room cosy and conducive to a long and sophisticated conversation. I felt my palms sweat. Was it just the humidity or the anticipation? At five minutes to three, I went out into Sabah Labaki Street, turned around the corner and dialled the mobile number that Alan gave me. It was answered after the second beep:

'Dennis?'

'Dudley? What a pleasant surprise!'

'Indeed, long time no see. Well, where shall I go?'

'The Private Hotel,' I dictated the address. 'I shall wait in the lobby. Will you be alone?'

'Yes, all by myself. Nobody will disturb us. OK, I shall be there in fifteen minutes or so.'

I sat down at a table in a café across the street from the hotel: from here, I could observe the entrance and the surroundings, unnoticed. Soon I saw a white Rover 820 with Beirut number plates. Only the driver was visible inside: he drove slowly along the street, looking for a place to park. Having spotted a space about fifty yards from the hotel and pulled over, the driver got out and walked towards the entrance, unhurriedly, swinging a fat briefcase in his right hand. Dudley! Just like the good old times! The briefcase contained a recording device, most probably; clearly, he would want to have our 'chat' on the record, to the minute. I did not mind. Rules are rules.

I waited till the heavy door closed behind him, then followed. On the way, I peeped into the parked Rover: no one there. The street was deserted at this time of day; how reassuring.

I entered the lobby. Dudley, a broad smile on his face, rose from an armchair to greet me. I shook his hand firmly. The Office knew whom to send to the rendezvous: I had always liked Dudley.

Once in my suite, Dudley took the armchair by the coffee table that I pointed to, and fished out of his briefcase an old-fashioned cassette recorder. He was connecting a hi-fi microphone to the device, while I was busy hanging the Do Not Disturb sign on the outside door handle, then locking the door and blocking it with a chair from inside the room. Having finished, I sat down opposite him and poured two cups of coffee.

'You have hardly changed at all, Den. How long has it been since we have seen each other? About three years? Four?`

'Yes, Dudley, trying to keep in mint shape. You as well, I can see.' I did not know if he was expecting to see me in a disguise; before the meeting I had taken off the wig, and shaved off the moustache and the budding beard.

'Well, déjà vu again, is it not?' Stephenson smiled and nodded towards the microphone, 'Just like good old times. How long have you got? Shall we start right away?'

'As long as we need, Dudley. You did not waste your time coming over. Just a minute, I shall turn the TV set on. Let the eavesdroppers enjoy that.' I turned on an elderly Sony and moved the TV stand closer to the entrance door.

A couple of hours later, Dudley turned off the recorder and asked for a drink, looking exhausted. I made two Bombay and tonics, being sure that inside the cassette recorder there might well be concealed another one, which carried on recording. That was our old KGB ploy, too: you make a show of switching the recorder off for a break; the client relaxes and spills their guts 'off the record'. Dudley knew that I knew of such ploys; but just in case, why not try it? We always did.

I pretended to have believed him. Sipping our G&Ts, we spent a good forty minutes remembering the old times, and battles long ago. I 'let my guard slip' and, looking worse for wear, confided to Dudley, even swore to him, that I had not even tried to contact the Traveller's controller since 1991, when my country and my organisation started falling apart. And that I was never a double after that. I hoped that it all sounded convincing and logical; the more so given that it was almost true. Of course, I did attempt to contact my controller, but I did not play a double game. There was no one to play games with in Russia, at that time.

In any case, those who wanted to believe me, would not be ashamed to do so. The tapes were convincing enough. In the labyrinth of mirrors of the intelligence world, objectivity is quite frequently substituted with impression. If it is impossible, or politically undesirable, to verify the facts (which is often the case), one has to rely on the multiple images reflected from one another….

We had some coffee, washed our faces, and re-started the session, with the recorder turned on. Dudley asked my permission and called his colleagues to tell them he was all right, but likely to be late. That was obviously a code phrase.

If they wanted to play cowboys, they would have done something by now. I thought they still might try after the meeting. At the very least, they would attempt to see where I came from, that was for sure.

We finished well after midnight. Dudley shoved his recorder and mike into the briefcase and leaned back in his armchair, clearly tired.

‘Come on, one for the road?’

I poured whiskey for both of us.

'Sorry, there is no ice. What next?'

Stephenson shrugged his shoulders:

'You know as well as I do. The recording will be analysed; the data correlated with whatever we received from Derby, and from you during the debriefing; they will raise all the files relevant to your good self; they will give any audio materials to psychologists… Security shall have their say, of course. It is their primary concern, after all. As for me, I am inclined to believe you, but my word is not the last one, as you know.'

'What shall I do while you are thinking, do you think? Am I still a wanted man?'

'Oh no, you are definitely off, for the time being. There is a paper from the Interpol. I brought it along for you to see.' Dudley passed me a letter with an official Interpol logo in the right top corner, complete with a sprawling signature and a blue round seal. I skimmed through it; put it back on the coffee table. I could only hope that it was genuine and not prepared by our experts. A trifle for them; but what was the point? In any case, I was not going to rely on it and relax.

'Wait one week exactly. Then call this number.' He gave me a piece of paper with a London number on it, 'Ask for me. Don't you want to give me Bruce's passport now? And the dossiers that you took from the Geneva safe?'

I shrugged my shoulders:

'Sorry, Dudley, I left them behind. But do tell my Friends at the Office that I shall return everything. Do you, by any chance, have a draft agreement on you?'

'The Service's proposals shall depend upon the results of the examination of all the materials pertaining to the case,' Dudley slid into the formal, bureaucratic language. Then a quick change: 'Between you and I, the draft will be ready by our next meet, next week.'

'Excellent, Dudley. I shall choose the next site, all right?'

Makes sense. Let us do it this way.'

Stephenson stood up, took his briefcase and extended his hand:

'Thank you, Den. Until next time. Thank you for your frankness and sincerity. You fooled us then, well done. No offence taken, you are a professional and you did your duty. *C'est la guerre.* The main thing now is to make sure that everything was above board after you came over to Britain. My instinct tells me that all shall be well.'

I squeezed his palm forcefully and saw him to the door. He looked at me over the shoulder in the doorway, nodded and walked towards the staircase. I checked the room, put the TV and the chair back in place; then glued on the moustache, put on my wig and spectacles. Waited another twenty minutes or so, then left my mobile handset on the coffee table, turned off the light and went out into the corridor. It was empty. I walked down the stairs to the ground floor, past the buzzing restaurant, via the service room, full of carton boxes; and opened the service exit door that led to a different street. I'd spotted it earlier today, before checking in. The skeleton key that I always carried when on business trips unlocked the battered old door without a problem.

Once in the street, I looked around. All quiet. A few parked cars, otherwise desolate. I walked in the warm, starry Lebanese night along my anti-surveillance route, towards the Albergo hotel. No tail, if you do not count those of a couple of homeless dogs who followed me in the vain hope of getting a sausage. This round was a success, my mind and heart were telling me. The future was still obscure, but now I could afford to wait and see.

Janis the Greek made it to the king-size bed in his hotel room and collapsed, drained of all energy. He slept like a log. In the early hours, a nightmare made him jump up in his bed: the room was on fire, and he couldn`t see where to run.

Chapter 7. THE CHANGE

Tempora Mutantur

Times change. Exactly one week later, I rang the London number that Dudley left. 'Can I help you?' a polite female voice enquired, having first dictated back to me the number that I dialled. 'Who is asking, please?'

I introduced myself and asked her to pass me over to Dudley Stephenson.

'Just one moment, hold the line.'

What melody! What intonation! Oh, yes, the Service was conservative and demanding when it came to the language of its staff. No regional accents, no dialects. Politically correct trends could not break through the defences of the bastion by Vauxhall Bridge. Besides, it was very important to speak clearly, so that every caller could understand and be understood. A couple of minutes later Dudley was on line.

'Den, I have everything ready. The draft agreement. When can we meet?'

'Can you make tomorrow?'

'Depends on where, old boy. Can you come over here?'

'Dudley, please be a tourist once more. For the last time, hopefully. We shall sign the agreement, I reckon.'

'So do I. Well, where shall I go to now?'

'Not very far this time. Tunisia.'

Stephenson laughed:

'Oh fabulous, we could go for a swim afterwards. The routine stays as the last time. I can come over the day after tomorrow. Call the number that you have got. We shall discuss business, close the deal, and relax a bit. I shall bring along Paul, our lawyer; you know him. So that we can do away with any legal issues that may arise, on the spot.'

'Good idea. In that case, I shall bring mine,' I put in, 'and we can solve everything there and then.' (I was bluffing. I did not have a lawyer handy, just said it in case the boys weren`t thinking of doing something stupid.)

‘Go ahead, but you understand what we are going to discuss. Some things are not for outsiders to hear.’

‘Never mind. He will close his ears when we tell him to.’

‘All right, the day after tomorrow, then. One more thing: don’t forget to bring along what we mentioned last time. This is important.’

He meant the operational passports and other cover documents for Donald Bruce, as well as the Global Capital files that I had removed from the Geneva office.

‘OK, will do,’ I said and turned off my mobile.

I had everything organised for the meeting: I was flying to Tunisia the following day, to get ready, using the Beirut scheme. It was necessary to think through, once again, the details of my proposed agreement with the Service, and try to be realistic about what I could count on, what the

Friends could possibly want from me, besides control and predictability.

I drafted some points that I wanted to be included into the agreement, thinking of today and also of my long-term prospects. I hoped that the Friends would be honest and that there would be no hidden traps or dodgy small print in their draft.

……………………

The two pages of legal text which we signed after a whole day of negotiations pre-determined my life for years ahead. All the household issues: finances, housing and such, were solved to my satisfaction. There was nothing to distract me from the main thing. From our cause, serving the national interest and keeping my mouth shut and my profile low.

Yes, my work for the Office would continue, but on a different basis and in a different manner. Previously I lived in a grey zone, like most of my ‘mainstream’ colleagues; from now on, I moved into the world of shadows. Not the afterworld; too early for that. I simply became a shadow, silent, light and inconspicuous. And extremely dangerous. All my official ties with the Office had been severed; I ceased to exist even for my SIS colleagues. I had to part with the world that I used to inhabit, all links to it cut off. There was no more Dennis for my acquaintances or relatives, without exception. Part of the deal. They had no entrance tickets to my new reality: I walked in alone.

Unofficially, informally, my work continued, but there were only three or four people in the Office who would know my true identity.

I returned to England under a new name; Dudley brought me the new passport; the Service quickly helped to create my new identity with all the supporting documentation. My new home was in Turners Hill, West Sussex. I used the money from the sale of my Old Windsor flat (the Office filtered it through cut-off bank accounts). Turners Hill is a sleepy village in the commuter zone not far from London: plenty of air, beautiful landscapes. The area is mostly populated by City types: bankers, lawyers, managers. Thus, when a new chap appeared in the local pub and the fitness club, it raised no eyebrows. William Anthony Dennis, financial and legal consultant. No more Dennis Antonov or Den Bates.

The place swarmed with his type.

Life was quiet and uneventful, generally. Even relaxed, as I no longer had office hours. From time to time my telephone rang and, having heard a familiar voice or a code phrase, the following day I caught a train to London.

Close to the Citylink station in Holborn, bordering on the City of London, there was a small safe flat. A safe studio, rather. Here I used to meet with Roger. He was my only remaining contact from the Office. I did not know his surname; his name was hardly genuine either. I felt sure it was an alias. But so what? This was our way.

He was of medium height, with greying temples, fit, agile, smartly dressed and composed: all this pointed to a military background. Most likely he'd entered the Office from the Special Forces, SAS or SBS. We did not waste much time talking; Roger would give me a file to familiarise myself with, sometimes thin, sometimes fat; always accompanied by photos. I read it very carefully, memorising the slightest details and the faces in the photographs. With his permission, I made some notes on a sheet of paper; they had to be in my hand. Then I returned the files to Roger: I was never allowed to remove them from the safe flat.

Afterwards, he would give me a brown envelope with cash, usually five thousand pounds: expenses. If I needed more, no problem. Then followed a glass of wine or a tumbler of whisky, depending on the time of day, small talk, and departure: first I, then Roger.

A few days later I would leave London for two or three weeks, or for a month, sometimes. As long as needed. Once out of the UK, I checked into a faceless hotel and made a phone call. Soon my room was visited by an equally faceless man, who would hand over a sealed envelope with documents – usually a passport of a third country, insignificant enough not to attract attention. He would also leave the tools of the trade necessary for the job, everything I'd requested from Roger. That was all; from then on, I was on my own.

Having done the job, I usually checked the news on the TV. Sometimes, my work made headlines. Often there were no reports at all. And once every quarter I checked my offshore HSBC account in Jersey: had the bonus arrived? Money was always credited on time; the amount would vary, according to the complexity and the importance of the job done.

I don't want to go into the details of my new work. To rake over the cold ashes, to open cans of worms or to bother the dead can be extremely dangerous: it mortifies one's soul and destroys one's mind. This is the domain of maniacs. Do your job well and forget all about it; wash it all away with water from your body and alcohol from your conscience. It is hard at first, but as you go along, you get used to it. However, if you do not manage to kill, or at least quell, your conscience, the cure stops being effective. No matter how hard you drink, it won't help.

Conscience did not trouble me at the beginning of my new career. The shadow spy did important work, serving the elevated interests of national security…

My private life was like a long tunnel without a light at the end. Somewhere, far away, my son was growing up; to be exact, he had grown up already, was in his twenties and graduated from Moscow University. A mathematician. Elena lived with her second husband, my former KGB colleague and classmate turned businessman. He owned three car dealerships and a travel agency. I hoped she was happy. We were not in regular touch; from time to time, mostly through my parents, we exchanged standard good wishes for Christmas or birthday. I had to do it clandestinely, using an alias; the Service must not know, because we were bound by agreement and officially Dennis Antonov no longer existed. My family was advised of a tragic boat accident off the Portuguese coast…

Contracts and treaties must be fulfilled. *Pacta sunt servanda.* But there are always small exceptions, the notorious small print people usually overlook…

I did have a girlfriend, though. Her 'candidacy' had to be approved by the Office after we made love for the first time, liked it and decided to carry on. At the end of the day, if a man is a complete loner, he can go off the rocker and do something incredibly silly.

I suspected that she, Nicola, my sexy and gorgeous girl, was actually introduced to me by the Service. They did it subtly enough not to expose the Service's involvement; it was done in a sophisticated manner and looked natural, so that I would not have an adverse reaction, or reject her on reflex.

Despite my suspicions, I did not mind it at all. Nicola was just what I needed, in all respects. Beautiful, clever (and clever enough not to show it too often), educated, accomplished. A cook in the kitchen, a lady in the sitting room and a nymphomaniac in bed. And no strings attached, no commitments or demands or attempts to dominate my life: what more could I wish? I could not care less that Nicki reported regularly to the Office, so I pretended not to notice or understand. Living with someone you can`t trust, sharing your pillow with her –

but never your true thoughts: was it what they call a professional deformation of personality? It never occurred to me just how naturally it would happen to me.

I lived like this for two years. Slowly, I came to realise the change in me: I had become a different man. *Tempora mutantur, nos et mutamur in illis.* Times change, and we change with them. How true. Something that I had shunned, had tried to avoid all my life, had become an everyday part of it. I was so used to it now; the only thing missing was a collection of scalps on the wall. The silent hunter could not afford to brag about his triumphs.

Although there was no scalp collection, I had a more useful one: a collection of the unused items from my inventory list, things that I was supposed to destroy after the mission, but did not. Instead, the collection was added to after each job. Who knows when and for what purpose they could prove to be handy? I kept all this stuff in a waterproof hiding place that I had prepared in the woods, not far from home. To have a cache at home was silly and dangerous: no matter how well hidden, it would be discovered by professionals sooner or later. Since the contents were totally illegal, they were damning evidence. There could be no escape if I was caught in possession. The park, on the contrary, was safe: even if it was found, there would be no evidential, no provable, link to me. *Not mine! I know nothing*. And that would be that.

This collection contained some very interesting samples of special devices and chemical agents not available even from the best spy shop in the world. Neutralising and soporific sprays and drugs; also those that loosen tongues or make the victim die without a warning, leaving no trace for an expert to see.

This ampoule I hid, having returned from Montreux. A Sheikh from Saudi Arabia came to this picturesque Swiss town to enjoy the July Jazz Festival, as he did every year. A typical sheikh, who stayed, as one would expect, at the Fairmont Montreux Palace hotel, with a stunning view over the Alps and Lake Geneva. He enjoyed the festival, listened to his beloved jazz, and minded his own business.

Yet it was him, who (together with his partners, also identified) financed the training and the preparation of those fanatical Muslim kamikaze pilots, who, on the 11th of September 2001, navigated their hijacked airliners full of terrified, screaming passengers, right into the Twin Towers of New York… A nightmarish, grandiose, incredibly spectacular, cruel and bloody act of terrorism to glorify Allah; over three thousand dead.

Intelligence regarding the Saudi came from our agent source and was re-checked, and found to be one hundred per cent correct and genuine. Officially, neither us nor any law enforcement body in the world had anything on him. He was clean, untouchable. On top of that, he was in with high society, friends with some Royals… And Saudi Arabia was, of course, our main ally in the region and the multi-billion-pound contractor for our defence exports. The Sheikh was a prominent figure at home; a scandal was out of the question. This is why he had to die of a sudden heart attack, sleeping peacefully in his hotel room in the quiet Swiss town.

Fair enough. The night before, when the Arab was out having supper, surrounded by beautiful hookers, I entered quietly his luxurious bedroom and emptied one ampoule of the colourless liquid into a bottle of his favourite Perrier water, standing on the bedside table… So, he exited this world cleanly as he came into it; the autopsy showed no signs of foul play, no traces of any poison. The second, reserve ampoule, I brought to England.

And here is one more toy that served me well. This time near Amalfi, an Italian town to the south of Naples, where one criminal billionaire type had built a palatial villa on a cliff.

Apart from drug trafficking and money laundering, he had a few hobbies. Fine art was one; the man was a well-known collector of Old Masters. He (let us call him Alex for convenience's sake) sponsored famous orchestras and art museums, and rubbed shoulders with some prominent figures: politicians, bankers and aristocrats from major European countries and the Americas. It was for them that he set up a network of exclusive luxury brothels, offering a complete service to satisfy the most discerning, not to say perverted, clients.

He loved to see his face in the glossy magazines' society gossip sections. With such connections, he was practically unapproachable, beyond reach. But he got carried away: decided to blackmail a high official from a major NATO country in the interest of his main businesses. He needed this fellow to keep a blind eye on his new supply channels. The hook was the official's sado-masochistic pursuits, duly videoed, photographed and documented at one of Alex's brothels, the Nice branch. Having done this, Alex overstepped an invisible borderline.

His target was no less than a minister of internal affairs, who had been nominated as the next NATO Secretary General. How could such acts against him be tolerated? They needed to be nipped in the bud, quickly and discreetly. Alex the scoundrel had gone too far; he had overreached himself this time. But blackmailers are all alike: where he had tried once, he would try again. Apparently, he had been collecting compromising stuff against VIPs for some time, and now he began to put it to use.

Alex loved his Lamborghini Diablo: the high speed was like the narcotics that he liked to sell to other people. The adrenaline went to his head, made him high. The Amalfi Coast, *Costiera Amalfitana*, is all steep cliffs. The road along it is all hairpin turns and seems to be suspended five hundred yards above the sparkling sea. Incredibly beautiful, stunning. But also very dangerous. It only took a little time and effort to research his habits and favoured routes.

I waited till the right moment came: Alex left his beloved Diablo in a car park near the Cathedral of St Andrew. This ancient twelfth-century *Duomo* is actually the resting place of St Andrew's relics. Amazing, but this individual, totally immoral and with a form miles long, was a believer. There was also another possibility: he was just superstitious and prayed in case there was a higher force that could alleviate, if not forgive, his sins. In that respect, he was not unlike us spies. My research showed that whenever he went to the *Duomo,* his bodyguards stayed at home. It was very close to his villa, and he was very confident. One only had to descend about half a mile down a steep slope.

It took me around sixty seconds to unscrew the air valve cap on his front right tyre and to spray the agent inside it. I fixed the cap back and vanished. All one had to do now, was to wait till the car was driven long enough for the air inside the tyres to heat up and expand. Then the agent from my spray would be activated, causing a spontaneous and violent expansion, so that the tyre blew up. There we have it: an accident. On a narrow, serpentine road and at a high speed, chances are that it would be fatal…

The following morning I was sitting in a small café in the *Piazza del Duomo* overlooking the Cathedral. Sipping at a cup of perfect espresso, I opened the local newspaper. There we go. A large photo of Alex, followed by a few more, taken from the cliff: the remains of his yellow Lamborghini three hundred yards down. The prominent businessman and local benefactor lost control as he accelerated. There was at least a hundred-yard freefall before the Diablo hit the rocks below. They found a body of a young girl next to him, not yet identified. Pity, but this was her fate. She was seeking her happiness with a dangerous partner.

The spare spray bottle complemented my collection.

One Friday a call came in from Roger. It was unusual, as that meant that the meeting would be the following day, on Saturday. Weekend meetings had never happened before. It had to be something urgent. I hated emergencies, but they were part of *bushido*, the Way of the Warrior. There was no escaping them.

It was 2002. The preparation for the invasion of Iraq was in full swing. The invasion was a US idea and initiative, readily supported by Great Britain. Lately, London readily, and slavishly, supported any American adventures. As far as I knew, there was no reason at all to invade Iraq, except our lust for its vast oil reserves and the weakness of Saddam Hussein's regime. There was no legal reason or pretext for any military intervention; but the attack on Iraq had to be justified somehow. The allies had to create legal and moral grounds, to make the act of aggression look like a noble act justified by international law and humanitarian rights.

A massive propaganda campaign bordering on hysteria was whipped up in the USA, the United Kingdom and in Western Europe. Iraq was accused of allegedly producing weapons of mass destruction; Saddam was said to possess the means of delivery of chemical and biological weapons, and purported to have the capacity and the intention to launch the first strike. It was ludicrous, there was no proof whatsoever; nobody cared.

The US and UK governments fabricated the alleged intelligence reports ostensibly received from their respective services, which purported to 'confirm' and 'prove' the existence of weapons of mass destruction in Iraq. They tried their utmost to pull through a United Nations Security Council resolution that would sanction the planned invasion, but in vain. The UN International Atomic Energy Agency sent in its teams of professional and independent inspectors: they found no trace of WMD. Whatever Saddam had before was destroyed years before, under international supervision. Stop right there? Oh no.

President George W Bush and Prime Minister Tony Blair could not wait: the troops had already been deployed to Saudi Arabia and Kuwait and were just waiting for the attack signal… Who cares about what the UN says?

Before the invasion even started, American and British oil and construction corporations were busily sharing huge Iraqi resources and the large amounts of taxpayers' money that was allocated to rebuild the infrastructure of the sovereign state that still existed, that was still independent…

I was holidaying in Sharm El Sheikh, Egypt in February 2003, happily snorkelling and making underwater films; my Controller from London called me and told me to get out by March, even if I had to cut it short. No explanation offered, none required.

The invasion was to be carried out no later than spring 2003: everything was ready, the dogs of war were straining at their chains and howling impatiently. One simply cannot restrain a fully deployed and primed army for a long time; besides, from May on, the heat in the desert would be such that it would render combat most uncomfortable. So, screw the Security Council resolution. The US–UK coalition was decided. And nonetheless…

If, at this very moment, information was made public that would provide a detailed disclosure of the falsifications, of the fictional pretext of the weapons of mass destruction, of the manipulation of the public and the Parliament by the government; if such an exposure, substantiated by facts, came from a very reliable government source, it would be a disaster.

A publication *post factum*, after the attack, would not have any practical effect, but it would still be politically damaging and have potential legal consequences. But right now? It could really ruin all the plans, frustrate the colossal efforts of the war machine, and indeed snatch a delicious sandwich from the salivating mouth… A worldwide anti-climax.

That is why, when the real threat of such revelation emerged, it made our great leaders panic.

The threat had concrete names and faces. One was Doctor David Kelly, a scientist and expert on weapons of mass destruction, formerly a UN weapons inspector in Iraq. He worked at the Ministry of Defence and knew the situation in that country thoroughly. Kelly knew full well that there was no WMD in Iraq. But what was much worse for the powers that be, apart from expert knowledge he also had conscience and courage. He could not just watch the disaster come, he must act. Kelly started writing reports and memos to his superiors. All of them were ignored. Nobody wanted to know the truth, the machine steamed ahead, the vast oil reserves beckoned…

Having realised that he would never get anywhere through official channels, Kelly contacted the news media. He began to leak information, at first anonymously. However, he was uncovered very quickly. They managed to shut him up at that crucial stage; later though, after Iraq fell to the aggressors and no traces of WMD had been found in the devastated country, Kelly broke his silence once again and started making damning public statements.

According to international law, there are only two legal ways to send foreign troops to a country: a sanction by the UN Security Council, or a formal invitation from the legitimate government of that country. Anything else is aggression, an international crime. Those guilty must be criminally responsible, according to the same law. That is Tony Blair and George W Bush; the military command; the special services… All those, who gave orders and who knowingly participated in the aggression.

And so it happened that the courageous Dr Kelly, a hounded man by then, branded a traitor of national interest and fired from his job, left this world very conveniently. In July 2003, he was discovered dead in the woods near his country home, where he used to go for walks. Apparently, he'd cut his veins open, right in the woods. The coroner's court delivered a 'presumed suicide' verdict. The forensic scientist's examination report remained classified. The potential witness, capable of giving devastating evidence in the International Criminal Court, of exposing the illegal aggression, was dead!

The political elite breathed out with relief. One irresponsible journalist had the temerity to ask the Prime Minister at a news conference: 'Mr Blair, is there blood on your hands?'

The question was ignored and the hack was shushed by his colleagues and shut up by his employers. So much for the freedom of speech.

But here I have put the cart before the horse, just to make clearer the circumstances of the times. The events that I am writing about happened in 2002. At that point, Dr Kelly seemed to have been brought to order. However, quite apart from him, we had a problem that was much more acute, much more serious.

This problem's name was Hugh. The same good old Hugh, the head of the SIS non-proliferation group. Weapons of mass destruction in general were also his remit. And, like Dr Kelly, he had a twinge of conscience, too.

No matter how knowledgeable, Dr Kelly was a man from the street, that is to say, not an officer, nor a career civil servant; not really an insider. Hugh, on the contrary, was our man, one of us: a career SIS officer with access to a large quantity of secret data. Potentially he was a bomb that could blow the Service and the government itself, to smithereens….

Hugh was an experienced and professional man, but romantically inclined. He still believed in good and bad. This trait let him down. He carefully selected a *Sunday News* investigative journalist who was renowned for his brave, insightful, revealing stories. Hugh met with him covertly, using all the tricks from our arsenal. He told him exactly what material he had access to. Publication of this stuff could really knock the UK out of the anti-Iraq coalition with the USA. It would have been a tremendous scandal.

Hugh understood perfectly well that he would be prosecuted under the Official Secrets Act. He was prepared to become a martyr; it was acceptable to him to suffer for the cause of the truth and in the name of the true national interest of the country that he dearly loved.

What Hugh could not possibly know (but should have suspected) was that the hack he turned to, despite his reputation as an intrepid and upright exposer of secret manipulations by the government and its secret services, had been our asset for a long time. The Service fed him some juicy pieces of sensational news, thus making public whatever scandalous material it wanted, while remaining in the shade. This hot stuff also blew up the hack's reputation ever more; the grateful pen pusher, in his turn, dutifully reported back anything that could be of interest to the SIS. So, having learned about Hugh's dossier on Iraq, which he wanted to have published, the journalist informed his Office controller the following day.

Two days later, on Friday, I received the summons from Roger.

Hugh's fate was decided at the very top and very quickly. To procrastinate in this matter would be lethal, they knew it well. The *Sunday News* source reported that in mid-January, after Hugh returned from his holidays, he would receive from the officer top-secret material concerning the mishandling and the direct falsification of intelligence on Iraq by Tony Blair's government and the SIS top brass. Such a revelation would mean the end of many a brilliant career and the failure of ambitious plans. In short: a fiasco.

'This man must be silenced forever. But it must look natural. Needs to be done quietly, without drawing anyone's attention. A tragic accident…You will see to it, Den. Oops, sorry, William. You can decide how. Your bonus will be doubled: this is a special case, with so much at stake.'

Christmas was near. Roger told me that Hugh and his wife were going to Megeve, in France, for two weeks to ski. This was an opportunity not to be missed: I read very carefully the detailed reports on his planned route, the hotel he'd booked, his habits and ways. Roger, my greying controller, watched me intensely. I knew Hugh well personally, of course. This fact could also be useful for the mission. I felt nauseated inside, but struggled to keep a straight, professional face.

Having finished with the dossier, I handed it back to Roger. There was no way I could refuse the assignment, or I could well end up next on the list. Hugh was a dead man anyway. He was sentenced, and there was no avoiding the execution: if not I, somebody else would do it.

'Any questions, Will? All clear? Good. The Chief relies on you. The traitor must be punished.'

'What if I need support?'

'You have done pretty well on your own till now. It's too sensitive to involve somebody else. Here is something for expenses; more than usual. Christmas, you know. Tickets will be more expensive, and Megeve is not a cheap resort, either. Do your job and have a holiday – two weeks in the Maldives, right? The Office will be happy to pay. For your girlfriend, too, should you wish to take her along.'

Roger gave me an envelope. Fifteen thousand pounds cash. He poured two glasses of wine.

‘Here is to success, as our tradition demands. Good luck, and see you the other side of Christmas.’

I raised my glass, silently.

We parted as usual, I was the first to go, then Roger. Ten days left to Christmas. There was a lot to do…

Two days later, I flew to Malaga, in Spain. I rented a flat for a month in Marbella, on the Avenida del Mar. On the way there, I dropped in on the British Consulate in central Malaga and collected a sealed envelope from one of the clerks. A British passport, a driving licence, a credit card. All in yet another name. Norman Foster this time. Everything as usual. The plan did not foresee the use of any tools this time: I would improvise.

A few days later I caught a Swissair plane to Zurich, Switzerland. Then a train to Geneva. It felt odd to revisit the city that I had fled from in a hurry a few years ago. A full circle of destiny.

I made a point to direct the taxi driver to pass by the exact place in Quai du Mont-Blanc where, at the traffic lights, several years back, I had been stunned by that powerful premonition, which I now knew was a sign from above. *Would I feel anything this time?*

My heart missed a beat when we reached the spot. The sign was imprinted deeply in my mind; I had ignored it then, and now what? *What had become of my life? Who am I, where am I going to?* Why could I not just have forgotten that idiotic idea to revenge myself on Otto: this was what I was warned about, was it not? Well, too late now. That is how it goes; that is life. And this will pass before long, too.

There was just over an hour's drive to Megeve from Geneva. Hugh and his wife were supposed to arrive two days later. I rented a car and drove to the site. I needed time for the reconnaissance on the ground. A thorough look around.

On the ground, it all looked straightforward.

In the woods on the mountain slope, above the town, there were several aparthotels. The chateaus were scattered picturesquely across the slope; each chateau had two or three apartments. Hugh rented one of them. The place was quiet and desolate. The woods were criss-crossed by walking paths, some of them verged on precipices. From Hugh's personal file I knew about a habit that he never changed, wherever he was: a morning jog. First thing he came to the Office, he always disappeared in the shower room to wash the sweat off and change. Well, the plan emerged by itself.

I returned to Geneva for the night. I intended to encounter my 'client' the day after next, after they had arrived, checked in and Hugh had fallen into his daily routine.

Meanwhile, I needed to prepare. There were a few things to buy…

In the morning of the 23rd December I left my car in a car park about five hundred yards from the aparthotel, among a few dozen other cars: most holiday makers had arrived and were getting ready for the celebrations.

I was clad in a light grey jacket that blended well with the white-greyish background of slopes and pines and firs, all covered in snow. I waited in the trees on the edge of the wood and watched Hugh's chateau through my mini binoculars. Half past seven. I was beginning to get cold and swallowed some strong tea from a pocket thermos flask. Where the hell was he?

At eight sharp the door to the chateau flew open and there, in the doorway, emerged a slight figure in a padded red windcheater and a knitted sports hat. Hugh breathed in the clean cold mountain air and jogged along the path leading towards me. I retreated behind the furs. Let him carry on for a couple of hundred yards; the path ahead made a sharp bend around a cliff, which hid it completely from any observer from the hotel. Not a soul around. There were no more jogging fans who would venture out so early in the morning, like my client. The situation was just perfect for my plan.

I waited some more for the red windcheater to disappear around the bend and then jogged after it.

Chapter 8. GOING PRIVATE

...Nos Et Mutamur In Illis

...And we change with them, with the times: this part of the Latin proverb was ringing in my ears, like a mantra.

I turned around the bend and ran faster. There was a precipice on the right, firs grew thick on the slope, branches heavy with snow. The path here straightened and led gently uphill until the next bend: there, right behind it, I would catch up with Hugh.

A few more seconds... He was not there! I accelerated, ran another hundred, two hundred yards: no Hugh. Nonsense! What on Earth...? I stopped and looked around carefully. There were no footprints on the path, the snow had melted and the surface was a mixture of small stones, gravel and earth. Could he possibly have dashed forward and outpaced me? Hardly, this geek was not strong enough. So where was the bloody client?

He could not have climbed up the mountain, not here. It was too steep to climb without special gear.

I turned around and slowly walked back down the path, intensely focused, inspecting the precipice. It was steep, maybe sixty degrees, and thirty to forty yards deep. I almost made it back to the bend when I spotted what seemed to be a splash of red on the white snow below. A jacket? I took out my binoculars…

Hugh was lying face down, his right arm twisted awkwardly. His fall had been broken by an old tree stump fifteen yards down the slope. It was so still around. No wind, no movement at all. The silence was humming. I swore and, holding on to fir branches and bush, carefully descended to Hugh.

He was dead. I felt for a heartbeat, his throat and wrist: nothing, there was no throbbing. There was no blood, either; it looked like his neck was broken. But how could he fall from a wide path like that, when it was not slippery at all? Carefully, so as not to slide downhill myself, I moved forward. About thirty yards away there were footprints in the snow: they led from above, and disappeared below, somewhere near the bottom of the precipice.

I suddenly felt hot, my hands trembled in an attack of rage. *They forestalled me! Fooled, I was fooled! The bastards played it safe!*

Breathing heavily, I climbed back onto the path. It had started to snow; now, there would be no footprints left to see, neither theirs, nor mine. Here we have it: a classic 'tragic accident'…

But it meant that I was being watched. Not everywhere, of course: I would have detected the surveillance. The must have done it only in some key points. The car rental in Geneva. Megeve, Hugh's chateau. Here I am, watching him. And here he is, dead. Any investigator worth his salt would put two and two together and take me down. I was framed. What a set up! But why? This I would learn before long; for now, I needed to vanish into thin air, no one must see me. Apart from those who had already done so.

I caught a flight to Malaga from Geneva; prior to that, I made a phone call to London. A lovely, moderated female voice answered. I left a message for Roger: Merry Christmas from William and added: 'and a Happy New Year.' This meant that the mission was fulfilled, but not everything went according to plan.

In the rented flat on Avenida del Mar in Marbella I drank myself into stupor and slept for three days. The sparkling sea was not welcoming; the *fiesta* below, on the splendid promenade, did not cheer me up. When I finally sobered up, I felt cleansed, calm, and confident.

On the eve of the New Year 2003, I went to the *Plaza De Los Naranjos*, the Orange Tree Square, in Marbella's Old Town. Here I mixed with the joyful crowd and drank champagne, swallowing grapes for luck, one for each strike of the clock on the old town hall building. I called Nicola and told her I would bring a nice surprise present to compensate my absence…Business, damn it.

Now I knew what to do next. All would be new in the new year.

On the tenth of January, I flew to London.

There were no reports about Hugh's death in the media, except one local rag that published a brief notice about a careless English tourist who fell down the slope and broke his neck. Roger showed it to me when we met right after my arrival.

'Well done, William. A very professional, clean job.'

'Roger, he fell down himself. I was chasing him, he probably noticed, panicked and slid off the path. I did not touch him, did not have to…'

(It was necessary to say all this. Roger knew the truth, of course; but I said nothing about the footprints that I found: let them think that I was ignorant of their involvement.)

'Listen, Will, what is the bloody difference? Thank you for being honest, but it is the result that matters. Whatever you did, or didn't do, you produced a good result. Everyone is happy. You did your job; Fortune assisted you a bit. To be brief: you get your double bonus. Now collect Nicola and off you go to the Maldives. As promised. As soon as you find the hotel, let me know and send me the reservation invoice. The tickets, the final bill – the Service is happy to pick them all. You have two weeks to fuck your brains out, you lucky devil.'

We shook hands and I went outside. It was drizzling in the street: your normal January day in London.

I bought *The Times* in a kiosk on the corner and found a pub nearby, where I could nurse my pint and read my paper, unbothered. There was nothing new in the news, the same old scares about Saddam Hussain being poised to strike the British military base in Cyprus with chemical warheads. What rubbish. However, this nonsense was allegedly confirmed by intelligence from reliable sources: one story carried a title referring directly to SIS as standing behind the information. The war was nigh…

Poor Hugh. Would there be someone else, brave and knowledgeable enough, who could put an end to this bloody rampage?

An intelligence service has in all times and ages served its political masters, in the sense that it obtained the required objective and trustworthy secret information, upon which sound political and military decisions could be made: how to act, or not to act at all, in the interest of the nation. The primary duty of a service has always been to make sure that its product was solid and reliable, accurate and true to fact.

So how could it be that the Service, even under pressure from the political leadership, the Prime Minister himself, falsified its own intelligence reports and then presented them as genuine, and allowed them to be made public and referred to by the media as coming from reliable 'SIS sources'. Unprecedented. To turn the most respected intelligence Service in the world into a prostitute and to gag all those who disagree… The Chief had not resigned in protest: this meant that he agreed with our new role.

How I wished I could share these thoughts with someone! But who? Jeremy? Out of the question. Nicola? She would report it the next day. A friend I could fully trust? Did not have any. A bartender at a pub (but not a local one) seemed to be the safest choice. Best keep it inside, this is what normally people of my profession do, until they blow their tops off.

Something like this happened in the USSR in Joseph Stalin's times. The heads of the intelligence services were so afraid to fall into disgrace with him that they did not dare to displease the cruel dictator by correctly reporting the inevitable Nazi Germany invasion in 1941. Instead they reported anything that would coincide with Stalin's own view of the situation, or, better yet, confirm it. Of course, there were courageous people who dared to say the truth, but they were all executed, shot by the paranoid tyrant….

But surely Britain was not the USSR and Tony Blair was a far cry from Stalin? Nobody would have been shot, would they? So, what were they afraid of? Of being demoted or fired? Of losing their pensions? Petty, was it not…?

Of course, I was not going to eliminate Hugh: he was not one of those scumbags whom you remove to make the air cleaner; to rid the world of whom is a noble task. He is a good man, a man of integrity. Or was, rather, poor thing. My plan was to warn him of the imminent danger and offer to place him in hiding. If he'd agreed, I wanted to move him and his wife, covertly, to the Marbella flat first; there, in relative safety, he could play for time and work out his next move. I would provide all the help and support.

Hugh turned out to be a man of dignity, a man of conscience, which is so rare in our system. His death shocked me profoundly, and kicked me out of my mental and spiritual lethargy, where I had been dwelling for the past two years.

This death meant that someone in the Office had considered the option that I would possibly let Hugh live. Bob, the former deputy, and now the new head of security and counterintelligence? It was his style, and he was right this time. He had always treated me with suspicion, if not with poorly hidden distaste… So they had decided to hedge their bets.

They killed two birds: one literally, and the second one, that is I, was now firmly under control. Should the Service wish, it could always blame me for Hugh's death, have me prosecuted as a murderer; they had irrefutable proof, hard evidence. I was there, right over Hugh`s dead body. I was tied hand and foot.

OK, let them think so. But I beg to differ. I was hoping that my colleagues would not guess that I had seen through their game.

Now off home, to Turners Hill. I'd ring up Nicola and we would do something pleasant for a change: choose a hotel in the Maldives and buy airline tickets. I was sure that the Office had alerted her to the forthcoming holiday already; but she was bound to pretend to be surprised. Interesting just how convincing she could be. I'd play along, and call the tune, discreetly. It would be boring to go alone; besides, I did not want the Office to suspect what was going on in my head.

A week later, a British Airways Boeing 777 brought us to Male, the capital of this incredible country in the Indian

Ocean. The Maldives consists of dozens of atolls and thousands of islands, some as tiny as a football pitch. The whole affair stretches four hundred miles between the Tropic of Cancer and the Equator and even below.

In just forty minutes a luxury speedboat took us tourists, dazed after our ten-hour flight, to Rheeti Rah Island, which is the home of the One & Only hotel. Spacious, stylish villas hid in the tropical greenery along sparkling white coral sand beaches. The Garden of Eden was here, we had found it! Our home for two weeks was on Turtle Beach, a wide strip of very soft sand five hundred yards long. The villa, complete with a swimming pool, stood in the shade of palm trees about thirty yards from the unbelievably blue lagoon waters.

It was so comfortable and serene here that body and mind relaxed completely, in harmony with each other and the Creator, under skies of the purest blue. I will not describe in detail all that we did on Rheeti: we derived maximum pleasure from the welcoming water, the sandy beach, the honey-scented air and from each other's bodies.

My mind kept on working though, in the background, like a computer in 'sleep' mode. To help it find the correct answers and decisions, I meditated: all around me was conducive to it.

So, where was I exactly?

`Hey look at these tiny sand crabs!` Nicky was jumping with joy, pointing at the little creatures staring at us from the water edge. I hugged her affectionately and picked up a shell as a present. Crabs aside, the nagging thought returned.

First, why did the Office want to hedge their bets?

There were two reason for this:

- They did not trust me completely, knowing that I used to be fond of Hugh, as well as because of the Traveller revelations. Besides, I seemed to have a serious enemy in the Office. The elimination of Hugh was potentially so explosive that the executioner had to be fully deniable (a scapegoat ready, if needed). I was the ideal candidate for the job. By using me, they also tightened their hold over me, just in case.

- I was needed in my present role and they had plans for my future use. For this, they wanted guarantees of my controllability and predictability. They believed they had them now. Otherwise they would have locked me away in some asylum or simply removed me. They could simply not let a man like me be on the loose. Things like that happened, but were dealt with swiftly and harshly.

The first reason called for extra caution; I was always alert, anyway. The second was reassuring, as it meant that I had time to do what I was planning to do. I hoped I had time enough to carry it out…

The question was, what did I need to do in order to make myself safe and secure when my plan had been fulfilled?

The solution here was more complicated than it appeared on the surface.

To start with, I needed documents. I had hidden the Janis Sokratos passport in my cache, but it could not be used for a prolonged time. I was not hundred per cent sure that my Friends had not worked out this identity after Beirut and Tunisia. It was hardly likely, but there was still a chance that they had. I could not tolerate such a risk. Besides, this identity would definitely be blown once I had completed my private mission. Thus, I had to create a new cover story, a biography supported by proper paperwork, obtain a whole set of cover documents.

Next, money: the lifeblood of operational fieldwork. My accounts in the UK and Jersey could not be touched; the Service watched them. However, throughout my life as William Anthony Dennis, I had been stealthily squirreling away cash that I hid in my cache. What I did to avoid being detected was simple: I visited a few London casinos. Each time I withdrew a thousand or two from my accounts and played for several hours. Sometimes I won; what mattered was that I did not lose, and all the 'liberated' cash went into my hiding place.

Slowly, step by step, this innocent and Office-controlled gambling habit brought me about fifty thousand untraceable pounds. Sufficient to cover all the overheads of the plot that I'd hatched, but not enough to keep me afloat for a year, which I might need, should Plan B become necessary. I had a two-year-old Range Rover

Vogue that I could flog off quickly and at the last moment, without the Service noticing. That would bring about thirty-five thousand. The money could be paid into the Sokratos bank account that I had opened in a Geneva Canton bank a few years ago; there I could easily collect the whole amount into cash.

This would be done closer to D-day; I would need extra cash for the new passport, too. There was a wonderful place one could obtain a new passport in a new name, completely genuine, and supported by a birth certificate. Genuine in this case means that the data would be introduced into the police computer, making the papers check-proof. This excellent service was available, in those days, from the flexible authorities of the Former Yugoslav Republic of Macedonia. Strictly for cash. Just in case, I'd buy a Ukrainian passport, too; that document could be dodgier, but came even cheaper. The police in that country treated their government jobs like a private business, anything was possible and had a price tag. I'd cross the Channel as Sokratos the Greek, where the trail would go cold. After the French border, this fellow would disappear. No way they could trace me to Macedonia, provided I went by train and coach or hiked, and paid my way in cash only.

There would be no reason for me to stay in Europe, whether I succeeded or not. It wasn't safe. A careful study of many options produced Brazil or Argentina as the best ones: far away, inexpensive, good climate and, most importantly, not very fond of the UK and the USA. These countries were semi-rogue, in the sense that they did not automatically cooperate with Big Brother (like the US or the EU) and would not do as they were told, even under pressure. Being careful, avoiding exposure, one could live happily and die in peace over there, like thousands of Nazi fugitives after World War Two.

All pieces in place now, I could indulge the tropical Paradise and my Eve to the full. (Let her write a report to the Office later; it will read like an erotic pillow book)

Once back in Turners Hill, I would work out and refine every detail of my plot. The Mission, with a capital M. I needed to prepare the logistics, and do the reconnaissance extremely carefully, timing every move to the minute. If I get it right, all the passports and Brazil would be irrelevant; if I make a mistake, or run out of luck, I would hardly ever need anything else, any time at all.

Back home in England it was grey and chilly, as it usually is in winter. Excellent weather to work! Having received my 'back home' report, the Office did not bother me further.

I found a small bungalow in a quiet parkland area not far from Great Windsor Park. This I rented for a year in the name of Janis Sokratos and paid for six months upfront, to avoid providing references, bank statements and answering silly questions. Cash is cash, it talks.

Then I bought a very used, faded green Land Rover Discovery, also in this name. Not smart, shabby even, but roomy and inconspicuous: just what I needed.

I also bought a used motorcycle, a powerful black Kawasaki, and stored the vehicles in the bungalow garage until the time came. Expenses, of course; but fully justified by operational requirements.

Once a week, on average, I had a date with Nicola. Apart from being a pleasure it was also a necessity: I wanted her regular reports of my mood and behaviour to keep the Office happy.

In March, Roger rang me up: a new assignment was coming my way. That suited me perfectly: during this short trip to the Continent, I rented a tiny one-bedroom bungalow with a basement, north-west of Paris, for six months. It was a very secluded, if not romantic, place.

All the overheads had set me back considerably, so in late May I sold my Range Rover for thirty thousand; the money was paid by transfer to the Sokratos account in Geneva. The countdown began.

June was approaching, and I was ready. I bought tickets for every day of the Royal Ascot races well in advance.

Sergei Vladimirovich Lapin, aka Otto, aka Derby, did not receive his latter operational codename by chance. He adored horses and adored equestrian sports. That is why they named him after the famous race. He liked it.

England for a horseman is like cream for a cat. I knew about this passion of Derby's from his dossier, which I myself carefully put together when the Office was cultivating him as a target for recruitment. I also knew that he always tried to schedule his business trips to England for mid-June, to coincide with the races at Royal Ascot, which always take place just before the Henley Regatta and Wimbledon. And now he lived here full time. That was the only hook that allowed me to find Otto and to track him to his home.

Unlike the previous time around, now I was not guided by revenge. Admittedly that would be sweet, too; but only as a by-product of the main plan. My former controller was the only man who could testify for me and tell all about Operation Traveller. He would never do this of his own free will: I needed to 'convince' him.

This was my last chance if not to return to Russia, at least to clear my name before my parents, my son, Elena, my former friends and colleagues, and to help them. And the more I watched Russia's rebirth in the last few years, since President Putin had taken office, the more I wanted it. I saw my country being revived, rising from its knees, after a decade of being robbed, humiliated and tramped on by the clique of thieves and traitors who had clung to power – with a little help from the West, that is.

Hugh's assassination made up my mind and helped resolve the split loyalty issue that had been bothering me lately.

The Iraqi adventure and the death of Hugh shook me to the core. I came to despise the greed, the arrogance, the hypocrisy, the insolence and the naked cynicism of Western politics, thinly disguised by the veneer of 'democratic values', 'human rights' and suchlike. The new Russia attracted me; it was on the right track at last; it needed support and help. That is how I was thinking at the time: silly and naïve thoughts, probably. At the end of the day, politics are determined not by high principles, but by mundane, economic interests. England, Russia, China, the USA – everyone wants his piece of cake, his profit; the rest is just talk, to keep the public happy.

All the words and statements about democracy, human rights etc., are no more than games, information campaigns to achieve political goals; or noise to conceal the ugly truth. Nothing new here: it was like this in the last century, and in the last millennium, and before. Only the wording was different. Notwithstanding, I remained a romantic in the sense that I still believed that one should fight to make the world a better place. Or at least to prevent it from becoming a worse place. Perhaps, deep inside, I simply invented this motive to justify my adventures. *Or was I just an idiot?*

Be it as it may, in the beginning I simply wanted to pot Otto. It twisted around the other way: Otto, albeit inadvertently, nearly potted me. Then I wanted to find and kill him; but now everything had changed: he was an asset that I needed alive, until he had served his purpose. The task was more complicated, but the game was worth the candle.

I had been to Royal Ascot twice before. It's one of the key events of the English Season. For lovers of races, and for the rich, the famous and the highborn, it was unmissable.

I did not belong to either of those groups. The first time I was invited to Ascot it was by the Office, right after my defection, as part of the familiarisation programme, an introduction to the best the island could offer. The second time was work. Here, on the so-called Parade, a fenced circle where they show off horses before and after the race, I saw Her Majesty, in the flesh, for the first time. She was so close to me that I could touch her. Queen Elizabeth II, accompanied by the Prince of Wales and a couple of courtiers, left her Royal Box to admire the horses. I was stunned then to realise that there were no tough fellows from Security anywhere nearby to shield the Sovereign. Perhaps they were so professional that they remained invisible; however, it might just have been a banal oversight.

The Parade was the spot where I hoped to see Otto. Horse owners always come out here to show off; to mix with the connoisseurs, spectators and admirers.

Everything was ready for the meeting, a long-awaited one for me, and a totally surprising one for him. I only had to count the days to the seventeenth of June, the first day of the five-day races. Destiny would come full circle then…

I calculated that, as Otto was a multi-millionaire, he would be enjoying the event from the Royal Enclosure. Apart from the Royal Box, there were several private VIP boxes and stands: members of the enclosure and their guests only. The Royal Enclosure was served by two dedicated car parks, numbers one and two; there was a separate entrance directly from the car parks to the boxes. I could not possibly get in there as I was not a member, and all guests were vetted by Scotland Yard Special Branch and the Security Service. I did not need to anyway, as I had to work covertly. Instead I bought standard tickets to the general public stands; before each parade I would come out and watch the guests from a safe distance. I would wear a disguise, in case my client happened to be near. If he recognised me, there would be no second chance. Glasses, a moustache, a wig…

In the morning of the 17th of June, I arrived at the Royal Ascot Racecourse on my black Kawasaki bike. The queues on race day were always huge; a car would be useless for the job. I left my bike in car park three, close to the first two. In any case, all the exits from the car parks joined the A-329 road; there was no avoiding that. The main thing was not to lose Otto when he came out from the enclosure and went to the car park. I brought my powerful, compact Minolta binoculars, to make sure I would not.

I picked out a tie and a jacket from my saddlebag (the general public stands have a dress code, too, although not as strict as the Royal Enclosure), and merged with the crowd of spectators hurrying towards the main entrance.

The first two races drew a blank. No Otto. There were four more to go, so I kept up my vigil. At about two in the afternoon, the cheering crowds announced the arrival of the Royal cortege. Her Majesty Elizabeth II and her entourage approached the racecourse in open carriages from the direction of Windsor. After the Queen had disappeared into the Royal Box and the spectators had calmed down, a new race was announced through the loudspeakers.

I watched it for a while, indifferent. When the dashing horses with tiny jockey figures glued to them raced by the stands, I walked out towards the Parade. I positioned myself at a distance, having mixed with a small crowd of excited people waiting for the horse presentation after the race.

Soon I noticed two elegant couples coming from the Royal Enclosure. The men were attired in the prescribed morning suits: tailcoats and top hats; ties, no cravats. The ladies wore extravagant hats, like everyone at Ascot.

They came closer. Look who was there, in a smart light grey top hat, a matching tailcoat, radiating self-confidence and contentment: none other than Otto himself! He was exactly as I knew him from the dossier, but was now sporting a stylish goatee. He was engaged in a lively conversation with his companion, who turned out to be Bob, the SIS director for security and counterintelligence; on Otto's arm was a beautiful, thoroughbred lady not unlike the magnificent horses on the Parade: our Anna, the one and only!

Well, so much water had passed under the bridge, and these two were still together. Did they get married, I wonder? Does she still work for the Office and report on her dearly beloved? Bob was accompanied by his wife Lisa: she must have returned to him after the divorce, when he was promoted to so high a position. The foursome discussed something excitedly; by their gesticulation I assumed the subject was one of Otto's thoroughbreds. Why not, he could afford such a horse.

One final race of the day was left. I hurried out to car park three, to my Kawasaki, in order to move closer to car parks one and two and my observation point, from where I could watch the exit from the Royal Enclosure. I must not miss Otto.

I could see through the lenses of my Minolta as he and Anna left the racecourse, said their goodbyes to Bob and Lisa and walked to their car. It was a black Bentley Continental R. The chauffeur who, judging by the way he moved, was also a bodyguard, held the door for the lady and his master. The car started moving, and I sat astride my bike, all set.

Riding in traffic, two cars behind with my headlight turned off, I followed the Bentley all the way to Virginia Water. It turned into a quiet, empty country lane that reminded me of a tunnel because of the tall old beeches on both sides, whose branches merged into a green ceiling high above. There were no cars in front of me now to hide behind. I increased the distance between us. The Bentley slowed down and indicated left: I had no option but to ride past it, in order not to be detected. But there it was! I saw what I wanted to see. Otto's car paused at a slowly opening gate. It opened into a long driveway: his home! Judging by the wrought iron, crested gate and the solid red-brick fence, a very serious mansion.

I kept riding for a while and stopped at a local pub. In my saddle bag, I had a miniature video camera with very high resolution. I bought it the other day in a spy shop not far from London Carlton Tower, just off Sloane Street. I turned it on and checked the sync with the receiver, which had 120 gigabyte memory storage. Should be enough for a week. The devices were weather proof, of course.

I returned to Otto's mansion and stealthily fixed the camera to a tree across the road from the gate, and the receiver to a post about a hundred yards down the road, within direct view. During the whole process, which took fifteen minutes or so, the lane remained empty. Just what I needed: a quiet spot, devoid of people, no potential witnesses. A week later I would return to change the memory card.

The week lasted a very long time, as often happens when one longs for something. I was dying of impatience, but decided to give it three of four more days, just to be sure.

To while away the time, I called Nicola. We went to London and spent a fabulous night out (and in): first *Macbeth* with Sean Bean and Samantha Bond, then a late dinner with a splendid view over London from the large windows of the Oxo restaurant on Southbank, followed by a tempestuous night at my place. Let her tell the colleagues that all was well. I needed them comfortable and happy now.

I said goodbye to my girl at noon and spent the rest of the day recovering. The following day I began writing these notes for posterity – maybe my son will get hold of them somehow. Hours and days move faster when your mind is busy, and soon it was time to go and pick up the memory card from the recorder.

First I went to my base, the rented bungalow. I went by train, then took a taxi and then got out and walked. Just in case. I brought with me a flash drive containing my notes, my memoirs: it would be dangerous to leave it behind. It was about a thirty-minute ride from Great Windsor Park to Virginia Water, so the whole business took an hour and a half. I removed all the devices that I had installed before near Otto's mansion. I reckoned that if necessary, they could be re-installed; if not, that is, if there was enough information on them, I would not have to return for them and risk being discovered. They must not be left behind, as they would be traced to the spy shop and from there, to me. The Service or the 'Sisters' from MI5 would be on my tail in no time at all.

Having returned to base, I turned on my laptop and watched the recordings from the camera. It took around four hours, but the result was encouraging: to my satisfaction, Otto's life was organised, he lived to a routine. Noblesse oblige, it would seem.

Twice a week, on Tuesdays and Thursdays, his chauffeur-driven Bentley came out of the gate at ten in the morning, sharp. The car turned left, towards Windsor. I did not know where he went, but that did not matter (in fact, he visited the Royal Guards Polo Club, where, enjoying a cup of tea, he watched the players train: he was the patron of several players and owned a few polo ponies). What mattered to me was to know the exact time and day, as well as confirming that it was just him and his chauffeur in the car, no one else.

I finished working and re-checked the necessary equipment. All was in place, ready – some interesting, very special items, not available commercially. As I mentioned before, I had a collection of those toys, the reminders of my missions over the past couple of years. Now I transferred the collection from my cache in the park to the new base. Some of the items I would use for the Mission. The rest had to be destroyed; it was a shame, but I could not possibly take them along with me.

The base was ready to receive a VIP guest. In exactly one week, next Thursday.

D-day came at last. I loaded a bicycle into my shabby Land Rover. Put on my disguise, patted down the pockets of my sports jacket: all in order, ready to go.

There was a small lay-by approximately five hundred yards from Otto's mansion. I left the Discovery there and rode my bicycle the rest of the way. Five to ten. Very close to the gate; three minutes, two... The gate moved, opening! The long black Bentley rolled smoothly onto the road, right in front of me.

The chauffeur could not react in time as a stupid, startled cyclist lost control and hit the shiny radiator grille, falling off his bike right in front of the Bentley. His reflexes switched on: the driver jumped out of the car and rushed towards the moaning idiot, bending over him – only to receive a spray up his nose, from the bottle that I was holding ready in my hand.

The chauffeur shook his head and dropped on the asphalt. Otto, whose head showed from the open rear door, clearly did not grasp what was going on. It was happening too fast. I jumped to my feet and reached him in two strides, before he managed to shut the door that he was just starting to pull close. A spray in his bewildered face. Done! Excellent stuff, this spray; but don't forget to take an antidote pill one hour before use.

I pulled the heavy chauffeur-bodyguard into the car, putting him on the rear seat next to Otto, and threw my bicycle into a ditch. Then I drove up the road to my waiting Land Rover.

Change once more. Now Otto was sleeping peacefully in the rear seat of my Discovery, and the chauffeur remained in the Bentley that I left in the layby. They would remain asleep for another hour or so. I knew that I took an additional risk leaving the chauffeur alive, but did not want to kill him: the bloke was innocent and I was not an animal. Yet.

Back at the base, I stopped in the driveway and carried Otto inside the bungalow. Here I put him on a chair and tied his arms and legs to it securely with a cord. Then I pressed a strip of sticky tape over his mouth. I checked the windows and the doors: they were safely shut and locked. No one would disturb me. Then I prepared my video recorder for the forthcoming interrogation. Let Otto rest for a while; I wanted him to wake up naturally: he had to survive more chemical agents today and I did not want surprises such as a heart attack. I made myself a cup of coffee and sat in an armchair opposite my former boss. Strange: I felt nothing at all. No hatred, no aversion, no desire to hurt him. He was no more than a tool for me now, to achieve my goal.

About forty minutes later his breathing became more frequent and erratic. He stirred and opened his eyes. His vision must have been blurred at first; he gazed at me, clearly bewildered, without recognising my face. He could not grasp where he was: a rude awakening indeed. Otto tried to say something, but could only make small muffled sounds through the tape. He attempted to raise his arm and to move his body: in vain.

I sat there, contemplating Otto, silently waiting for his brain to clear. Five minutes later I saw fear surfacing in his now focused eyes. He stopped shifting on his chair and was now staring at me. Oh yes, he recognised me, all right.

'Well, hello there, Sergei Vladimirovich. Good morning, Comrade Colonel. Or is it General? I can see you have recognised me. If you have, and if you understand me, nod.'

He nodded.

'I have been waiting for this for such a long time… Now that we have met again, at last, you must tell me a few things that interest me. If you answer all my questions, I shall let you go. Promise. And now you promise me to behave and not try anything stupid. Then I shall remove the tape from your mouth and we shall start working. The sooner we finish, the sooner you will return home. Nod if you agree with me.'

Otto nodded once, then again. I tore the silvery tape off his mouth; he grimaced in pain, snorted, then coughed. I took a glass of water to his bleeding lips. Otto gulped greedily and caught his breath.

'Dennis? Oh, my word, but how? I have been looking for you, tried to find you and help you out of the mess…'

'That's enough crap, my dear Otto' I cut him short. 'Don't let us waste precious time. Just drop the theme. I am turning on this camcorder; you look into the lens and answer all my questions, fully and frankly. When I am satisfied, I shall release you.'

'What guarantees do I have?' *They all ask this question*, I thought. As if there were any guarantees in this line of work.

'Well, I haven't killed you, although I could have done so, easily. You shall have to rely on my word. We must trust each other: this is what you taught me long ago. Besides, you have no choice. If you decide to be difficult and stubborn, I shall extract the truth from you, notwithstanding. You know what the truth drug can do, and you know the consequences.'

To convince him, I put a syringe and an ampoule on the table, in Otto's line of sight.

'So be it, damn you. Have it your way. Ask your questions. But if you kill me, the Service shall find you, wherever you are.'

'This is my concern, not yours.'

'Listen, maybe you need money?' Otto's face lightened, he sounded hopeful now, 'Just name the amount.'

Silently, I turned on the camcorder.

The Otto interview lasted till six in the evening, with short breaks for coffee and sandwiches and a visit to the loo (the latter was not so easy as I untied his feet only). He told all about Operation Traveller, his KGB exploits, his business affairs, and all about his career as an SIS agent. The material was pure gold.

As I thought, the Deputy Chairman of the KGB who had given my mission a blessing, was fired and arrested after the coup attempt in August 1991; he had wholeheartedly backed the wrong horse in this game. He was released soon afterwards, but the stress and the dishonour were too much for him: he died of a heart attack.

Otto had resigned of his own free will and had gone into business, hook, line and sinker. He had control over serious money, the Communist Party funds squirrelled away by the KGB, as well as serious connections. He had done well for himself as a trusted member of the special team in charge of setting up a network of front firms and banks, where Soviet leaders secretly channelled the wealth of the nation. A good start-up for his private enterprise.

My liaison Andrei vanished in 1992. The Deputy's aide who had access to the Operation Traveller material put a bullet through his head, that black August 1991. Thus Otto remained the only man who knew what had really happened. That is, if you don't count his controllers in the

SIS, whom he had enlightened dutifully; but these were unlikely helpers.

So, I had in my hands video recordings of Otto's full confession, which proved my innocence; as well as the confession of Otto the defector and agent about his work for the SIS, complete with a detailed account of the damage done: everything he had ever divulged, everybody he had ever shopped. And let's not forget all his knowledge of the SIS itself, all his Friends included. Invaluable stuff: two disks worth a fortune, and my life. All I had to do was to deliver them to the destination. If possible, with the source attached. I made two more copies of the disks.

'Well Otto, or shall I call you Derby? Thank you for the enlightening chat. Exhaustive information. Truly exciting. We did not even need an injection to get it out; well done.'

'OK Den, do as you promised` He started twisting in his chair, his voice now raised, demanding. `I told you everything, now I want to go home. I am sure they are looking for me very hard, already.'

‘Oh yes, yes, General. But the promise given was a necessity of the past; the word broken is a necessity of the present,’ I said, simultaneously thrusting a needle in the side of Otto’s neck. He started to protest, but thirty seconds later his eyes rolled and his head dropped. He was fast asleep. The sleeping drug I injected was powerful; five to six hours guaranteed for a man of his weight. That should suffice.

I quickly tidied up at the base, erased all the fingerprints. Then I loaded a bag with everything I might need into the Discovery. Otto went in last into the roomy baggage compartment, camouflaged with a suitcase, clothes and a blanket. He did not even stir once. On the way, I posted an envelope addressed to my solicitor Jeremy; this contained a letter, a flash card, and a DVD. Twenty minutes later I reached the M4 motorway and turned onto the M25 south. An hour and a half later, I rolled into Dover.

I shunned the Eurotunnel as the security there was too tight, and I could not risk being searched by customs. A ferry would be much better, albeit it took ninety minutes to get to Calais as opposed to Eurotunnel's thirty. At the port they just looked at your passport and nodded you through to boarding. Cars were selectively searched only on the way back from France, mostly for excessive booze and cigarettes, and illegal immigrants. Otto would be dead asleep for four more hours, so I did not foresee any problems, unless I was very unlucky.

I crossed the Channel without a hitch; the ferry was packed. The summer holiday season was just about to begin. Just what I needed: it is best to lose oneself in traffic, that way you do not stick out.

I could not know at the time that I'd had a narrow escape with my crossing. Otto was important enough that his abduction triggered a nationwide alert. The police and special services were scrambled, and all air and sea ports were alarmed and controls enhanced. This happened at half past nine at night: Otto's bodyguard, when he came to and was able to tell his story to the local police, was not a very useful witness; it took a while for the cops to contact the Special Branch, and several hours passed before the news reached the SIS. The bureaucratic machine was set rolling sooner than I thought, but with a delay that was vital for me.

My ferry left the English shore at eight forty-five p.m.

It took three and a half hours to reach Pontoise, a small town near Paris, where my French base awaited me: a small bungalow, hardly visible from the street for overgrown trees. I had to stop once on the way to give an additional injection to my prisoner, who was beginning to wake up. A tiny dose this time: this trophy must be delivered safe and sound.

The trophy woke up in the small hours; I was awake already. He was disorientated, understandably. Where was he? What was happening to him? Never mind, he would get it soon enough. I took him to the loo and gave him a sandwich, then handcuffed him to a pipe in the cellar. There were no windows here, the wooden door was heavy and there was a fair distance to other buildings in the area; it was unlikely that anyone would hear if he shouted. I put a plastic water bottle on the floor next to him and left, dropping casually over my shoulder that I would be back soon to let him go. Just to keep him quiet. I locked up the bungalow, checked all the windows: it looked reliable.

I made my way to Boulevard Lannes in Paris. Here, close to the Bois de Boulogne, the Boulogne Woods, was the destination for my parcel: the Russian Embassy. In my pocket, I had a sealed envelope containing a letter and the first disk of Otto's interview. Part one only, regarding Operation Traveller and a few more titbits about his recruitment. The envelope was addressed to Victor Zverev, officially a Counsellor at the Embassy; in fact, he was Head of Station of the SVR, the Russian Foreign Intelligence Service. What seemed to be a century ago, we were classmates at the KGB Red Banner Andropov Institute, the Soviet intelligence training establishment, known as the Academy of Foreign Intelligence nowadays.

Several months ago, reading diplomatic news on the Internet, I learned by chance that he had been posted to Paris. This was my chance. He would listen: we had always liked each other, and Zverev was an insightful, discerning and decent type. He was at his office today, I checked it with the embassy duty officer, pretending to be a newspaper reporter seeking a comment. I parked half a mile away from Boulevard Lannes and walked, casually, towards the embassy compound.

I worked on the assumption that it was watched, as was always the practice. There had to be a DST (the French Security Service) stationary surveillance post somewhere near. To change my appearance, I put on a baggy jacket that concealed my figure, and stooped slightly, supported by a walking stick; locks of grey hair were hanging from beneath a beret. Glasses and moustache, as usual.

Calmly walking past the metallic grille fence, just opposite the entrance to the embassy that was sunk deeper inside the grounds, I dropped the envelope through the gap, blocking the view of DST watchers with my body. I was certain that the guards on duty could see it: the small package was directly visible from the entrance, besides, there were CCTV cameras everywhere. The guards were chaps from the Russian Security Service, reporting to Zverev.

Keeping the tempo steady, I walked on, past the fence, and crossed the street in a hundred yards, turning into a lane.

I had to make sure now that I had not grown a tail, courtesy of the DST.

After two hours of dry cleaning I was positive that I was no unwelcome company. It was lunchtime and I was hungry as a bear, so I went to Le Grand Café Capucines. Enjoying the fabulous mussels in white sauce, accompanied by light white house wine, I tried to visualise what was happening at the moment in the Russian Embassy.

The duty guard would have noticed my drop all right. I pictured him walking, leisurely, towards the gate, as if checking the perimeter. As he was walking past the envelope, perhaps a newspaper fell out of his hand. Naturally he would bend to pick it up and as he did so, pocket the envelope, now covered by the paper.

The guard would continue his check for a while and, looking satisfied, return to his post, from where he'd immediately call the Head of Station, the SVR *Rezident.* Knowing Zverev, he'd send down a technical expert to check the envelope for anything untoward, such as poisons or explosives. Having made sure that it was clean, Zverev would dismiss the officer and, alone now, open the package.

It would be perhaps be a couple of hours before he, having finished with the recording, summoned the cypher clerk; in my mind I followed the urgent coded message, marked top secret, eyes only, winging its way to the SVR Centre in Yasenevo, Moscow.

Two more hours had passed when I, walking in the Tuileries Garden after lunch, received a call on the burner phone that I had bought on my last business trip. I recognised his voice at once, as he did mine.

The caller's number was not identified, of course, and why should it be? The *Rezident* said a code phrase, confirming a rendezvous in the Boulogne Woods at six thirty p.m.

I walked to the meeting point as if to my first date. *Déjà vu again*. How many times have I experienced this condition? My heart raced, my head was slightly dizzy. It was hard to keep a steady pace thanks to my disguise, complete with heavy walking stick. There, just ahead, behind the bush, was a garden bench.

Now I will see him.

Zverev was sitting with his back towards me. He did not move as I approached him from behind. Presumably he had posted one of his men on lookout, who signalled to the *Rezident* that I was approaching. I came up to the bench and sat down next to him, in silence.

'Hello, Dennis,' Zverev said, without turning his head.

'Hello. Had fun reading my letter? What does the Centre say?' I replied, without looking at him.

'Huge interest. It is like putting a stick in an ant hill: everyone's excited. They said they will examine it in every detail. From what I managed to read and view, I can say this: I am glad for you. I am sure all will be well. But you must wait a bit. You do have something else, more info, don't you?'

'I do indeed. And how long do I have to wait?'

'They will decide at the very top, you know. The official word for you is to lie low for a short while. I believe one week, not more. Keep the same number for contact?'

'Yes, and the code phrase: "It looks like rain." The meet will be on the following day, at seven thirty p.m. This place. OK?'

'That's great, Dennis. And now come on, spill the beans. Tell me what else you have brought. Anything will give you more credit.'

I handed over to Zverev a set of keys on a ring and a note with an address.

'What is it?' He looked genuinely surprised.

'Surprise, Victor. My gift to your colleagues, if you like. The former Colonel and Member of the State Duma

Sergei Vladimirovich Lapin, none other. He is sitting in a cellar, waiting for you.'

The *Rezident* was clearly shocked. He made an effort to pull himself together and turned to me at last:

'Did you kidnap him?'

'Yes, I did,' I shrugged, matter-of-factly. 'The client is all packed and ready to go home.'

A silent scene followed. A few moments later Zverev shook his head:

'Den, this is amazing. Incredible. Bloody James Bond, damn it. Sorry, I need to rush to the Station. What a fucking surprise, and a pain in the ass you gave us… Well done, man!' He gave me his hand and I squeezed hard, with hope. It was sweaty: Zverev must have been very nervous.

'I'll be in touch.' He nodded and walked briskly towards the exit from the woods.

I now had to go to Geneva to withdraw my cash from the local Canton bank, the thirty thousand pounds from the sale of my Range Rover; then on to Macedonia, to get my new passport.

Although I was almost sure that the SVR colleagues would clear my name and that I would be rehabilitated and restored, there was always the other possibility, and one had to consider one's personal safety and security. Besides, my SIS colleagues who were searching for Otto, could at any time come up with my name as a prime suspect. They could find the house rented in Sokratos's name, too; thus, the Greek cover story would soon become dangerous to use.

The following morning I was in Geneva, where I emptied my bank account. Having bought the morning papers, I drove on to Macedonia right away; it was a long drive, about twenty hours.

Having passed the endless Mont Blanc tunnel, I popped out on the Italian side and kept on going. Near Como, tired, I stopped at a café for an espresso. The weather was brilliant, I was enjoying the strong brew on the roadside terrace and, feeling smug, opened a copy of the

International Herald Tribune, which I had bought in Geneva.

'Terrible Blaze in Pontoise: No Survivors' – a heading on page three sent shivers down my spine. 'The body was badly burnt; identification impossible… The police are looking for the house owner… The cause of the fire is unknown, arson not excluded.' And a photo of the smoking ruins: all that was left of my base.

I paid quickly and went to my Discovery, threw the paper into the bin on the way.

What the hell was that? Did they not accept my present? Was Otto not wanted in Russia? Could he be in somebody's way, spoiling somebody's game? Perhaps he knew too much about those who prefer to stay in the shade?

And most importantly, where does that leave me? What's my position in this game? Am I a marked man? After all, now I could be framed for two murders that I had not committed: Hugh's and Otto's. I hated Otto, true; but I did not want him dead. And to die such an ugly death… Whoever set fire to the bungalow clearly did not bother to shoot him first. They let him roast alive, chained to the pipe. I just wanted him locked up in jail… But one thing was clear: whoever did this would stop at nothing.

My revenge had made a full circle, unexpectedly. Like a boomerang, it had returned to me, wounding the avenger. 'If you embark on a journey of revenge, dig two graves' – the ancient wisdom helpfully came to mind: why now, when it was far too late?

My trusty Land Rover was swallowing mile after mile on the motorway, going at the maximum allowed speed – I could not afford any problems with traffic cops at the moment. *Will Zverev try and contact me? No, I cannot let him. I shall try to reach him myself, later on. What if they only need me roasted, potted, like Otto? Think, Den, think...*

First thing to do was to get rid of my French mobile phone and the Discovery. Here, in Italy. Right away. All they were doing was creating a treacherous trail, making me traceable.

Ahead lay Macedonia, where my new documents would give me a new name and a new life. But would I make it there? They would hardly search for me officially, using the police. An arrest, all the buzz, a trial: nobody needed that, albeit for different reasons. The Janis Socratos track would lead them to Pontoise and Geneva; one set of pursuers or two, English, Russian, or all together: it made no difference to me whatsoever. Should any of them catch up with me, that would be my end.

'By the pricking in my thumbs, something wicked this way comes' – the Second Witch's words from Macbeth, which I suddenly remembered, seemed appropriate. To think that I had watched this play in London just a couple of weeks ago…

In another world, in a different reality that I had left forever. I cursed and crossed myself, eyes steady on the road.

The dashboard clock was ticking away minute after minute. How many did I have left? My death could be just a few short hours away.

Chapter 9. BIG WAVE SURFING

The huge mountain of water, roaring, relentless, rushed towards the shore. I was riding before it, my surfboard just below the crest. The tension was mad: you lose your balance, you're dead. You lose you nerve, you're dead; one wrong move and the mountain will crush you. I was only safe as I was, terrified, my feet glued to the surfboard, riding at a crazy speed before the monster. No way I could stop this, not until the big wave broke and I was safe in the shallow waters so close ahead, but so out of reach….

I opened my eyes with a huge effort. The same nightmare again, a repeated scare I kept seeing every other night; always open-ended: I woke up neither crushed, nor safe. As if someone was knocking at the door to my mind, trying to deliver a message. Now I was awake; *cogito ergo sum.* I can think; therefore, I am alive, I exist. But my headache was splitting.

The room was turning grey, light filtering through the heavy curtains. Morning… I hated it; I did not want the morning to come. I rolled my eyes, which seemed to screech in the rusty sockets, to see the bedside clock; I strained my mind, trying to stop the time. Or at least to slow it down. Exhausted, I fell asleep again; or, rather, lost consciousness. I came to again, with a start: a quarter past nine. It was five to eight when I'd checked last. Bollocks! Time had moved on, my attempts were miserable, futile… Slowly, I rose from the cramped bed with red stains all over the sheets, feeling as if I had been hit by a truck. I stumbled towards the window; every movement was echoed by a flash of pain in my head.

I opened the curtains and opened the frame. The room was instantly filled with greyish morning light and fresh, cool air. I strained to focus my eyes and looked down to the street: nothing to see, except the flaky blind wall of the house opposite.

I turned around and whistled. Or, rather, tried to: my dry, swollen lips would not let the sound through. On the table in the middle of the bedroom there were two empty wine bottles, one finished bottle of Dimple and half a bottle of Blue Label. Only one glass. Next to the devastated bed stood a bottle of beer, cap on, put there by a caring hand. There was a wardrobe in the corner, and further, a door; to the bathroom, perhaps?

I sat down heavily on the edge of the bed, opened the Heineken and, greedily, took a large gulp. Then I listened to my body: it was beginning to resurrect itself, gradually, bit by bit. The headache dulled; now I could try and remember the night before…

The main question: where was I? The room seemed unfamiliar; a hotel room, judging by the furniture. At that moment, the rest of my knocked-out senses started switching back on. Smell first: I don't smoke, so I can smell tobacco a mile away, stale butts especially. I crawled to the other side of the king-size bed: yes, there it was, an ashtray. Three butts in it, one had a distinctive red stain. Lipstick. Next to the ashtray, there was an empty wine glass, red lipstick on the rim. Oh dear. It was beginning to dawn on me now.

There was a ribbon or something, showing from below the bedside drawer. I pulled it and my inflamed eyes could see a bra, beautiful, black laces with Bordeaux cups. It was heavily scented with some arousing perfume: the aroma of Agent Provocateur.

Drained, I fell back onto the pillows and closed my eyes. My tortured brain was humming, like an overloaded computer. At last, it began opening images, one after another. Aha, here she was, my lady guest. A brunette, around thirty-five, perfect, voluptuous body, sensual lips, but what was her name? I could not recall. Something with a 'C'. Cornelia? No. Caroline? Christina? Yes, Christina she was. And we had got acquainted in…

From that point on, the previous day began to roll out before my mind's eye, until all the pieces, isolated and uncertain, fell into their place: the mosaic was complete, clearly readable.

A bar in La Rambla, Barcelona. What was it called? No matter. And I was suffering from a hangover at the Catalonia Hotel in the Old Town.

Bugger! I panicked; cold sweat pricking my skin. I jumped from the bed and rushed towards the wardrobe. There was a safe built in: I dialled the password without pausing to remember, muscle memory sending the right impulses to my fingers. The door buzzed and opened. I sighed with relief as I took out a maroon booklet: my passport; then an envelope containing a green one – another spare passport; then a wallet and a thick pile of fifty-pound notes. Thank God, everything was intact. Despite my being semi-conscious last night, my well-trained body hadn't forgotten the elementary precautions and had done the right things automatically.

I opened the maroon passport: Adrian Goranovich. Former Yugoslav Republic of Macedonia. Aha, that is why she had called me Andres, Spanish style. All right, all in order. *You got away with it this time, Adrian of Macedon.*

Another gulp of beer, cold from the minibar. My brain worked like clockwork now. Shower first: hot, cold, hot again, followed by strong coffee. My strength and reflexes restored, I sat in an armchair, nursing a cup of Espresso from the machine and sorting all the facts that I knew, or insights that I could deduct from what had happened in the past few days and weeks.

So, I was right when I thought that they did not need me in Russia. They were not interested in knowing what I knew… Well perhaps not 'they' but someone very high up, someone important enough to order intelligence officers to eliminate people overseas. Just like the old times: 'KGB Removals' at your service. Who could it be? As far as I could see, that was the level of the Director or his deputies, no less.

Unless it was someone even higher, who had the power to give orders to the SVR itself. The Government? Hardly. Although the Service director was formally a member of the cabinet, in fact he reported to the Presidential Administration, a body that had much more real power. Yes, that's what it looked like it. The Administration supervised the so-called *silovoi blok*, the departments that had powerful muscle: defence, police, intelligence and security. It was likely that over there, at the very top, sat a VIP bureaucrat or two who needed Otto's tales, as well as my life story, like a hole in the head. I could not be sure, of course. But it all looked very bad; my comeback was postponed indefinitely. Returning to England was out of the question, forever. I had to watch my backside now, and run for my life. What a bloody mess!

The only way to help myself and sort it all out was to solve a riddle: what was it that poor Otto (I even felt for him after his terrible death) and I could know that could be so damaging to the Russian establishment? Damaging enough to cost them a career, or even their liberty? Or their life? How could I figure out who they were, or he was, or she was?

I had to analyse all the events of the past few years: a massive volume of information. I had to concentrate and recall, day after day. I had to study the balance of power in modern Russia; in particular, the composition of the Presidential Administration, if that was at all possible.

But right now, I needed to vanish, go to ground, and lie low. I needed breathing space and time to work everything out. My enemy was very powerful and he would not let go until he had made sure he was completely safe – which meant, by implication, that I was dead.

I'd rung up Victor Zverev, the SVR Head of Station in Paris, from Athens, five days ago, on the way from Skopje, the capital of Macedonia. Although I had already decided everything for myself, I still wanted to corroborate my deductions. Maybe all was not lost yet?

'*Da?*' (Yes?) He answered the call, curtly.

'Hello. I say, it looks like rain.' This was the code phrase that we had agreed on: a call for a meeting the following day.

'Not here, it doesn't. You dialled the wrong number,' said Zverev dryly and rang off.

That was it. No rendezvous; Plan B activated. The bastards… But all credit to Zverev: he did not take the chance to shop me to his superiors. All he had to do to pot me was to reply: 'Yes, if the forecast is right.' I would have come to the meeting in the Boulogne Woods, and joined Otto in hell…

Alternatively, the SVR could have shopped me to the SIS and let them do the dirty work; or simply put the police on me, as the Pontoise arsonist and murderer: enough for life imprisonment. So many things they could do to prevent me from appearing in Moscow. I did not wish to think of all the unpleasant options… But Zverev I could rely on, to an extent. He had saved me. *But why?*

Adrian Goranovich flew to Barcelona the same day. The die was cast.

I spent a few days there. Worked on my notes, organised a few things, got ready for the next move, wandered around this beautiful gem of a city, deep in thought: I was saying goodbye to my former life and to Europe.

Solitude gripped me, suddenly; it was suffocating. I realised, acutely, that I was alone in the Universe: no country, no home, no friends, no family. No support; nobody I could safely turn my back to; and no one I could turn to for help, unless it was a paid service. I could not even make a telephone call without jeopardising my safety, my life itself.

No real name; no real past; the present was a quagmire, and the future all fog. All that was genuine was well hidden, very deeply, hermetically sealed; it could not be touched, as that would be fatal. *Mister No- One of Nowhere*. I almost lost touch with the world around me; it was real only nominally. I felt like I was inside a sphere made of armoured glass: my prison and my protection at the same time.

Subconsciously, I had tried to break out of this sphere last night: getting plastered and shagging my brains out with Christina, a girl I met in an Old Town bar. I had not succeeded. The only good thing was that I hadn't broken my neck in the process. The lesson was clear: safer to stay inside the sphere for the time being.

Gradually, though, the sadness left me and my natural optimism triumphed. I started thinking of the positive elements of my circumstances. Just like Daniel Defoe's

Robinson, I took a sheet of paper and wrote down all that was bad on the left, and all that was good on the right.

I have already mentioned the bad; the only thing to add was that I was wanted by two of the most powerful and dangerous intelligence services of the world.

What about the good?

I was alive, well, in a great physical shape; only suffering from a residual, post-piss-up headache.

Just over forty, but I looked younger. I had 'clean', that is reliable, cover documents. I had enough money for a fresh start; once established, I could earn what I needed.

And I was completely free! One could start a new life in a new reality with such preconditions. Would the past reality let me go? Would it not try and drag me back, like a crocodile drags his victim into a swamp? This depended on me alone, and no one else. If I let go of the past, forgot about idiocies such as revenge and justice, accepted my new situation and withstood attacks of nostalgia and depression; if I cut off the tentacles of the octopus called my past life: anything might be possible, with time.

A new me, a new life in a different world, on the bright, sunny side. Enough of being a shadow of the bygone epoch.

Thus, thinking and feeling encouraged, I reserved an airline ticket from Lisbon to Sao Paulo, Brazil; a TAP Air Portugal flight leaving in two days. Where else to start a new life but in the New World? I packed quickly and caught a train to the Portuguese capital.

As I was busy making the last arrangements before the leap across the Atlantic, on the other side of my armoured glass protection, things were happening fast.

The case of the abduction of Otto was being handled by Scotland Yard's Special Branch in tandem with the SIS and supervised by C, personally. The first day brought no results: Otto's chauffeur could only give a description of the disguise that I had been wearing. However, the next day after the Virginia Water events, the Office started interviewing all the SIS officers who knew Otto or had come across him for any reason, at any time.

Clearly, I was on the list, albeit not at the top: officially, I had dealt with him quite some time ago. The Office tried to contact me by phone, but there was no reply either on the landline, or on my mobile. Nicola, my girlfriend, had no idea where I was, and could only say that we had seen each other a week ago. Having learned all this, Bob, who was the SIS man in charge of the investigation, ordered a covert search for me.

They checked my car by number plate, and saw that I had sold it in May. The new owner, a Swedish businessman from London, readily told the investigators to what bank account and in what name he had transferred the money. That was how the Janis Socratos identity emerged for the first time.

The Driver and Vehicle Licensing Agency in Swansea reported that a Mr Janis Socratos had bought a green Land Rover Discovery, in the same month. The car was put on the wanted list immediately, all the police forces alerted throughout Europe.

Simultaneously, an official from the Swiss Federal Prosecutor Office, who had also been a valuable SIS agent for many years, visited the Geneva Canton bank. The visit was unofficial and highly confidential. Two hours later, Janis Socratos's bank statements and a copy of the photo page of his passport were on Bob's desk in London. They showed that this gentleman had withdrawn all his money a few days previously, and closed the account. And that he also looked very much like a certain William Dennis, aka Dennis Antonov. Then data from CCTV cameras in sea- and airports began to arrive. One recording showed the Discovery that belonged to Janis Socratos boarding a P&O ferry on the evening of Otto's abduction. Interpol and Europol were alerted to the fact. The car was found two weeks later, in a long-term car park at Malpensa Airport, Milan. Apparently, Socratos had abandoned it there, having paid a month in advance. This is where the trail had grown cold.

In the meantime, the French police had found the owner of the house that had burned down in Pontoise. To be exact, he showed up himself, having learned of the fire from newspaper reports. Thus, the lawmen were at a loss: if the scorched body was not that of the owner, who did it belong to? The tenant? From the rental agreement, it followed that it could be Janis Socratos, Greek citizen. They had his passport details.

The French sent an enquiry to Greece, where the authorities were less than helpful: his last known address was fifteen years old; other people lived there now, and nobody had the slightest idea as to Socratos's whereabouts. He had no relations to turn to. The Greeks sent his details to Interpol, only to find out that he was already on the wanted list.

The French police closed their file on him with relief. The matter was clear as daylight: he had burned to death, end of story. They didn't need to go looking for loose ends.

London was a different story. Over there, they knew what their colleagues across the Channel did not. Bob learned about the Pontoise blaze and about Socratos, who had allegedly died there, from Interpol, and did not believe the report for a second. He did not believe that the dead body belonged to some unidentified person, either. He finally had his answer as to what happened to Derby. Up until this point, he had believed that Dennis Antonov had either killed him and hid the body in England, or kidnapped him; if the latter was the case, where had he taken him?

Now it became apparent that he had taken him all the way to France. And killed him over there, having disguised the murder as a fire. But why?

`Antonov was not a maniac, he was not crazy; his purpose must have been rational` Bob muttered.

Most likely he was trying to extract information from Derby chemically, and, inadvertently, gave him an overdose. Or tortured him. The prisoner could have died of a heart attack, concluded Bob. Why would Antonov want to interrogate Derby? *Only one reason: he wanted to give the Russians a present, and get a pardon in return, along with the possibility of returning home and even being decorated. Yes, that was it! The puzzle was complete.*

Serious questions remained unanswered, though. What, and how much, did Derby tell Antonov before he died? Where was Antonov with his treasure now? In Russia, already?

Would our man in Moscow have time to react and neutralise him, thus ensuring the Service's own safety? Or did the Service need to exfiltrate him, bring him back from the cold? He must be warned immediately…

In the end there was no need to send a warning: on the same day, Bob received a message from Stingray, a source in Moscow. Antonov had contacted the SVR in Paris and attempted to hand over Derby. However, Derby was removed on the orders of the Moscow Centre, which Stingray himself managed to initiate. *What the hell does he mean, initiate?* Bob thought. Antonov had vanished into thin air; he did not contact the SVR again.

The immediate danger of Stingray being blown was over; however, to be on the safe side, Bob decided to switch communication with the source to Quarantine mode for the time being, until the coast was definitely clear. This meant that Stingray would, once a fortnight and until further notice, make a small correction to a fake identity profile on Facebook. This meant that he was safe and sound. No correction meant trouble.

'How pleasant it is to work with a professional,' Bob smiled to himself, muttering, re-reading the message. 'We must look after him as best we can. Not the slightest risk will be tolerated now; you get an agent like that once in a hundred years. Never mind. The government will cope without his intelligence for a couple of months.'

But where should they look now for this damned Dennis Antonov? Mister bloody Bates? Or whatever alias he would be using now? Wait until he attempted to contact the SVR again? No, he must realise by now the danger he's in. Derby's murder would be proof of that.

Bob switched on the Dictaphone and cleared his throat. 'Dennis clearly possesses some important and damaging material. Obviously, he understands that this material is damaging to someone in Moscow, too; that he is extremely “hot”. Antonov -Bates, an experienced officer, can surely see that this person might not just be involved in large-scale crimes, but could also be a Western agent, CIA or SIS. In the nineties, many officials yielded to the temptation to grow rich on the ruins of the old Soviet system… Who else would need Derby dead? Speaking objectively, the Russians would give a lot to capture Derby alive. You’d have thought it’d be in their national interest.

‘We have to find Bates, come hell or high water.’ Bob pushed a button, summoning his secretary.

‘Sue, please invite my deputy. And the head of the special action team.’

Let us have a brainstorming session…

Meanwhile, in Paris, Victor Zverev, the SVR Station Head, was confused. On the one hand, the orders from the Centre were to be executed no matter what. There was no place for doubt or reflection: they know a lot more in Moscow, and their decisions were based on intelligence received from dozens of Zverevs around the world. On the other hand, Dennis had provided very valuable information, had proved his innocence, and even handed in the traitor Lapin / Otto to crown it all, who himself should have been a source of information of the utmost interest to the state.

And only to be treated like this. They had eliminated Lapin / Otto. The job had been done by a reactivated illegal agent who had been a 'sleeper' in France for twelve years, bypassing Zverev. He had been told of the murder *post factum.* And to get rid of Dennis, they wanted to shop him to the SIS! Zverev had been instructed to call Dennis to a meeting and ensure the Friends knew the time and place.

Zverev had knowingly committed a crime when he failed to reply to Dennis's code phrase correctly, thus letting him know that he could not count on the SVR. Get lost! This was the clear message. The *Rezident* reported to Moscow that Antonov had not attempted to contact him, and that he was out of contact, apparently alarmed by the news of the Pontoise blaze. They had to wait for his next move, or for a lucky break.

Zverev could smell a fish. He wanted to understand what was going on, to shed some light on the situation. He kept a copy of the disk with Otto's interview in his safe, in spite of Moscow's orders not to make any.

Now, having turned on the electronic noise generator to frustrate any potential eavesdroppers, the *Rezident* was carefully studying the DVD in his office; from time to time he made coded notes that made sense to him only.

In faraway Moscow, two middle-aged men were walking casually along the paths of Neskuchny Gardens, a beautiful park on the banks of Moscow River. Judging by their expensive, conservative business suits, one dark grey, another dark blue, almost black; and by the fact that they were followed by two bodyguards wearing similar suits, who kept at a discreet distance but close enough to react to any threat; judging by this, the men were either big business types, or important government officials.

Their discussion was clearly serious enough that it couldn't have taken place in the car, or the office, or any other confined space. Two black Mercedes with chauffeurs inside and official number plates had been waiting for them for half an hour by the park entrance.

'Dmitry, you reacted just in time. By no means could he be allowed back here. I can see it now,' the grey-suited one said.

'Well, Vitaly, you have done well. Good job the Service managed to survive the chaos of the nineties and preserve the best professionals.' Tall, grey-haired Dmitry Griaznov, Aide to the President of Russia charged with oversight of the intelligence services, patted his confidant on the shoulder. The latter was Vitaly Sindeev, First Deputy Director of the SVR.

These two went back a long way: classmates at MGIMO, the elite college producing Soviet, now Russian, diplomats; then at the KGB Andropov Institute, equally elitist, turning out intelligence cadres. Sindeev was a Muscovite. In the nineties, he had stayed at the Service's headquarters, and Griaznov, from St Petersburg, went back there and became head of the local branch of the Security Service, the FSB. Later, when the FSB Director was unexpectedly appointed Prime Minister, Griaznov was transferred to Moscow. When the Prime Minister became President, Griaznov was invited to join him in the Kremlin. That was how he ended up in the Presidential Administration. A key post, very low profile, but with a lot of clout. Sindeev owed him his job.

Both men shared huge experience and an impressive track record, details top secret.

'Well, with a huge effort we managed to stabilise the country. But this stability has not settled in yet. And this Lapin fellow could have blown everything up, changed the balance, the status quo. Too many would have suffered; a huge, nasty scandal. Over the past ten years, many people had their fun: it is time to forget this now. Let bygones be bygones. Let the buggers work hard to compensate for their mischief.'

You had some fun, too, Dmitry, did you not? thought Sindeev. He knew that the late Lapin took part in organising the flight of Communist Party's money abroad; he was aware that Griaznov was also implicated. It followed, logically, that Griaznov was one of those who did not need Lapin / Otto alive and in Russia. Who knows what he could tell his interrogators in Lefortovo prison? You couldn't gag all of them; there were principled ones, too, who would not yield to pressure or money.

'However, Antonov disappeared. Zverev reports from Paris that he did not contact him after the fire. The only thing we know about him from sources is his alias, Den Bates. Which I am sure he had discarded already' Sindeev said out loud.

'This is bad. Do you trust this Zverev? They were classmates, right?' Griaznov stopped abruptly and looked Sindeev in the eyes.

'Yes, I do. He has an excellent reputation, both in the field and as a *Rezident.* I do not think that he would be capable of…'

‘Do not think? Indeed,’ Griaznov interrupted, ‘we must not exclude any possibility. This is our job. And men are men. Sometimes, they are capable of things they would never imagine themselves… If I only knew what Lapin told Antonov before he died…’

‘Well, we have the video recording that Zverev sent.’ Sindeev shrugged his shoulders.

‘Yes, and I watched it carefully. What is on it is bad enough. But Antonov is not enough of an idiot to give away all he has, correct? Without withholding something, keeping a little something close for a rainy day? I am sure he has a second disk! You think it’s possible?’

The spy chief grunted:

‘Quite. He is a smooth operator and nobody’s fool. Top marks both in the KGB and the SIS, as far as I know.’

‘Indeed. So, what shall we do with this fucking chap? Where shall we look for him?’

‘He will be on the alert now, surely. He’ll have changed his identity and gone somewhere safe. Blow it! ` Sindeev barely avoided a skateboarder who swished by.

‘Oh yes, with a nuclear bomb of information on his hands. If he manages to bring it here, he can even publish it…We have no right to let that happen.’

‘Dmitry, do not get on so. First, who says he has anything? It is only an assumption. Well, he probably does; we always use the worst-case scenario. But the SIS are looking for him, too. He is like a thorn in the flesh for them. Knows too much, and a suspected murderer. This means he is wanted by their CIA cousins, as well. And we are watching, worldwide. The boy is in deep shit. He will not get away. It’s only a matter of time.’

‘Do we have the time? While we are waiting for him to get caught, he has the initiative. The ball is in his court, and he can play it next, Vitaly. We must be proactive!’

‘He is not crazy enough to play his last remaining trump card, if he indeed has one. Not anytime soon. And slowly but surely we will tighten the noose around him. We shall figure him out: wherever he goes, he is bound to keep away from Russian and English-Speaking communities. He's no fool; he wouldn't want to run into a planted agent or an informer. So, we shall search in other ex-pat communities; starting with Third World countries, far away ones with good climates. This is just one option.'

Sindeev took Griaznov by the arm; he spoke reassuringly:

'He is a pro, which means his moves can be calculated, the way he thinks can be worked out. Calm down; we shall find him. You know how good our specialists are, and we will use the best analysts, too.' The two men kept on walking slowly down the path.

'Please, Vit, I rely on you. We must also forestall our overseas competitors. When you find him, capture him and interrogate him, if possible. All materials for my eyes only. Afterwards, eliminate. Erase, remove. If capturing alive is not an option, eliminate. A fatal accident.'

Griaznov chewed his lips, wrinkled his forehead; then bent towards his companion:

'Tell you what: forget about capturing him. I want an accident. Plain, straightforward. No fuss. Report on your progress weekly.'

'Will do. Don't worry,' Sindeev assured his comrade and superior. They walked towards the exit from the gardens.

Look how scared you are. I have never before seen you panic, Dmitry. So, what is it that you are concealing? the old spy thought, watching Griaznov get into his shiny Mercedes, glimmering in the setting sun.

He returned to the SVR Headquarters in Yasenevo and locked himself in his office. Forty minutes later, he summoned his aide and gave him a message to send to Zverev, the Paris *Rezident.* The message was coded with Sindeev's personal code: even a cypher clerk could not read it.

At the same time, far away across the Atlantic Ocean, a Portuguese TAP Boeing 777 was on its final approach to Sao Paulo international airport. On board the airplane, battered in turbulence over the Brazilian coast, a passenger called Adrian Goranovich was filling in his immigration forms.

He could still vividly remember the nightmare that made him wake up in a cold sweat during the flight: he was surfing a huge wave that was about to crush him.

He couldn't stop. He could only ride it, to the end.

EPILOGUE

A shabby, heavily dented Mitsubishi Pajero was moving slowly, tiredly, manoeuvring to avoid the numerous potholes that peppered the country road, which went on forever, until it merged with the sky at the horizon. Three hours of such driving exhausted both the man at the wheel and his passenger. The latter, a youthful, black-haired fellow in a khaki safari suit, was trying to pour coffee from a Thermos bottle; he spilled some on his lap and cursed.

'Shit! They call this a road? It looks like someone`s bombed the crap out of it. How much longer?'

'Patience. At least an hour more,' replied the driver, a phlegmatic, tough man, as he deftly escaped another gaping car trap: that one would have been deadly for the suspension.

They stopped at the roadside to relieve themselves. All around them, there was wilderness, mostly flat, with small copses of strange looking trees here and there and clumps of bushes. The grass was tall and green; in the distance, they could see herds of free-grazing cattle, also strange: they looked more like large antelope than cows.

'Don't go far and watch your step, there may be snakes in the grass here,' the tough man called to the dark-haired one, who was stretching his legs near the bush. The latter shivered, and briskly returned to the Pajero: he feared snakes and creepy-crawlies. That was, possibly, the only thing he feared in his life, and he had been through a lot, faced things that would have terrified most people.

They were travelling from Cuiaba, the capital of the central Brazilian state of Mato Grosso. The emptiness around them was almost oppressive: on the way, they had seen neither a single car, nor a single human being. Only massive herds grazing on the wide, wild wetlands; vultures high above and funny toucans, bright with oversized beaks, who flew a few times over the crawling four-by-four, curious.

It was July; midwinter in these parts. The daytime temperature was around thirty Celsius; quite tolerable, even comfortable.

Almost exactly two years had passed since the memorable summer of 2003; when our hero disappeared; now the tough man and his companion were driving along this so-called road, from Cuiaba to a small provincial town with a long and proud name: Sao Jose Dos Quatro Marcos. They were Marcio and Pablo: the tough one Brazilian, the other Colombian; at least, according to his passport. Between themselves they spoke neither Portuguese or Spanish, but English, for convenience's sake.

Their destination, Quatro Marcos, was famous for its large slaughterhouse and a meat factory that exported the wonderful, lean Brazilian beef and meat products to countries around the world. Lately, the exports to the Middle East had grown very considerably: both to the Arabs and to Israel. But the biggest export increase was to Russia. The company even had to employ two Russian-speaking immigrants, one from Bulgaria, another one from the former Yugoslavia.

Marcio and Pablo operated according to a shopping list they received from their controller, together with generous expenses. The list contained eleven Brazilian companies spread over eight different cities. Their target could be employed by one of them. The man they sought was an immigrant from Eastern Europe, who was granted indefinite leave to remain and a work permit about a year ago.

The controller gave them the target's photo and several names: aliases he was likely to use. One of them was Adrian Goranovich. The two men have been cruising Brazil for almost two months, ticking off company after company, town after town. Quatro Marcos was number seven on their list.

They had no need to know that similar tasks were being carried out by teams in Argentina, Uruguay, Venezuela and South Africa. The Centre had acquired very serious assets in those countries' immigration services and police forces, even before World War 2, and continued cultivating them ever since. This helped a great deal, whether one had to find a fugitive or a traitor, or to create a well-documented operational identity and a solid cover story for an agent.

According to his papers, Pablo was an official representative of an Israeli meat importer in South America. The cover for his visit was a formal inspection of the slaughterhouse: the meat imported to Israel absolutely had to be kosher. This meant strictly observing certain rules and rituals: the poor creatures must be drained of blood while a rabbi said prayers over them, et cetera. Otherwise the meat would be considered unclean and could not be eaten by the Jews. Unless the procedures were followed to the letter, the meat could not be exported to Israel. Similar procedures applied to exports to Muslim countries, by the way, albeit they came under a different term, halal, and the prayers were said by a mullah instead of a rabbi.

Using this cover story, or 'legend' in the Centre's professional parlance, Pablo and Marcio were to meet the company director and inspect the export department. If their target was employed by the company, these two specialists would surely find him. Child's play. Once they'd found him, their instructions were to report to the controller and wait for instructions. If this was not possible, they should eliminate the target.

The Mitsubishi made it to Quatro Marcos at dusk. Having spent the night at a local hotel, the following morning the pair were enjoying strong, aromatic coffee in the offices of the company director. The middle-aged Brazilian was hospitality personified, and readily answered any questions posed by his important clients.

He spread a few booklets over the conference table: all the information about the firm, its clients and management. Marcio was paging through one, when he stepped on Pablo's foot slightly, under the table. The latter glanced at the photo of the manager in charge of exports to Russia and coughed.

Adrian Goranovich said the caption over the smiling, dark-haired man, photographed full size.

‘By the way, Mr Santos,’ Marcio interrupted the director, who was just beginning to explain another diagram, ‘we have brought a small parcel for one of your employees. His cousin sent it. She works at our Head Office in Haifa. Is he around?’

‘But of course. What is his name?’

‘Goranovich, Adrian Goranovich.’

The director’s smile faded away; suddenly, he looked sad.

‘Gentlemen, I am awfully sorry. Bad business… It is not possible.’

Marcio and Pablo looked at each other, baffled.

‘He is no longer with us.’

‘Left the company? Never mind, just give us his forwarding address, and we’ll make sure he gets what’s coming to him.’ Marcio winked at Pablo.

‘Worse than that, I’m afraid. He died.’ Mr Santos sighed, tragically: ‘A fatal accident two months ago.’

‘Oh Lord, what happened? What do I tell his cousin? They have not seen each other for five years, since she had emigrated to Israel.’ Marcio looked appropriately, genuinely grieved.

‘He lived in a rented house on the edge of the town. A butane bottle blew up at night. We use bottled gas for cooking here… The fire was so strong that it only took half an hour to burn down to ashes.’ The director dropped his head, ‘We buried Adrian’s remains in the local cemetery. Not much was left. Such a pity, he was a good man and an excellent manager. Lonely, though. He never said anything about his family.’

‘They were all killed during the civil war in Yugo, that is why. Only his cousin survived and emigrated to Israel. He might not even have known that she was alive. She only learned a month ago about Adrian. Wanted to surprise him, poor thing,’ Marcio sighed.

‘Oh yes, a surprise indeed, only a black one. We shall have to tell her the bad news,’ put in Pablo grimly. ‘Well, pity, but what can one do? Life goes on. Can we have his death certificate? His surviving relative might need it?'

The director nodded his agreement. The silence felt thick.

'So, back to business?' The director made an awkward gesture towards the coffee pot, trying to change the scene.

When the working day was over, Marcio and Pablo visited the local cemetery to pay their respects to the untimely dead. Afterwards, they locked themselves in the hotel room.

A coded message went to the Centre with attachments: a picture of the grave with a cross on top and a simple notice saying 'A. Goranovich. 1960 – 2005'; a copy of the company booklet with his photo, as well as a copy of Adrian Goranovich's death certificate.

The following morning, they received instructions from Moscow: task over, return to base. The long search had ended.

A week later, copies of the same messages were on the desk of the SIS head of security and counterintelligence. Agent Stingray reported from Moscow. Bob noted that the body of Dennis /Adrian was burned beyond recognition; and that it was buried without a DNA test done. Those Brazilians! On the other hand, why should they bother? Who was he, a mere immigrant, a humble employee of a meat factory…

There was enough proof of the target's death. Bob reported to C that Case Traveller had been closed due to the death of the object, and archived.

This was a rare occasion: the eternal adversaries in London and Moscow both felt huge relief and were equally pleased. They both believed what they wanted to believe so badly.

That a troublesome shadow of the past had been put to rest, forever…

Just before Christmas 2008, the police of the Brazilian city of Manaus closed the seemingly hopeless case of the stolen Piper Cherokee airplane that crashed in the rainforest several years previously. The dead pilot`s French passport turned out to be a fake; the colleagues from Paris established it immediately. There were no other leads at all to the pilot`s identity. Well, it looked like the end of the road, but then, a few months later, what was thought to be just a wild guess, turned up gold.

DNA test results of the pilot`s remains came at last from the Central registry of the Federal Police: they were an exact match of the DNA of the notorious Rodrigo "The Bat" Santana, also known as "The Sky Fox". He was a much-wanted man; the narcomafia courier and the intrepid flyer, whom most of Latin America`s police forces and border guards had been trying to hunt down for years!

This time his favourite low-flying, radar-avoiding trick did not work: the plane hit the treetops. Happens even to the best of the best.

Christmas 2008 promised to be a jolly affair for the Manaus detectives.

Far away, in Cape Town, a Ukrainian emigrant was also in a joyful pre-Christmas mood. Pavel Boyko came here almost three years ago. About fifty years old, fit, sporty, not a grey hair yet, he lived a secluded life and made his living by translations from English and Russian. Every morning Pavel checked the news on the Internet, mostly from the UK and Russia. What he saw today made him, a very reserved man, to smile broadly.

He re-read the announcement from the London law firm Ashton Miles LLP and could not help laughing happily. The serialization of the memoirs of a Russian spy and renegade double agent was to be launched over the weekend.

Good man, Jeremy. He kept his word.

Printed in Great Britain
by Amazon

50141584R00251